PACIFICA

H. P. OLIVER

MYSTERIES IN HISTORY

HPO Productions
Mysteries In History
8698 Elk Grove Boulevard
Suite 3-271
Elk Grove, California 95624

Printed in the United States of America

ISBN-10: 0988833107

ISBN-13: 978-0-9888331-0-4

DEDICATION

In memory of Uncle Bob, whose photograph of the Pacifica statue gave me nightmares as a kid and, years later, provided inspiration for the setting of this story.

ACKNOWLEDGEMENTS

The author wishes to thank the following people for their valuable assistance during the writing of Pacifica: Margaret Warren for access to her collection of memorabilia from the Golden Gate International Exposition; Tim McCoy for helping me see San Francisco as it was in 1939; the many friends and family members who went to the fair and shared their experiences with me; Richard Rheinhardt for his book, *Treasure Island*; Patricia F. Carpenter and Paul Totah for their book, *The San Francisco Fair—Treasure Island 1939-1940*; and Suzanne Cox for making sure my commas behaved themselves.

PACIFICA

ONE

⋏⋏

San Francisco - Tuesday - April 11, 1939

After more than twelve hours on U.S. Highway 101 between Los Angeles and San Francisco, I was tired, irritable, and generally out of sorts. It didn't help my disposition any when I finally arrived at 2308 Third Street and found the Tang Fan Trading Company locked up tighter than a drum.

I'd even taken the time to stop in Salinas and call Mister Tang to explain I'd been delayed by road construction and would arrive later than expected. Tang said he understood and would be waiting for me no matter when I arrived. Hogwash!

It was now eight-thirty, and Mister Tang was nowhere to be found. To make matters worse, I was in a dark and deserted industrial part of town with no public telephones, few streetlights, and not much of anything else. Welcome to San Francisco!

When I finally got tired of pounding on the Tang Fan Trading Company's front door, I stepped back a few paces and craned my neck to search the two-story brick building's dark upper-floor windows for some sign of life. Nothing. I was about to give up on the whole deal when I heard two muffled bangs about ten seconds apart from somewhere in the building. They weren't signs of life, though; they were signs of death. I know gunshots when I hear them.

Pressing myself against the building to be less visible, I felt the day's heat stored in the bricks and listened for the rest of the story. Before long an automobile engine cranked to life. I cautiously moved to the corner of the building and took a peek. A light-colored four-door sedan roared out of the alley behind the Tang Fan Trading Company and squealed its tires turning up the side street in my direction.

I jerked back out of sight as the sedan slewed through a left onto Third Street. A decidedly Oriental face behind the passenger-side window stared at me intently as the car passed. It was only natural the sedan's occupants would be curious about who the hell was banging on the front door while they were

1

inside taking care of business. It was the nature of their business that worried me. Business involving guns is almost always a cause for concern.

Fully expecting the sedan to return, I ran to my car at the curb and grabbed the Smith & Wesson Police Special stashed in the glove compartment. Revolver in hand, I stood there next to my car for several moments waiting for whatever was going to happen next to happen. When nothing at all happened, I figured the sedan was gone for good.

I walked cautiously down the side street to the alley behind Tang Fan's warehouse. Mostly the alley was dark and deserted, but there was a narrow stripe of light spilling across the pavement next to the rear of the building. I moved past a large roll-up door designed to accommodate the loading and unloading of trucks. It was pulled down tight. The light was coming from a man-door left ajar a few feet further down the alley. I peered through the opening warily, expecting the worst.

The worst was about twenty feet or so inside the door. The single light bulb suspended from the high warehouse ceiling didn't give off much light, but it was enough to make out a lumpy shape on the concrete floor. From ten feet away the shape became a man. The guy had taken two shotgun rounds—one in the face and one in the chest. I didn't need to get any closer.

Based on what was left of him, the victim appeared to have been a gray-haired Oriental man in an expensive, custom-tailored suit. I wondered if I was looking at Mister Tang, the man I'd come here to meet. I didn't know Tang and had no idea what he looked like. For that matter, even someone who knew him well would be hard pressed to recognize the guy on the warehouse floor in his present condition.

By this time it was apparent that the corpse and I were quite alone in the warehouse, so I slipped the revolver into my coat pocket and looked around for a telephone with which to perform my civic duty. I found what I was looking for on the desk in a tiny office with windows looking out into the warehouse. I dialed "O," and the friendly operator connected me to the not-so-friendly San Francisco Police emergency dispatcher. I explained the situation. The guy on the other end of the line ordered me to stay put; officers would be arriving in a few minutes.

I decided staying put in the alley was preferable to keeping the dead guy company, so I went outside and lit a Lucky Strike. The night air had gotten damper and chillier during the short time I was in the warehouse, or maybe it was just me.

Wisps of lacy fog were now sinking into the alley, and a skulking cat in search of dinner moved slowly along the opposite wall until he noticed me. He scurried off in a furry blur, eager to be far away from the evil invading his domain. The cat had better sense than me and I wished I could follow his example.

I was exhaling my last drag on the fag when I heard the sirens—at least two of them. About three minutes later a pair of headlamps accompanied by a bright red light turned into the alley. The black and white Chevrolet sedan pulled up at an angle so the cruiser's lights lit the area where I was standing next to the warehouse door.

Squinting into the glare, I watched the cruiser's sole occupant open his door and step out. From behind the relative safety of the patrol car's open door, he yelled over the sound of his engine, "You the guy who called in the shooting?"

I hollered back in the affirmative.

At that point a second cruiser turned into the alley, but the first cop never took his eyes off me. Finally, with reinforcements on the scene, he moved in my direction, his hand on the butt of his holstered revolver. The cop was about my height—around six feet—but bulkier. There were sergeant's stripes on the sleeve of his uniform jacket. When the guy was close enough to be heard in a normal voice, he asked not entirely pleasantly, "Who the hell are you?"

"Johnny Spicer. I'm a licensed private investigator from Los Angeles."

"You got some ID?"

"In my wallet, left hip pocket."

By this time the two officers from the second patrol car were standing a few feet behind the first cop. Their hands also hovered near the butts of their revolvers. Over his shoulder the sergeant said, "Watch him." To me he said, "Let's see that ID. Take it out slow and easy."

I removed my wallet as instructed and opened it to the photostat on which the great state of California proclaimed to anyone who cared that Jonathon Anthony Spicer was authorized to operate as an investigator-for-hire within the state's boundaries.

After giving my license the once-over, he handed my wallet to one of the other cops. "Jot down this guy's info."

Facing me again, the sergeant said, "I'm Bailey, Homicide Division. Where's the victim?"

I gestured toward the warehouse behind me. "About twenty feet inside the door."

"Johnson, grab a flashlight and come with me. Carter, you keep an eye on Mister Spicer here."

Bailey and Johnson disappeared through the Tang Fan Trading Company's back door while Patrolman Carter finished copying the information from my license. Carter was just handing me back my wallet when Sergeant Bailey returned. He looked about like you'd expect a guy to look after encountering a particularly gory corpse. To Carter he said, "Johnson's calling the coroner. You stay here and copy down Mister Spicer's answers to the questions I'm going to ask him."

Then Bailey gave me the tough cop, look-'em-in-the-eye stare for a moment before asking, "Okay, Spicer, what's your story?"

I offered the sergeant a Lucky, which he accepted. We lit up and I said, "I drove here from L.A. today to meet a client by the name of Mister Tang Fan at this address. I got here about eight-thirty and found the front door locked. I banged on it for a few minutes with no result, and then I heard two gunshots from inside the building."

Carter held up his hand in a gesture to stop for a moment while he caught up on his note taking. I puffed on the Lucky until he looked up and nodded. I continued, "I took cover and waited to see what was going to happen next. After a minute or so I heard an engine start up back here somewhere. I looked around the corner of the building and saw a car shoot out of the alley at high speed. It turned right onto the side street, left onto Third Street, and disappeared."

Bailey said, "You got a description of the car?"

"It was a light-colored four-door sedan—white or light gray. It looked like a Ford, but might have been one of those new Mercurys. They look a lot alike. I think there were two guys in it. I couldn't get a tag number, but my impression is that it was a current California plate—yellow numbers on a black background."

Bailey was still watching me intently, looking for some sign I wasn't the law-abiding citizen I was trying very hard to be. After a moment's pause he asked, "You get a look at the guys in the car?"

"Not a very good look. I couldn't see the driver, but the guy on the passenger side was staring at me when they went around the corner onto Third. He was definitely Oriental, but I can't tell you much more than that."

Still showing me his tough-guy cop face, Bailey said, "You're pretty good at this, Spicer. Reported a lot of dead bodies down there in Los Angeles, have you?"

I gave him a sour look. "Not that many, Sergeant. I'm just trying to be thorough so we can get this over with and I can get some sleep. It's been a long damned day."

I hoped he'd take the hint and speed things up a little, but the sergeant went on at the same plodding pace, apparently intent on being thorough. Or maybe he just had nothing better to do. Casually he asked, "So, you know that guy in there?"

"Best I can tell from what's left of him, I've never seen the fellow before tonight."

Cocking his head to one side, Sergeant Bailey faked a pretty convincing surprised expression. "That strikes me as kind of strange, Spicer. His driving license says he's Mister Tang Fan, the client you claim you came up here to see."

"Mister Tang was a new client. Another fellow named Liang Chao came by my office yesterday and set up this meeting with Tang." I looked over at Carter and said, "That's L-I-A-N-G-space-C-H-A-O."

"So what did Mister Chao want you to investigate?"

"Technically that would be Mister Liang. The Chinese custom is to put last names first. To answer your question, I don't have all the details yet, but it has to do with a Chinese woman who was working at your World's Fair. She's apparently disappeared, and Mister Liang would like to find her. He sent me to see Mister Tang because Tang made the arrangements for the missing woman to come here and he knew more about her."

"I see. What's the missing dame's name?"

"Sun Ling."

"And why does Mister Liang want to find this gal?"

"I imagine he's concerned about her welfare. Miss Sun just came here recently from China, and she probably isn't familiar with the city and our ways. Mister Liang seems worried that something bad might have happened to her."

"So, if this dame's missing, why hasn't he called us?"

"I can't answer that one, Sergeant."

"You can't or won't answer it?"

"Can't. I was told only the information Liang thought necessary. The rest of the story was supposed to come from Mister Tang."

Bailey scowled in an ugly way. "You know, Spicer, guys like you really get my goat. Here we professional cops are, barely making a living wage, and hot shots like you get paid a bunch of money for the same job, except you usually get us to do all the work for you."

Given my current frame of mind, it seemed wiser not to reply, so I kept my mouth shut. When I didn't rise to the bait, Bailey said, "Earning that fat paycheck is gonna be a little tough now with Mister Tang out of the picture, huh?"

"Could be. I'll call Liang in the morning to find out how he wants me to proceed."

Still smarting over the "fat paycheck" I was getting, Bailey glared at me a moment longer before saying, "Okay, Spicer, I guess we've got everything we need from you for now, but don't leave the city until I give you the okay. Where are you staying?"

"I have a reservation at the Sir Francis Drake Hotel on Union Square. I imagine that's where I'll be."

"You'd better be there. I don't want to have to go looking all over creation for you if I need you."

I wished the sergeant and his two patrol officers a most pleasant evening and hiked around front to my car, thinking Bailey was actually pretty good at what he did. I followed Third Street to Market, the main drag through downtown San Francisco. Jogging over to Powell Street, I turned right and a few minutes later pulled up in front of the Sir Francis Drake Hotel.

Now don't mistake my description of the route I followed to the hotel for an indication that I know my way around San Francisco. I don't. Even though I've been to the "City by the Bay" many times, the wacky layout of the streets still befuddles me. I sort of find my way around San Francisco by accident.

Fortunately the Drake is right in the heart of town across from Union Square, making it pretty easy to find. I pulled to the curb at a loading zone next to the hotel's snazzy sidewalk marquee, and an equally snazzy doorman outfitted in a bright red conquistador costume quickly arrived to help me with my bags. Since I only had one suitcase, there wasn't much for him to do but hand my car key over to a valet parking attendant. For that he received a quarter tip.

I carried my bag through swanky double glass doors, each decorated with the Drake's emblem in gold, and walked across an overdressed lobby that thought it was entertaining royalty. At the registration counter I gave a clerk with a stuffed-shirt attitude my name and he produced my reservation paperwork with a flourish. They do everything with a flourish in this town.

A bellman, also outfitted in red, insisted on carrying my bag up to room 422, which was on the Powell Street side of the hotel overlooking Union Square and the other high-class hostelries that surround it. The room's furnishings and décor were posh to the point of absurdity. I guess we who inhabit the southern regions of California tend toward a more casual and practical approach to our accommodations.

After crossing the bellman's outstretched palm with silver, I hung my jacket in the closet and did the same with the two additional sport coats I'd hastily stuffed into my suitcase last night. Hopefully the wrinkles would hang out.

Then I removed my tie, kicked off my shoes, and flopped onto the cushy bed to contemplate my situation. I wasn't yet sure how Tang's death affected my mission or, for that matter, if it was even related to the Sun Ling kidnapping caper. Also worthy of contemplation was the fact that I wasn't completely forthcoming with the local constabulary. Contrary to what I told Bailey, I knew exactly why Mister Liang had not sought the San Francisco Police Department's assistance in locating the missing Miss Sun Ling. It had to do with the woman's real reason for coming to the U.S., which involved a good deal more than simply working at the fair.

Those thoughts brought to mind memories of my Monday meeting with Liang Chao. It had been an interesting conversation to say the least.

TWO

⊥⊥

Hollywood - Monday - April 10, 1939

It was a typical Monday morning in the detective trade, which is to say sheer boredom was my highest expectation for the day. The most exciting item on the calendar was hand-delivering my final report to a big-shot movie producer who hired me for some keyhole peeping. It seems he doesn't trust one of his partners, and so he had me follow the guy around for a week to find out who he was seeing and why he was seeing them.

I'd already hunted-and-pecked my way through the typed report and it was tucked away in an envelope on my desk, ready to go. I'd also filed my copy of the report—under "W," if you must know—and had absolutely nothing to do until I delivered the report at one-thirty. Since it was only a few minutes after eleven, I was pondering how to most productively spend the next two hours when the telephone on my desk sounded off. Hoping the caller might be a new client, I answered in my most professional voice.

"Spicer Detective Agency, Johnny Spicer speaking."

"Hello, Johnny. This is Agent Tom Kendall with the FBI. Remember me?"

I remembered Kendall, alright. He's one of J. Edger Hoover's Junior G-men I encountered on a caper about six months ago. It was damned hard to forget a professional lawman who flummoxed up a case as badly as he had.

Wondering how I'd been so careless as to attract the FBI's attention, I replied warily, "Yes, Tom, I remember you. How are things in the federal crime-solving business?"

"Everything is fine here; how are you doing?"

"I'm getting along. What can I do for you?"

"I called to tell you about a visitor who will be knocking on your door soon."

"You've added fortune telling to your crime-solving skills?"

Kendall laughed. "No, I know about this particular visitor because I sent him to you."

"Why? Does he have some sort of contagious disease?"

"Come on, Johnny; don't be so suspicious. This guy could be a client for you."

Being naturally wary of G-men bearing gifts, I said, "When did the FBI start referring clients to private detectives?"

After a pause that made me think he was trying to figure out how to make what he was about to tell me sound better than it really was, Kendall said, "Before I tell you about this guy, I need your word that you'll keep what we discuss under your hat. This is a touchy matter with international implications."

International implications? He'd piqued my curiosity, so of course I told him his secret was safe with me. Kendall responded, "I know I can count on you to keep that promise. Have you been following the newspaper stories about what's happening in China?"

"Yeah, more or less. H. V. Kaltenborn was talking about the situation on his show the other night—something about the Japanese stepping up attacks on Chinese cities."

"Right. Then you probably also know that the Chinese have been fighting the Japs off for several years now—actually since 1931. In a nutshell the Japanese want to control China so they can get their hands on the country's natural resources—rice, petroleum, minerals, and stuff like that."

"Yeah, I've got the picture. What I don't get is why all the hubbub in China concerns the FBI. Foreign wars are the State Department's bailiwick."

"I'm coming to that. Intelligence reports tell us the Chinese are holding their own against the Japanese Imperial Army, but just barely. China is much larger than Japan, but the Chinese military isn't nearly as well-equipped or well-trained as Japanese forces, so the Chinese appealed to the League of Nations for help. Beyond censuring Japan for a few specific incidents, however, the League has done nothing. So now General Chiang Kai-shek is seeking United States military assistance in fighting the Japanese."

"I've heard that, too. Washington doesn't seem very eager to get involved."

"It isn't. Our official policy in this is neutrality. The politicians want nothing to do with another war."

I was growing a little weary of Kendall's current events lesson. "That's all fine and dandy, but I still don't understand what any of it has to do with the FBI—or with me, for that matter."

"We're interested because something happened in San Francisco yesterday that is directly related to the Sino-Japanese War."

"Oh?"

"Yes. It seems that the Chinese government is trying to start a grassroots movement among people of Chinese descent living in this country. Most Americans aren't aware of it, but the Chinese in this country have quite a bit of influence, especially in financial circles. Chiang Kai-shek wants to put that influence to work lobbying for U.S. military support.

"With that in mind he sent a highly respected Chinese citizen to San Francisco for the purpose of starting such a movement. Over the weekend that citizen turned up missing, possibly kidnapped."

"Okay, I see your interest in all this now. What's mine?"

Kendall paused again. "Put simply, the FBI needs your help finding the missing diplomat." Before I could get my mind fully around that revelation, Kendall changed his story slightly. "No, that's not quite right. It would be more accurate to say I want your help. Officially the FBI wants nothing to do with any of this."

I didn't know what he was up to, but whatever it was stunk to high heaven, and I started to say so. "Kendall, I know you don't have much respect for my intelligence, but . . . ."

"On the contrary, Spicer, I have a great deal of respect for you. During the Ernest Bellman incident last year, I checked you out and learned some interesting facts about one Jonathon Anthony Spicer. For example, I learned that you graduated from Occidental College in 1929 with a degree in social sciences and that after graduation you enlisted in the Army and served in the elite Corps of Intelligence Police until you were discharged in 1932. That part of your background is a little sketchy, but it seems you served with distinction, so I underestimate neither you nor your intelligence."

Ignoring his interesting facts about yours truly, I said, "So if you have so much respect for me, why are you handing me a load of manure about needing my help to investigate a kidnapping? The mighty FBI is far better equipped to handle a case like that than I am."

"I told you, Johnny; Hoover wants nothing to do with this."

"Why the hell not?"

"Officially the reason handed down to me from the top by my boss a few minutes before I called you is that the missing diplomat is in this country under false pretenses. Agents of foreign governments conducting missions in the U.S. are required to register with the State Department. This person came here as a private citizen for the stated purpose of representing China at the Golden Gate International Exposition up in San Francisco."

"Whoa, hold it right there, Kendall. Coming here to talk with American citizens is in no way a diplomatic mission. What are you guys trying to pull here?"

"Like I said, Johnny, that's the official reason we aren't getting involved. Unofficially Hoover wants to avoid becoming embroiled in a touchy political situation on which the U.S. has taken a firm hands-off position."

The manure was getting deeper and deeper. What Kendall wasn't telling me about this touchy political situation would fill a book. For one thing, there was something odd about the way he referred to the subject of his call as a Chinese "diplomat" and "this person" without actually identifying the guy. "Tom, just exactly who is this missing Chinese citizen?"

Once more there was a pause before Kendall answered. "Her name is Miss Sun Ling."

"Come on, Kendall; stop tryin' to kid me. Women don't have the social status in China to become diplomats."

"They do if they happen to be a very attractive and well-educated relative of Sun Yat-Sen, the founder and first president of the People's Republic of China."

"Yeah, but Sun died more than ten years ago. Chiang Kai-shek is running things now."

"All true, but Chiang is impressed with Sun Ling's efforts on behalf of the Nationalist Party, and so he chose her for this mission."

"So he sends this hoity-toity dame over here on a secret mission in the middle of a damned war, huh? Didn't they send any bodyguards with her?"

"Oh, they sent some bodyguards over with her, but they apparently weren't very good at their job. Sun Ling disappeared last night without a trace."

"I see. So tell me how I got to be the lucky so-and-so on whom you're trying to dump this mess."

"That was my idea. This whole situation developed very quickly. You were the best option I could come up with on short notice."

"Gee, thanks." Since I needed a moment to mull the situation over, I kept asking questions. "So how did you come to be involved in this?"

"When I arrived at the office early this morning, a gentleman by the name of Liang Chao was waiting to see me. If you don't recognize his name, Mister Liang owns a couple of large shipping companies along with several other ventures. He's easily among the top ten wealthiest and most influential men on the west coast. Liang also seems to be the man on this side of the Pacific who was chosen to head up Chiang Kai-shek's grassroots movement seeking U.S. involvement in the Sino-Japanese War."

I concluded Liang must be one of those guys who ran things from behind the scenes because I had only vague recollections of occasional references to him in the papers. "So this Liang character showed up on your doorstep wanting you guys to find his missing princess or whatever the hell she is?"

"More or less. Liang told me his story and said he wanted the FBI to find Sun Ling and do it discreetly without a lot of press coverage. I called my boss, and he called his boss, and so on up through the chain of command until the man at the top said no dice. I told Liang we couldn't help him because of the irregularities of Sun Ling's entry into the U.S. He said he understood and asked if I knew of anyone else who could handle the case the way he wanted it handled. I gave him your name and told him I would set it up with you."

"I see. So when am I supposed to meet Mister Liang?"

"He was going straight from here to your office, so he should be there in about five minutes."

"Tom, I've got to say I have some serious reservations about . . . ."

"I figured you would. Of course, whether or not you take Liang's case is up to you, but I will tell you this: I'm pretty confident the U.S. will have to become involved in the Sino-Japanese War eventually, and when we do, it will be on the side of the Chinese, so finding Sun Ling would be a service to your country as well as a profitable venture for you. There's some big money behind all this."

Kendall's story still stunk to high heaven, but I could also smell some long green mixed in with the stink, so I said, "Okay, I'll meet with your Mister Liang and hear what he has to say, but I'm making no promises. By the way, if I take the case, how much help can I figure on from you guys?"

Yet again, Kendall took a moment to phrase his answer. "Some, but not much. About all I can do is try to dig up background information you might need, but even that will have to be on the QT."

"So if something goes wrong, you never heard of me, right?"

"Right."

"Okay, Tom. I'll let you know what I decide to do."

"Thanks, Johnny. Oh, and good luck finding Sun Ling."

I hung up the telephone handset and was letting myself get irritated about Kendall's cock-sureness that I would take Liang's case when I heard my outer office door open. I went to the inner door and found two men of the Asian persuasion patiently waiting there..

THREE

In stature and dress the two men occupying my outer office were like night and day. One, clearly the leader of the duo, was tall and slender with close-cropped gray hair. The price of his snazzy dark blue suit might have fed the entire town of Barstow for a month, and the shine on his black shoes would have been blinding in direct sunlight. In his left hand he carried a thin, black leather dispatch case that looked like it cost more than all the furnishings in my office combined.

The second guy couldn't have been more than five-six and was almost as wide as he was tall, but I could tell at a glance it would be fatal to mistake his girth for flab—there was muscle there and a lot of it. He wore both a skinny Charlie Chan-style moustache and a permanent scowl on his face. His rumpled black suit looked to be at least one size too small. Guys who use shoulder holsters ought to wear looser fitting suits.

The distinguished guy in dark blue said, "You are Mister Johnny Spicer?"

"I am. I presume you are Mister Liang Chao?"

"I am he."

"FBI Agent Kendall said I should expect your visit. Please come in."

Liang said something in what I presumed was Chinese to the short guy, who nodded sharply and took up a position next to the hall door. Liang entered and surveyed my second-floor, secondhand office with polite distaste.

I invited him to take a seat in one of the slightly threadbare-but-comfy chairs facing my desk. After examining the chair briefly for contaminants that might soil his immaculate suit, he accepted my invitation, placing his classy black leather dispatch case on his lap. I dropped into my desk chair and said, "Mister Liang, before we begin, I want to make it clear that based on what Agent Kendall told me, I have reservations about taking your case."

With just the hint of a smile, Liang said, "As have I about offering it to you. Let us discuss the matter to see if our reservations might be put to rest. What did Agent Kendall tell you of our situation?"

Leaning back in my chair, I said, "Essentially he said a Chinese citizen named Sun Ling may have been kidnapped in San Francisco last night. He described Miss Sun as a person of some political importance who is in this country ostensibly to participate in the San Francisco exposition, but who is actually serving in a covert diplomatic capacity on behalf of General Chiang Kai-shek."

Liang's coal-black eyes watched me intently as I recited the condensed version of my conversation with Kendall. I paused, giving him an opportunity to correct any errors in my facts. When he said nothing, I continued, "Agent Kendall told me that because of Miss Sun's questionable status in this country, the FBI declined to pursue the matter of her disappearance. Is that about the size of it?"

Nodding his head once, Liang said, "Yes, as far as it goes, Agent Kendall's description of our situation is accurate. Did Mister Kendall also explain the nature of Sun Ling's true mission to the United States?"

"He said Miss Sun was here to encourage influential Americans of Chinese descent to urge U.S. involvement in the Sino-Japanese War."

"That is also correct. Now, please, tell me of the reservations you mentioned."

I studied Liang's impassive face for a long moment looking for insight into what he might be thinking. Finding nothing there, I leaned my elbows on the desk and said, "The first concern I have is the position taken by the FBI in this matter. Frankly, it makes no sense. The unofficial reason you've given for this woman being here doesn't qualify as a diplomatic mission by any definition I've ever heard. And even if it did, the FBI would still be obligated to find Miss Sun, if only to send her back to China as an undesirable person.

"So Agent Kendall was fibbing or, at the very least not telling me the whole story, and I'm not too keen on taking cases from clients who start out by lying to me."

Liang's expression remained impassive. "Your point is well taken, Mister Spicer. I can only respond with my personal assurance that I have been completely honest and forthcoming in my statements regarding this situation. I cannot speak to what motivations the FBI may have for the position they have taken."

His response was eloquent, but added nothing to what I already knew or didn't know. Given my natural distrust of Kendall and the FBI, however, I tended to believe Liang's claim that he really didn't know what the Junior G-men were up to. So leaving that matter for the moment, I moved on to a different question.

"Mister Liang, what makes you think Sun Ling was kidnapped? Since you haven't mentioned receiving a ransom demand or any other communication from someone claiming to have taken Miss Sun, isn't it also possible that having arrived in the land of the free, she simply decided to take off and leave all the political turmoil behind?"

Inscrutable is a word often associated with the Chinese, and Liang certainly fit that description, but I thought I detected a slight raising of his eyebrows in response to my question. After only a second's hesitation, he said, "Mister Spicer, I have not said I believe Sun Ling was kidnapped; however, the lack of a ransom demand does not negate that possibility. If Miss Sun was kidnapped, it would have been for the purpose of political rather than monetary gain.

"Put simply, the Japanese government would find U.S. intervention in the Sino-Japanese War most inconvenient at this time. That in itself is certainly strong motivation for someone supporting the Japanese point of view to take whatever steps might be necessary to prevent the success of Sun Ling's mission here."

"Yes, but wouldn't it be simpler to just kill Sun Ling instead of going to all the trouble of kidnapping her?"

"Not if any possibility existed of her death being blamed on the Japanese. That would make Sun Ling a martyr, and killing her on U.S. soil would be certain to have repercussions sympathetic to China. Causing Sun Ling to mysteriously disappear, on the other hand, leaves her fate open to speculation."

"Alright, let's say for a moment that Miss Sun has been kidnapped by Japanese agents. What would they do with her once they had her?"

"It is most likely they would murder Miss Sun and dispose of her remains in such a way as to preclude them ever being found. We accept that possibility, but you must understand it is crucial for us to know Sun Ling's fate with the highest degree of certainty possible."

After a momentary pause, Liang Chao added, "As for the likelihood of Sun Ling disappearing of her own volition, I can only say that I know her well through personal conversations and frequent correspondence, and I assure you her dedication to the cause of saving China from Japanese imperialism is steadfast. Sun Ling would never place personal aspirations above that goal."

Even though Liang had a ready answer for each of my questions, my mental picture of the case was still vague and full of more holes than a slice of Swiss cheese. Worse, I couldn't shake the feeling that was exactly what Liang intended. Or maybe I just wasn't asking the right questions. I tried a different approach.

"If you don't mind me saying so, it appears that by hiding Sun Ling's mission behind the guise of representing her country at China's exposition exhibit, you've played very nicely into the hands of whoever might have kidnapped her. The true purpose for her visit here is perfectly legitimate, and if it had been publicized, Sun Ling would have been in the spotlight, making it much more difficult for anyone to take her out of the picture. The same holds true for your decision not to report Miss Sun's disappearance to the San

Francisco police just as any other citizen would do under similar circumstances."

Liang gave me another of his one-syllable nods and said, "The issues you raise are quite reasonable. I will begin to address them by correcting an inaccuracy. While Miss Sun Ling was officially sent here by her country to participate in the Golden Gate International Exposition, the Chinese exhibit at the exposition is not sponsored by China. This may seem a minor issue, but it is quite important to the overall situation.

"You see, Mister Spicer, despite its geographical proportions, China is a relatively poor country, and what financial resources China does possess must be spent in defense of its borders against Japanese imperialism. Therefore, regardless of the many benefits associated with participation in the exposition, the country cannot afford to do so.

"For that reason China asked Americans of Chinese ancestry and some degree of wealth to do what it could not. Specifically, China asked us to finance a Chinese exhibit at the exposition. An informal organization was formed to raise funds for that purpose. The endeavor was quite successful largely due to the efforts of a young man named George Jue, a prominent San Francisco businessman who accepted the responsibility for overseeing the fund-raising and for planning a magnificent three-acre Chinese village on the exposition grounds.

"So as you see, Mister Spicer, the nature of Sun Ling's true mission to the United States is tied quite closely to the nature of the Chinese exhibit at the exposition. The people responsible for the exhibit are the very same people whose assistance Miss Sun seeks to enlist for the purpose of encouraging U.S. military aid to assist in defending China against Japan. If her mission became widely known, the efforts of many well-intentioned people would become suspect and viewed as propaganda supporting activities this country's politicians oppose primarily because advocating American involvement in a foreign war would have a negative impact on their chances of reelection."

Liang's response to that question left my head spinning. He must have been a whiz on his high school debating team because he was a master at making statements that sounded terribly reasonable while completely sidestepping the issues. I asked one more question—one that left little room for fancy footwork. "Mister Liang, if I accept your case, what specifically would you be hiring me to do?"

"Specifically, I would expect you to find out what has happened to Miss Sun and, if possible, regain her freedom. Moreover, I would expect you to do so without public notoriety."

That was the closest thing to a straight answer Liang had given me since he walked into my office. Leaning back in my chair, I drummed the eraser end of my note-taking pencil on the desk and gave a moment's thought to the pros and cons of taking Liang's case. After my conversation with Agent

Kendall, I thought the case stunk, and for all his eloquence, the Chinese gentleman sitting on the other side of my desk had done little or nothing to change that opinion. Even in desperate times I'd walked away from cases that made more sense than this one.

On the plus side of the ledger were the lure of international intrigue, my curiosity to know what the hell Kendall and Liang were really up to, and the prospect of fattening my bank account with a lucrative case. I decided to find out how lucrative it might actually be, saying, "I have to warn you, Mister Liang, fulfilling the mission you've described will be expensive." Fudging on the truth a little to see what the market would bear, I added, "My rate is one hundred dollars per day plus expenses, and I require a two hundred dollar retainer paid when I accept the case. And, of course, there are no guarantees. The most I can promise is a diligent and thorough investigation."

While I can't swear to it, I thought I saw some satisfaction in Liang's face—as if he'd impressed even himself with his powers of persuasion. Moreover, he didn't so much as blink an eye at my inflated daily rate. Liang just said, "Your terms are acceptable, Mister Spicer. How do we proceed with the investigation from here?"

I tuned out the little voice in my head telling me I was nuts and said, "We can take care of the financial details in a moment, but first I need all the details you have on the circumstances of Sun Ling's disappearance."

"I personally have little to tell you on that subject. The person you will need to see for those details is Mister Tang Fan." Removing an address book from his dispatch case, Liang added, "His office is located in San Francisco at 2308 Third Street. His telephone exchange is Garfield 7687. I will contact Mister Tang by telephone and tell him to expect you. When should I say you will arrive?"

"I'll start out first thing tomorrow morning. You can tell Mister Tang I'll be there late in the afternoon or early in the evening."

After completing our financial arrangements, I shook Mister Liang's hand, and as he left my office, he said, "I wish you good fortune in your investigation, Mister Spicer. Please keep me informed by telephone of your progress."

A moment later I was back in my chair contemplating the four fifty-dollar bills on my desk and the challenge of earning them. I also contemplated the photograph of Sun Ling Mister Liang provided so I'd know who I was looking for. It was clipped from a magazine printed in color on glossy paper. The photo caption was in Chinese characters, but Sun Ling would be a looker in any language. She was a stunning young woman with an appealing smile and black hair framing delicate features. Sun Ling also had dark eyes that seemed to belong on a face much older than her twenty-two years.

A City-Wide messenger bearing two envelopes arrived around 4:00 p.m. The first contained a typewritten letter of introduction signed by Liang Chao and addressed to whom it may concern. I presume the second envelope contained the same message, but I can't say for sure because its content was expressed in neatly hand-printed Chinese characters.

I finished my day in the office by calling Tom Kendall to tell him I'd taken Liang's case. Kendall sounded pleased as punch.

FOUR

San Francisco - Wednesday - April 12, 1939

The morning view of Union Square from my hotel room window was shrouded in fog and fit my mood perfectly. My lousy case had already gone from bad to worse. Not only had a man been brutally murdered, but I hadn't been in town an hour before getting into Dutch with the local cops. I didn't dare ask myself what else could go wrong.

Tang Fan was the guy I'd been told knew the details of Sun Ling's disappearance, and now whatever those details may have been might be lost forever. The possibility that knowledge of those same details might also be the reason he was now on a slab in the San Francisco County Coroner's morgue did nothing to improve my disposition.

It was a few minutes after eight when I finished my corn flakes, orange juice, and coffee in the Drake's dining room and headed out to the lobby. I ensconced myself in an elegant public telephone booth and placed a long-distance, person-to-person call to Mister Liang Chao at the Trans-Pacific Shipping Company in San Pedro.

"Good morning, Mister Spicer. I've been expecting your call."

"I take it, then, you've heard about Mister Tang?"

"Yes, Mister Spicer. We are a close community. I received a telephone call late last night informing me that Mister Tang was shot to death in his warehouse. Will you please tell me what you know of this tragedy?"

"I got to Tang's building a little later than planned—around eight-thirty. I was knocking on his door when I heard gunshots from inside the warehouse. I entered the warehouse from the rear and found Mister Tang on the floor. He was dead, killed by two rounds from a scattergun—a shotgun—fired at fairly close range. At that point I had no choice but to call the police because even in San Francisco they frown on licensed private detectives witnessing a murder and failing to report it."

"Very succinct, Mister Spicer. Tell me, did you see Mister Tang's killer or killers?"

"If we can assume the men in a car that sped away from the alley behind the warehouse right after the shooting were Tang Fan's killers, I can tell you there were two of them. The one I could see most clearly was Oriental."

"Oriental is a term that encompasses many. Can you be more specific?"

I mentally scored one for Liang. His implied criticism of my inability to tell one Oriental race from another was well taken. I said, "If I had to guess, I would say the man I saw was Japanese, but don't hold me to that."

There was no mistaking Liang's sarcasm when he said, "I most certainly will not."

Changing the subject, I said, "How do you want me to proceed from here?"

Liang was quiet for a moment before saying, "We must put you in touch with someone who can tell you something of Sun Ling's disappearance. Tang was the best choice for that, but as he is no longer available, we must settle for second best. That would be Mister Jeffery Yang. Mister Yang is the young man chosen to serve as Sun Ling's official escort while she is in this country. He is a U.S. citizen living in San Francisco."

"Okay, where do I find Mister Yang?"

"I know little about him other than his family owns a restaurant in the Chinatown district of San Francisco. If you will be so kind as to give me a telephone number where I can call you back within fifteen minutes, I will find out how you may contact him."

I read Liang the payphone number from the little round card stuck to the center of the telephone dial and sat back to wait for his return call. From the phone booth I could see a large white clock with black numerals on the wall behind the front desk. The big hand hadn't quite covered the distance from the seven to the ten when the phone rang.

Liang said, "Mister Spicer, I have just spoken with Jeffery Yang's aunt. She informed me that Mister Yang left only a few minutes ago to look after some business at the exposition. He is expected to be at the Chinese Village exhibit there for at least two hours, and since I am unable to speak with Jeffery Yang directly before you meet him, I recommend you introduce yourself with my letter of introduction—the English copy."

"Alright, Mister Liang, I'll drive over to Treasure Island and track him down, but tell me, does this Yang fellow know Sun Ling's real reason for being in this country?"

"He does. His father, Mister Yang Da, is a respected member of our community and was our original choice for Sun Ling's escort. Sadly, he was stricken with a grave illness and is now bedridden. We asked his son to take on the responsibilities of Sun Ling's escort in his stead."

"Got it. I'm on my way to Treasure Island. I'll be in touch."

"Mister Spicer, as I am sure you have already concluded, the murder of Tang Fan has exacerbated this already deplorable situation. Even worse, the local San Francisco police are now involved. I most strongly urge you to proceed with the greatest haste so that we might resolve this matter before the newspapers turn it into an international scandal."

Several responses to Liang's plea went through my mind, but since none of them would give him much hope that I would find Sun Ling quickly, I simply said, "Understood."

My next stop was the concierge desk in the Drake's lobby where I asked for directions to Treasure Island. Apparently it was a frequently asked question, because the man in the scarlet uniform behind the desk handed me a small map showing the route from Union Square to the exposition. I then stepped through the ornately decorated glass doors to the street and handed one of the valet parking attendants the parking stub I'd been given the night before.

When my chariot arrived, I slipped the attendant a quarter and nonchalantly made a circuit of the car to make sure the fenders were all still intact. My Chrysler Royal Business Coupe may be last year's model, but it's new to me, and because the automobile's gleaming paint and chromium plating represented what to me was a major investment, I was naturally concerned about its welfare.

A couple of months back I received an unexpected windfall for recovering the loot from a bank heist out in Santa Monica, and I used eight-hundred dollars of it to replace my 1934 Plymouth coupe, which had seen far better days. My search for an automobile befitting my image as a dashing Hollywood detective and with enough power to stay ahead of the bad guys led me to the local Chrysler dealership, where a smiling used car salesman introduced me to a Regal Maroon Royal five-window business coupe. While the car's luxurious interior appealed to my aesthetic side, its one-hundred-and-two-horsepower, six-cylinder engine and overdrive transmission were my justifications for parting with nearly half of my total savings account balance.

After determining that all of my Chrysler's shiny parts were still in place, I slid behind the steering wheel and set out to find Jeffery Yang. The map provided by the Sir Francis Drake's concierge routed me around the block and back to Market Street. A left turn on Market took me to Third Street where I made a right turn. All of that zigging and zagging eventually brought me to U.S. Route 40 and the approach to the new San Francisco-Oakland Bay Bridge.

Large signs informed me that a speed limit of 40 MPH was strictly enforced and that I was crossing a toll bridge, the privilege for which would cost me forty cents. There were no tollbooths in sight, however, so I assumed the toll was to be collected at the east end of the bridge. Since I was only going halfway across the bridge, as did all other fairgoers traveling to Treasure Island from San Francisco, it seemed I was getting a free pass. That left me wondering how the bridge authority overlooked the revenue they were missing by not collecting tolls at the west end of the bridge.

The marvel of modern engineering over which my tires rolled was completed back in November of 1936. The press made a big deal out of the bridge's opening—even the Los Angeles press. That wasn't too surprising when you consider that the state's taxpayers paid seventy-seven million bucks to build the damned thing. Based on what little I recalled from the news stories, the bridge is something like eight miles long and consists of two sections. The part on which I was driving was a suspension bridge, which means the roadway dangles from gigantic cables slung between four enormous towers. The second half of the bridge, between Yerba Buena Island and Oakland, is supported by pilings driven deep into the bottom of San Francisco Bay. In order to keep automobile traffic from mixing with the trucks and streetcars, the bridge was built with two decks—the six-lane auto roadway I was on and a lower deck with both a roadway for trucks and rails for the trolley cars, if that's what they're called.

From my perspective, which consisted of what little I could see between the guardrail posts flashing by my passenger-side window, it was a long way down to the water. I hoped the guys who put in the rivets, or whatever held the bridge up, knew what the hell they were doing. I will admit to feeling a certain amount of relief at being back on solid ground when I entered the tunnel they blasted through Yerba Buena Island to accommodate bridge traffic. Moments later another sign informed me that those heading for Treasure Island should take the turnoff to the right at the east end of the tunnel.

If all these islands are confusing, here's the lowdown I got from the exposition brochure thoughtfully left in my room by the Sir Francis Drake's management: Yerba Buena Island is a natural pile of rock partway across the bay between San Francisco and Oakland. Treasure Island, on the other hand, was manmade a couple of years ago from five-hundred-plus acres of fill dredged from the bay. Treasure Island is attached to the north end of Yerba Buena by a short causeway and was constructed at government expense to provide a location for San Francisco's municipal airfield when the Golden Gate International Exposition is done with the place. Pan American World Airways is already using docks at the south end of Treasure Island as a base for the Clipper ships they fly across the Pacific to places like Hawaii and China.

The freshly paved roadway I followed from the bridge took me around the south end of Yerba Buena where I discovered that the bridge authority had no intention of giving fairgoers from San Francisco a free pass. I stopped at a tollbooth and handed over my forty cents to a grumpy-looking fellow in a blue uniform shirt. I didn't blame him for his demeanor. I'd be grumpy-looking, too, if I had to spend my days collecting quarters, nickels and dimes from folks who were on their way to have a lot more fun than I was having.

From the tollbooth the road proceeded north up the west side of the tiny island and crossed an overpass above the Bay Bridge. Then the road began descending to sea level, and after rounding a final curve, Treasure Island and the Golden Gate International Exposition hove into view.

My first impression was one that included a hundred or so buildings of exotic architecture spread out across an absolutely flat island and interspersed with greenery, decorative ponds, and spire-like structures, all of which gave the place a mystical character like some mythical land from the Arabian Nights. Movement to my right caught my eye, and I turned to watch a huge, four-engine Pan American seaplane taxiing across the body of water separating Treasure Island from Yerba Buena Island. It was all quite impressive.

The isthmus connecting Yerba Buena to Treasure Island widened as it approached a five-lane tollgate with signage informing me that admission to the grounds was fifty cents for adults and twenty-five cents for children. That was all fine and dandy, but the tollgate lanes were closed and their booths were empty. Then a car passed me and pulled up to the last tollgate on the right where the driver was greeted by a uniformed security guard who, after looking at some sort of credentials presented by the driver, opened the railroad crossing-style tollgate barrier and allowed the car to pass.

I followed suit, and as I pulled up to the tollbooth and rolled down my window, the guard informed me the fairgrounds did not open until ten o'clock. I flashed my official-looking private investigator's photostat and said, "I have business at the China exhibit."

After a not very thorough examination of my license, the guard said, "Yes, sir," in an official-sounding tone. He then handed me a yellow card and said, "Follow this road past the Portals of the Pacific and the Northwest Passage to the taxi parking area. You can park there with this card on your dashboard."

Pleased with how smoothly I'd bypassed the fair's security system, I thanked the guard and proceeded according to his directions with absolutely no idea what the hell the Portals of the Pacific and the Northwest Passage were. Obviously I had a lot to learn about this mythical land called Treasure Island.

FIVE

⌒⌒

According to a map in the hotel information brochure, Treasure Island was constructed in a rectangular shape, except three of its four corners were truncated diagonally, creating a seven-sided polygon. The one remaining square angle of the polygon is at the southwest corner of the island where the isthmus connects it to Yerba Buena Island. This is also the location of the ticket booth through which I'd just passed.

From the ticket booths the road led straight up the long western edge of the island. I proceeded slowly, looking for the Portals of the Pacific and Northwest Passage mentioned by the gate guard. The only thing I knew for sure was they had to be on my right because the waves of San Francisco Bay were lapping the shoreline fifty or so feet to my left.

The first landmark I passed was a large, multi-story building shaped like a shallow U with its open end facing my direction. It looked for all the world like a modern airport terminal, complete with a glassed-in control tower perched atop its roof, so I concluded that was its intended purpose once the exposition vacated the island and San Francisco's municipal airfield moved in. In front of the terminal building a white sign with black capital letters read, "GGIE ADMINISTRATION—Official Vehicles Only."

Bordered on both sides by decorative planting areas filled with what I thought were called ice plants, the road continued along next to a stepped-roof building that seemed to go on forever, but didn't. It was interrupted by a wide opening that I took to be the exposition's main entrance. This opening was flanked on either side by huge structures extending out toward the road. They looked like giant stacks of children's building blocks that became progressively smaller toward the top, creating pyramid-shaped towers. These towers appeared to be made of pink stone with stairways and impressionistic elephants decorating their fronts. All in all, they gave me the feeling I was looking at a Burmese or Siamese temple as interpreted by a cubist sculptor.

What struck me as even more unusual were the tall, narrow, free-standing walls filling the entrance opening. There were nine of them aligned in a shallow V-shape with its open end facing my direction. As my vantage point changed, I saw that the walls overlapped with spaces between them, apparently to allow visitors entry into the exposition. Why the designers chose to impede the progress of fairgoers in this manner was a mystery to me.

The tallest of the spires I'd seen from Yerba Buena rose behind the mysterious walls. It was so tall that its topper—some kind of gold-plated bird—was almost lost in the layer of fog covering the bay. To the west the same fog bank still shrouded the city of San Francisco, obscuring most of its skyline. On a clear day, if there were such things in this part of the world, the view from Treasure Island would be spectacular.

On the other side of the elephantesque entrance structures, the long building with the stepped roof continued toward the northern tip of the island. Up ahead on the left, a set of four finger-shaped docks stuck out diagonally into the bay. As I drew adjacent to the docks, a sign informed me I was looking at the West Ferry Terminal. Another sign on the opposite side of the road pointed toward a second break in the long building on my right and identified it as the "Northwest Passage."

From that clue I cleverly deduced that the landmarks to which the tollbooth guard referred were the exposition entrances, which meant the opening decorated with cubist elephant towers must be the Portals of the Pacific. I guessed the Northwest Passage entrance was put here to serve visitors arriving by ferryboat. It was less elaborate than the main entrance, but they shared one feature in common. Another set of the freestanding, overlapping walls I'd seen at the main entrance also filled this opening. Then the light bulb finally went on over my head, and I realized why they were there.

Being perfectly flat and out in the middle of the bay, there were no natural barriers to protect Treasure Island from offshore winds. The architects anticipated the effect westerly winds would have on fairgoers and provided sets of manmade barriers to prevent the winds from whipping through the entrances. Clever fellows!

Another fifty feet or so feet further along the road I spotted a sign that read, "Taxicab Parking." The sign's arrow pointed to the right and I followed it, ending up in a rectangular-shaped parking lot that was completely empty. I pulled into a spot, stuck the yellow card on my dashboard, and climbed out into the cold, damp air.

Looking around to get my bearings, I saw that the long building paralleling the road ended a short distance to the north. Beyond it the tip of Treasure Island was covered by what the hotel pamphlet described as a 12,000-car parking lot. While I couldn't see the entire lot, what I could see left little doubt that it would, indeed, accommodate twelve thousand cars. The problem of moving those cars on and off the island in a timely fashion along the roadway I'd just taken would be another matter.

Figuring it to be the shortest route to the exposition's interior, I set out for the Northwest Passage. Once past the wind barriers, I found myself at one end of a long courtyard. To my right and some distance away at the south end of the courtyard stood the tall spire with the gold bird on top. Directly in front of me there was a large, round, decorative pool and fountain surrounded by leafy green trees. To my left was a gigantic statue of the ugliest woman I have ever seen.

She stood at least eighty feet tall in front of a background decorated with silver stars. Sculpted from white stone, the woman wore a snazzy deco-style headdress and she was draped in a long gown, but the strangest part of her— besides the fact that she was just plain ugly—was her posture. Her arms were raised in exactly the same position assumed by a dog's front legs when it stands on its hind legs. For that reason I would have called her Dog Woman, but the name sculpted into her base was Pacifica. What this big, ugly dame had to do with the Pacific Ocean escaped me, other than the possibility that the bottom of that ocean might be a better place for her.

But gawking at incredibly hideous eighty-foot broads wasn't what I was here for, so I hunted around for a directory or signage that would point me toward the China exhibit. Beyond the fountain, in an opening that led out of the courtyard to the east, I spotted what looked like an information kiosk. At that hour of the morning I had no expectation of finding a real, live person on duty, but I thought there might be a map displayed at the booth.

As I got closer, however, I noticed movement—a young woman was busy inside the kiosk restocking neat stacks of pamphlets. She looked up as I approached and I said, "Good morning."

"Good morning, sir. I'm afraid you're a little early. The exposition doesn't open for nearly an hour."

Nodding, I said, "Yes, I know that. I'm here on business. Can you direct me to the Chinese Village?"

"Certainly, sir." Pointing to my left, she added, "It's right over there, just past the Bank of America exhibit."

Thanking the young woman, I walked in the direction she'd indicated. Once past a building labeled in formal lettering as the Bank of America, I was on a wide north-south walkway called Nanking Road. It was bordered on the east by a long, ten-foot-high wall bearing large signs in English and Chinese characters. The sign I could read said, "Chinese Village."

The wall was interrupted by two entrances. I walked through the first I came to and found myself in a Chinese village or at least in what I imagined a Chinese village might look like. The rectangular space enclosed by the wall on all sides was large—easily the equal of two football fields in length and another two in width—and filled with an assortment of buildings that made me feel as if I'd stepped into a James Fitzpatrick travelogue on the mysterious Orient.

The colors were soft shades of off-white, turquoise and salmon-pink with contrasting details in glossy black and vivid crimson. Symbols of Chinese culture were everywhere—slate roofs with upturned corners and topped with dragons, square columns decorated with delicate artwork and stylized Chinese characters, and at the center of it all, an eight- or nine-tiered pagoda tower overlooking the entire village. This tower wasn't as tall as the monstrosity beyond the exposition's main entrance, but it was a close second at maybe 150 feet.

What I did not see, however, were any signs of life. Except for some distant hammering sounds, the place felt deserted. I headed toward the hammering, taking in the sights I passed along the way. These included a swanky-looking restaurant, a theater advertising daily acrobatic performances, an elaborate building housing a collection of rare and exotic jade, and a myriad of art and craft exhibits. Seeing the jade collection required the purchase of a twenty-five-cent ticket, but the rest of the exhibits and demonstrations appeared to be free.

The village designers had not overlooked the flora of China. Trees, shrubs with exotically shaped leaves, and brilliant flowers filled in what little empty space remained between the two- and three-story exhibit buildings. Approaching the base of the pagoda tower, I found the source of the hammering sounds—a couple of workmen erecting a wooden stage. I was planning to ask the carpenters if they knew the whereabouts of Jeffery Yang when a young Chinese man appeared in the doorway of a nearby building.

I placed him in his early-twenties, and he was the stereotype of a second-generation American dressed to make sure he was not mistaken for such. From his off-white-and-tan saddle oxfords and pleated khaki slacks to his brown houndstooth jacket and neon green tie, he was the image of an American hep-cat. Somehow I knew I was looking at Jeffery Yang.

He also noticed me—a stranger wandering around his territory before the exposition opened—and said in a cheerful but obviously curious tone, "Hello there. Can I help you?"

"Good morning. I'm looking for Jeffery Yang."

He turned the curiosity up a notch by cocking his head to one side. "I'm Jeff. What can I do for you?"

"My name's Johnny Spicer." I handed over Liang's English letter of introduction and added, "I'm a private investigator hired by Mister Liang Chao to look into the disappearance of Sun Ling. This letter should explain things."

He unfolded the letter and read it quickly. Then, his face bursting into a big grin, Yang said, "Well, isn't this a rip-snorter . . . a real, live gumshoe!" He handed the letter back to me and offered his hand. "Pleased to meet ya', Johnny. You packin' a gat?"

In addition to being a very hep cat, Yang was apparently a fan of gangster movies. Deciding to humor him, I shot back a slightly Bogartish, "Sure, kid. I never go looking for disappearing princesses without it."

Yang was clearly enjoying his encounter with "a real, live gumshoe," but he quickly corrected me on what to him seemed an important point. "Gotcha, man, but Sun Ling ain't no princess. We have a real-life princess—I guess she's an ex-real-life princess—here from the Dowager Empress's court, but Sun Ling is a modern, up-to-date woman of the Chinese Republic." He spouted the last part in a cadence and tone that made it sound like something out of a propaganda broadcast.

"Is that right?"

"You bet! No royal razzmatazz for that gal. She's strictly business."

"Well, Jeff, I need to know a lot more about that gal, and I hear you're the guy to talk to. You have time for some questions?"

He nodded and put on his wide grin again. "Sure thing, Johnny. Tell you what, let's go over to the coffee and doughnut joint where we can be comfortable. It's just across the Gayway."

I followed young Mister Yang to one of several smaller, but no less ornate, buildings tucked up against the village's east wall. We climbed some low steps leading to a pair of bright scarlet doors decorated with fearsome dragons and a neatly printed sign that said, "Employees Only." Yang selected a key from several on a ring he pulled from his pocket and unlocked one of the doors. He ushered me inside the building and locked the door behind us.

A ten-foot-deep entryway decorated with wall-hangings and tall Ming-style vases ended at a pair of thick, black velvet curtains. We passed through the curtains and came out in a carpenter's hell—a maze of bare wood two-by-fours and plywood panels extending in all directions. I had the immediate impression of a movie studio back lot with its makeshift facades. Apparently, the same approach was taken by the Chinese Village designers for structures into which fairgoers were not allowed. No sense putting money into places the ticket-buying public can't see.

The only visible clue that the interior of this structure was intended for human use was the carpet under our feet. It covered the plywood flooring of what would have been called a hallway if it had a ceiling and walls instead of being open over our heads and lined with bare studs. The thin plywood floor panels sagged and groaned under our weight as we made our way between bare-bulb light fixtures nailed to studs along our route.

We were about twenty feet into the building when the carpet marking our route dead-ended at a north-south carpet. The new carpet-way was bordered on its east side by a plywood wall that extended along the edge of the vast empty area to our left. Looking across the empty space and back toward the front of the building, I saw two more curtained entryways like the one we'd come through. Apparently the building was constructed to look like three separate structures from the outside.

Yang turned to the right, and a moment later we rounded a corner to the left into a short hallway that ended at a heavy door secured by an impressive deadbolt lock. Yang put his magic keys to work again, and we exited the Chinese Village into an entirely different environment.

It seemed the carnival midway, or Gayway as Yang called it, backed right up against the east wall of the Chinese Village. The doorway passed through that wall and deposited us in a narrow space between two Gayway attractions. The concession on our left was a souvenir stand, and the booth on our right appeared to be a skill game involving three balls for a nickel. Yang gave neither of these thrilling attractions a second glance, but strode purposefully across the Gayway to our destination, the none-too-cleverly named Doughnut & Coffee Restaurant.

SIX

Jeff Yang and I seated ourselves in a couple of chintzy wooden chairs at a wobbly table next to a filthy window with a collection of fingerprints that would have made the FBI jealous. There were no menus on the table, but a signboard over the service counter listed the bill o' fare. In addition to a half dozen varieties of doughnuts available for two bits each, the joint offered five beverage choices: Pepsi-Cola, milk, tea, Instant Postum, and coffee. The java cost twenty cents a cup with refills going for a nickel a pop.

With prices that steep, you'd think they could afford to wash their windows once in a while. The mom-and-pop doughnut shop a block east of my office on Hollywood Boulevard gets fifteen cents for fresh-baked sinkers and a dime for coffee with free refills. And their windows are clean.

A middle-aged cow in a stained green apron shuffled over like her feet hurt and leaned a well-padded hip against our table. The wood creaked in protest and she mumbled something that might have been, "Whatcha have, boys?"

Glancing up at the woman's official GGIE concessionaire name badge, which identified her particular species of bovine as a "Clara," I said I'd have a cup of coffee. Jeff ordered the same with a cruller. As Clara shuffled off to fetch our order, I pulled my notebook and a pencil from my jacket pocket and said, "Okay, Jeff, let's talk about Sun Ling. What kind of person is she? I mean, what are your general impressions of her?"

Yang frowned contemplatively for a moment or two. "Well, like I said before, she's strictly business. When Sun Ling isn't appearing in the village, she wears old-lady clothes—you know, loose-fitting blouses with long sleeves and high collars and long black skirts that come down almost to her ankles. She doesn't put on any make-up and pulls her hair back into a bun like an old spinster schoolmarm."

After another brief pause, he continued, "That's a shame, because when Sun Ling is all dolled up for her appearances, you can see she's a real dish."

"Appearances? What does Sun Ling actually do at the exposition?"

29

"She makes daily appearances in the Chinese Village between five and nine P.M."

Prompting Yang for more, I said, "And she wears costumes for these appearances?"

"Does she ever! They dug up a whole bunch of traditional ceremonial costumes for her to wear, with snazzy headdresses and the works—really colorful stuff! Plus, she puts on the traditional old-time makeup—white powder, lip rouge, all that. I'm tellin' ya, when Sun Ling goes out for an appearance, she looks like a real live China doll!"

"So what, besides looking spectacular, does she do during these appearances?"

"Oh, we make big productions out of them. First, we announce her over the loudspeakers, then we play traditional music while Sun Ling and her court form a procession and parade across the village from the base of the Pagoda Tower to this nifty booth we built for her."

"Who all is in this procession?"

"Well, there's Sun Ling, of course, and two local girls in handmaiden costumes, plus a couple of guys in ancient warrior outfits. Then when they get to the booth, Sun Ling sits in this elevated cane throne chair with her handmaidens on either side, and the warrior guys stand out front looking inscrutable and fierce. The whole show is really out of this world!"

"What does Sun Ling do while she's in the booth?"

"Mostly she just meets village visitors and answers their questions about China. They ask about all kinds of stuff about art and traditions. The subject doesn't matter—Sun Ling has an answer for every question. And she's really good at talking to crowds. I get all flustercated when I have to do that, but Sun Ling handles those people like she's been doing it all her life."

"What about the bodyguards who came over from China with her? Are they the guys in the warrior costumes?"

"Oh, no. The warriors and the handmaidens are just local kids who volunteer to help out in the village. Sun Ling's bodyguards are a whole different bunch."

Clara chose that moment to serve our coffee and Jeff's doughnut. The coffees arrived in cheap, chipped ceramic mugs that were probably white when they were new, but were now kind of a tan color. Despite the fact that my mug wasn't more than three-quarters full to begin with, Clara managed to slosh some of its contents on the table, creating a mess she didn't bother to clean up.

While Jeff took an enthusiastic bite of his cruller, I used a couple of paper napkins from a metal dispenser on the table to mop up the coffee puddle in front of me. Then, as I was about to taste the barely brown liquid in my mug, I noticed the lipstick stain on its rim. I shook my head, set the mug aside, and got back to my questions.

"Tell me more about the bodyguards."

He swallowed some doughnut and said, "Well, there are six of them and they work in pairs for eight-hour shifts. They're big palookas, all dressed in black suits—very mean-looking guys—and they never let Sun Ling out of their sight, even for a sec."

"Do you have any idea how Sun Ling feels about her bodyguards?"

"We never talked about them or anything, but I don't think she likes having them around very much. I mean, who would? She gets no privacy except when she goes to the john or turns in for the night, and even then there are always two of 'em just outside the door."

"Do you talk to the bodyguards much?"

Jeff shook his head. "Practically not at all. For one thing, only the head guy—he's called the Captain of the Guard—speaks English, and I don't savvy much Chinese. Even if I did, these guys don't have much to say about anything to anybody. They just hang around watching . . . kind of spooky-like. The funny part is when it really mattered, the big, bad bodyguards goofed up and somebody snatched Sun Ling right out from under their noses."

"What have the bodyguards been doing since she disappeared?"

"Good question. All six of 'em were here from just after Sun Ling vanished to sometime late Monday afternoon. I guess they were searching the exposition for her or for clues about who took her. Then I saw two of them in the village for a while yesterday morning."

"And since then?"

"I haven't seen hide nor hair of them."

"Okay, I want to talk with one of the bodyguards, preferably the one who speaks English, but it would probably be a good idea for me take along an interpreter just in case. Where can I find these gorillas, and who can I get as an interpreter?"

Yang frowned. "I don't know about that. I mean, I know where to find the bodyguards, and I know someone who'd be a good translator, but I don't know if those guys will even see you. Remember, they work for the Republic of China, and unless they have specific orders to answer your questions, you won't get anything out of them."

"I understand, but I still have to try. Where do I find them?"

"They're staying at a hotel near Chinatown. I'll call the place when we get back to the village and see if I can get you in for a powwow. As for an interpreter, my sister, Susie, can handle the job, no sweat. And Susie helps at Pop's restaurant, so she's already close by."

"Is Sun Ling staying at the same hotel as the bodyguards?"

"Naw, she's at a much classier joint up on Nob Hill, the Fairmont."

"Okay, I have just a few more questions before we head back."

Smiling as if he was enjoying our chat, Jeff said, "Sure, fire away."

"Besides the bodyguards, who else came over from China with Sun Ling?"

"Nobody. She arrived aboard one of those big steamers—the SS China-something—a week before the exposition opened last February. Mister Liang and Mister Tang and I were there with some others to greet Sun Ling, and the only people in her party were the bodyguards. If there'd been anyone else with her, I would have known about it."

Making a note in my book, I said, "I see. Does Sun Ling have any friends here that you know of. I mean, was she friendly with anyone at the fair?"

"My sister, Susie, is the only person I can think of who got kind of chummy with Sun Ling. Susie plays one of Sun Ling's handmaidens in the processions, so they're together quite often—or they were before Sun Ling disappeared. I saw them talking a few times, but mostly Sun Ling kept to herself."

"Okay. When you call Susie to ask for her help as an interpreter, please tell her I'd like to ask her some questions, too."

"Will do. What else do you want to know?"

I turned back a few pages in my notebook to review what I'd written so far. I was using my favorite witness interview technique—one I'd seen used very effectively by a captain in Army intelligence. He would start out by asking the witness a few opinion questions. The answers to those questions gave the captain the witness's point of view and sometimes uncovered prejudices to consider when evaluating answers to more pertinent questions. Next, the captain would ask about the lesser details of the case. These questions helped refresh the witness's memory of the incident and occasionally uncovered a previously unknown aspect of the case. Finally, the captain would get around to the big questions—the specific details about what the witness actually witnessed. In this instance, it was time for Jeff Yang to tell me what he saw the night Sun Ling disappeared.

I looked the young man across the table in the eye and said, "Now I'd like you to think back to when Sun Ling disappeared and tell me everything you can remember about that night."

Yang gave my question a moment's thought, then said, "Well, it was last Sunday night, and I guess the place to start is when Sun Ling finished her appearance around nine o'clock. As usual, Sun Ling, along with the kids in her procession and one of her bodyguards, left the booth and walked to the dressing rooms where they change into their street clothes."

I held up my hand in a stop gesture. "Where are those dressing rooms?"

"Oh, they're in the building you and I went through to get here. I can show you her dressing room on the way back."

"Good. Now, you said one of the bodyguards escorted Sun Ling to her dressing room. Where was the second bodyguard?"

"He went to get the Caddy we rented for them to drive Sun Ling wherever she needs to go."

"Was that unusual?"

"Naw, they do it that way every night. One of the bodyguards drives the Caddy from the parking lot to where Nanking Road—the walkway out in front of the village—ends at North Boulevard, which runs along next to the parking lot. That's just half a block or so from the village. I guess they do that so the car is warmed up and Sun Ling doesn't have to walk so far in the cold night air."

I nodded, made a note in my book, and said, "Okay, Sun Ling is walking to her dressing room. What happened next?"

"I closed up Sun Ling's booth and turned out the lights, and then I followed along to her dressing room. I do that every night. As her official escort, I'm always supposed to be on hand whenever she arrives or leaves the village. Anyway, when I got there, Sun Ling was already in her dressing room and her bodyguard was outside the door."

"Did you actually see Sun Ling go into her dressing room?"

Again he thought for a moment. "No, I didn't actually see her go in. The door was already closed when I got there. The bodyguard and the handmaidens would have seen her go in, though."

I nodded and he continued his story. "I waited around like always, but Sun Ling was taking longer than usual to change. I remember looking at my wristwatch at a few minutes past nine-thirty. Sun Ling is usually out of the village and walking to her car by then. My sister and the other handmaiden, along with the warrior guys, had already left.

"The bodyguard was getting antsy, too. Four or five minutes later he knocked on the door and said something in Chinese loud enough to be heard inside the dressing room. There was no answer, so he banged the door hard with his fist and yelled something else.

"Sun Ling still didn't say anything or open the door, so the bodyguard tried the knob like he was going to walk in regardless. The door was locked, and before I could get my key out, the big guy took a step back and hit the door with his shoulder. The second time he did that, the door crashed open.

"The bodyguard charged into the dressing room, and I looked in through the open door. Sun Ling wasn't there. Nobody was there."

Looking up, I asked, "Is there another way out of the dressing room?"

"That's the weird part. There's only the one door. There isn't even a window."

"What did the bodyguard do when he saw Sun Ling wasn't there?"

"Well, the dressing rooms are pretty bare inside, so when Sun Ling's was finished, we hung curtains to hide the plywood walls. That was classier than just painting the wood and cheaper than finishing the walls some other way.

"Anyway, the bodyguard ran around the room pushing the curtains aside to see if anyone was behind them. He didn't find anybody."

Still jotting in my notebook, I said, "From where you were standing in the doorway, how did the room look?"

"Well, there wasn't anything out of whack, if that's what you're getting at. The room looked just like it always does. We put one of those roll-around garment racks like department stores use in there for Sun Ling's costumes, and I could see her costume from that night hanging on the rack, so she finished changing before they kidnapped her."

"What else is in the room?"

"Not much. It's pretty small, so there's only room for a few pieces of furniture. There's a dressing table and mirror at one end of the room, and a couple of upholstered chairs with a small end table between them at the other end." Yang paused for a moment as if he was picturing the room. "The only other things in there are an overhead light fixture and a small sink next to the dressing table. That's it."

"Okay. What happened next?"

"The bodyguard was still searching the room when somebody started banging on the front door of the building—one of the three that go back out to the village. I always keep those doors locked. I ran over and opened it, and the second bodyguard pushed past me in a big hurry. It must have been quarter to ten by that time, and I guess he figured out something was up."

"Okay, hold on a minute, Jeff. You said you keep the outside doors to the dressing room building locked, but you also said that after the procession you closed up the booth and by the time you got to the dressing rooms, Sun Ling was already inside. How did she and the rest of her procession get into the building?"

"Oh, her bodyguards have one key to the building. The guy who escorts Sun Ling back to the dressing rooms opens the outside door."

"I see. But the bodyguards don't have a key to Sun Ling's dressing room?"

"Right. I'm the only one who has that key. Really the only reason we lock the dressing rooms is to protect the costumes when no one is around. They're worth a pretty penny."

"Okay, I've got it. Go on with what happened Sunday night."

"Well, when I got back to the dressing room from letting the second bodyguard in, the two of them were jabbering away in Chinese. Then the second guy ran back out, I think to call the other bodyguards because they all showed up about half-an-hour later. Meanwhile, the first bodyguard kept looking around the room."

"What specifically was he looking at?"

Yang thought about his answer. "Well, he went over the walls pretty carefully, like he was looking for a secret panel or something. Then he went through the stuff on the dressing table, but there didn't seem to be anything there that interested him. Finally, when the second bodyguard came back from making his phone call or whatever he went to do, the two of them moved the dressing table and chairs around so they could roll the rug back and look at the floor.

"When they didn't find anything there, the first guy sent the second bodyguard outside for something—maybe to look around the village—and the first guy started searching the rest of the dressing room building. He looked in the other dressing rooms and had me unlock the only other two rooms in the building—the two storage rooms. After that, he wandered around looking at the main part of the building—the big empty area with all the beams and stuff."

I stopped Yang again. "Jeff, how many ways are there to enter or leave that building?"

"From the village, it was made to look like three separate buildings, so there are three sets of doors on that side. Then there are two back doors leading out through the wall to the Gayway—the one we took to come over here and a second one at the other end of the building."

"What about windows?"

"There's a bunch of them facing the village, but none of them actually open, and none of them were busted or anything Sunday night. I checked."

"Alright, what happened then?"

"The other four bodyguards showed up around ten-thirty or so, and they all had a meeting in the hall outside the dressing rooms. The Captain of the Guard gave the other five guys instructions, and they all went running off to do whatever he told them to do. After that I asked the head guy if he wanted me to call the police. His answer to that one was a definite no.

"The thing is, I don't work for the Chinese government, so I went to my office and called Tang Fan to find out what he wanted me to do. I guess I woke him up because it took Mister Tang a few minutes to understand what I was telling him. When the message finally got through, he told me to just sit tight while he called Liang Chao. The phone rang about twenty minutes later and it was Mister Liang calling to give me my marching orders."

"Which were?"

"First, he told me in no uncertain terms I was not to call the police. That surprised me. It was like everybody wanted to find Sun Ling, but nobody wanted to do the most obvious thing that would help get her found.

"Then Liang told me to keep Sun Ling's disappearance quiet—like not talking to any newspaper reporters or anyone like that. Then he told me to go home and call him Monday morning with a report about what was happening."

"Did you go home like he suggested?"

"Yes, but first I went back to Sun Ling's dressing room and moved the garment rack into one of the storerooms so I could lock up the costumes. Like I said before, they're worth a lot of money, and some of them are on loan from people, so I didn't want to leave them in the dressing room with a broken door I couldn't lock.

"After that, I drove home. My sister and I live in a couple of apartments above Pop's restaurant, so I woke Susie up when I got there to tell her what happened. I asked her if Sun Ling was any different than usual that night or if anything strange happened. She couldn't think of anything."

With what Yang told me I thought I had a pretty clear picture of Sunday night's events. They didn't make a whole lot of sense, but making sense out of the clues was what I was getting paid to do.

I noticed a group of college-aged kids go by the doughnut shop window and looked at my watch. The Golden Gate International Exposition had officially opened for the day fifteen minutes ago. Closing my notebook and stuffing it and my pencil back into my jacket pocket, I said, "Okay, Jeff, I think I've got enough to get started now. I'll probably have more questions for you later, though."

Jeff Yang's grin was back. "Sure, anytime! What's next?"

"Let's go see if we can get in touch with Sun Ling's bodyguards and maybe take a quick look at that dressing room on the way."

"Okie-dokie. You know, this is actually kind of a kick."

Wherever she was, Sun Ling probably wouldn't agree with him on that score, but I didn't say so. Instead, I picked up the check Clara left on the table when she served our coffee and Jeff's doughnut. The total was sixty-five cents. I left a couple of quarters and two dimes on the table and pocketed the check for my expense report to Liang Chao. Clara was getting a five-cent tip she sure as heck didn't deserve, but I wasn't about to wait around while she did the complicated calculations required to figure my change.

As we headed for the door, Jeff thanked me for the coffee and doughnut, saying they really hit the spot. I couldn't speak for his doughnut, but the only way I could see that coffee hitting any spots was if you spilled it on your tie.

Outside, the Gayway was transformed from a ghost town into a lively hubbub of activity with jazzy music playing through the loudspeakers, barkers barking, and laughing folks having themselves a gay old time. But as we approached the door back into the Chinese Village, another sound threatened to drown out the Gayway racket. It was the rumbling throb of powerful engines somewhere to the east.

I stopped and looked for the source of the new sound. I saw nothing for a moment, but just as I was about to give up, a movement above a rollercoaster to the northeast caught my eye. There it was—a huge silver flying boat with four powerful engines pulling it aloft. I asked Jeff if it was the famous Pan American Airways China Clipper I'd heard so much about.

He said nonchalantly, "Yeah, that's it. They take off around this hour two or three times a week, and everybody on the island stops to gawk."

Being one of the gawkers, I could certainly understand the attraction. It was a sight you didn't see every day—a mighty silver miracle of modern technology gracefully whisking its passengers off to adventures in exotic foreign lands. Then just before the Clipper disappeared into the fog, it began a gradual banking turn to the west. I imagined its passengers pressing their faces to the ship's windows for one last look at San Francisco. In a way I envied them. It must have been quite a view.

SEVEN

Jeff led me along the north-south walkway in the dressing room building. We passed one closed door before arriving at a second that stood slightly ajar. The first thing I noticed when he pushed it open was the interior door frame. The section closest to the door latch was splintered and pulled away from the wall—the result of Sun Ling's bodyguard bashing the door in.

The rest of the room was in total disarray. The carpet was bunched up against the east wall and the bare plywood floor was littered with overturned chairs and small items that must have come from the top of the dressing table, which sat a few feet out from its original location against the north wall. Jeff told me nothing had been touched in the room since the bodyguard searched it Sunday night except that he'd moved Sun Ling's costumes to another room down the hall.

Of course I would do my own search of the room, but that could wait a while. Setting up an interview with Sun Ling's bodyguards seemed like a more immediate priority, so we left the dressing rooms, and I followed Jeff to a rustic building set against the village's south wall. It housed the Chinese Village administration offices, including the cubbyhole assigned to Jeff Yang.

What his office lacked in size, however, it made up for with a window overlooking a small garden full of exotic shrubbery and shade trees with lacy leaves. I plunked myself down in the room's only guest chair to enjoy the tranquility while Jeff dialed the bodyguards' hotel. The call was short and, judging by Jeff's end of the conversation, not very sweet.

He hung up the telephone and wearing a glum expression said, "Bad news. All six bodyguards checked out early this morning, and they didn't leave local forwarding address."

A stray thought crossed my mind, and I liked the idea so much I put words to it. "You know, we might have just watched those bodyguards leave the country."

Jeff Yang was a bright boy. It only took a few seconds for his brain to shift gears and catch my drift. "You mean the China Clipper we just saw take off?"

"Yes, if China is where that ship is headed."

"Well, yeah, that was the China Clipper and it goes to Hong Kong by way of Manila, but that doesn't make any sense."

"Why not?"

"For one thing, a one-way ticket to Hong Kong costs about a grand. Why would the Republic of China pay so much to bring those guys home when they could travel by ship for less than half that? Besides, why would the bodyguards go home now? They should still be looking for Sun Ling."

Jeff's points were valid, but experience has taught me following up on my hunches, as farfetched as they might seem, usually paid off. I said, "I can't answer your first question yet, but there are a couple of possible explanations for why the bodyguards might have flown the coop. One could be that they found Sun Ling. Another might be that they know they're never going to find her. Or maybe they were called home to face the music for losing Sun Ling in the first place. But speculating on why they might have left doesn't get us anywhere until we know for sure they're really gone, whether by clipper, steamship or rowboat."

"How do we find out?"

"It's a long shot, but let's start with the easiest thing to check first. Make a telephone call over to the Pan American Airways clipper terminal. Tell them who you are, and say you're checking to be sure some visiting dignitaries got there in time to catch the flight. You can even give them the names of the dignitaries. Oh, and add Sun Ling's name to that list just for ducks."

"You think Pan American will just give me that information over the telephone?"

"Jeff, one lesson I've learned about the detective business is when you're trying to root out hard-to-get information, it's usually best to go straight to the horse's mouth first because you never know what's going to work. In this case, we've got nothing to lose. The worst Pan American can do is not answer your question. If that happens, we just go after the answer another way."

Jeff looked skeptical, but he was game to give it a try. While he dug up Pan American's telephone number and placed the call, I went back to enjoying the view from his window. So far the day was going well. It wasn't even lunchtime, and I already had several notebook pages of details about Sun Ling's disappearance. While I didn't have any real answers yet, it was a good start.

When I heard Jeff say, "Thank you. You've been very helpful," I turned to see a grin on his face. He hung up and said, "I'll be darned! It worked!"

"And?"

"They don't have a passenger named Sun Ling on the flight, but all six of the bodyguards are on that Clipper right now heading for Hong Kong. How on earth did you know that?"

"I didn't know that. It was just a passing hunch until you nailed it down. Good job! You handled that call very well. Thank you."

"Oh, you're welcome. Playing detective is fun! What's next?"

"Well, I guess I can cross interviewing the bodyguards off my list of things a clever detective would do in a case like this, so that brings us to your sister. How about giving her a call to see how soon she can come out here and answer some questions?"

"You need Susie to come here to Treasure Island?"

"If she can. Being at the scene of the crime, so to speak, might help her remember more details about Sunday night."

While Jeff made the call, I contemplated the abrupt departure of Sun Ling's bodyguards. The kid was right; there had to be a good reason for somebody to cough up six Gs to get them back to China in a hurry, but would knowing that reason help me find Sun Ling any faster? Priorities are the challenge in a complicated case like this one. Metaphorically, I was standing at the intersection of several roads. One of them was the quickest route to Sun Ling, but which road was it?

Jeff finished the call to his sister and said, "Susie says she wants to help any way she can, but they're shorthanded at the restaurant this morning. She can't get away until after lunch, so she won't get over here until about two-thirty. Is that copasetic with you?"

"Sure, I'll find something to keep me busy until then."

"Susie said she'd meet you at the base of the pagoda tower. She's wearing a dark blue skirt and jacket with a light blue blouse today. That should help you recognize her."

"You aren't going to be here?"

"I've got to sit in for my father at a luncheon meeting today, so you'll be on your own until Susie gets here. I should be back by three or three-thirty, though. I'm sorry to skip out on you, but I kinda have to do this for Pop."

Before leaving me to my own devices, Jeff handed me a stack of stuff he thought I might find useful, including a Golden Gate International Exposition Participant Pass he said would get me through the main gate without having to pay the admission fee every time. The other items in the stack were an exhibitor parking permit, an exposition guidebook with a fold-out map in case I got lost, and a stack of vouchers good for free meals at the Chinese Village restaurant. Thus equipped, I set out to spend the next few hours exploring Treasure Island.

With the morning fog retreating back to the west from whence it came, the air warmed and I saw the exposition in an entirely new light. The most noticeable features revealed by the newly arrived sunshine were the flowers— Treasure Island was literally covered in brilliant blooms that were downright dazzling in the sunlight. There were thousands of them encircling fountains and statues, bordering walkways, and surrounding exhibit halls. What's more, the planting areas were so meticulously maintained, there wasn't a weed or wilting stalk to be seen anywhere.

Other features of the exposition also took on a new life in the sunshine. Ornate lampposts fitted with elaborate deco-style fixtures showed up, as did hundreds of colorful flags and banners fluttering in the breeze. Statuary, murals, and gracefully arched streams of water from decorative fountains appeared everywhere I looked.

The buildings of the fair also came alive, their lavish facades, columns, and other gewgaws standing out in vivid relief, as did the vast differences in their architecture. Far from expert in such matters, I was confounded by the mishmash of cultural styles embellishing the exhibit halls, restaurants, and other structures. Some of the styles I thought I recognized were Mayan, Burmese, Malayan, Egyptian, and Gothic—all modern recreations of ancient designs. I estimated at least a hundred buildings were built for the exposition on Treasure Island, and no one of them seemed to share anything in common with any other.

As I wandered around in wide-eyed amazement at the marvels of my first world's fair, however, I began to sense an underlying pattern—a method to the madness. Though well concealed, the exposition did have a theme, and it seemed to have something to do with trade across the Pacific Ocean. The clues that lead me to that brilliant conclusion were found in the nature of the exhibits rather than in the architectural styles of the buildings. The exhibits fit into two general categories: those promoting places and those promoting products.

Most of the place exhibits were sponsored by countries bordering the Pacific Ocean. Moving around the world map in a clockwise direction from the U.S., there were displays from the Latin American countries of Mexico, El Salvador, Costa Rica, and Panama. The South American continent was represented by Columbia, Ecuador, Peru, and Chile. Jumping across the Pacific from there, exhibiting nations included New Zealand, Australia, Johor, French Indo-China, Japan, and of course, China.

Not to be left out of the fun just because they didn't happen to have Pacific shores were the countries of Argentina, Brazil, Norway, the Netherlands, Scotland, France, Estonia, and Italy. As if determined not to be outdone by the rest of the world, the western U.S. states of Oregon, Washington, Idaho, Montana, and Utah, along with the Canadian province of British Columbia, were on hand with their own exhibits. As you would expect, the host state of California was also well represented, both by regional and county displays and by a large exhibit hall dedicated to the entire state.

In most cases, the country, state, and regional exhibits displayed the cultural traditions, products and vacation opportunities of the places they represented. As interesting as this international tapestry was, I must admit to finding some of the commercial exhibits even more absorbing.

In the Vacationland Hall, for example, an exhibit sponsored by General Motors showed us a see-through Pontiac on which the sheet metal panels were replaced with clear plastic so we could see all of the mechanical parts normally hidden under shiny paint jobs. Of course, Ford and Chrysler were also on hand, albeit in different buildings, to regale us with the comfort, performance, and convenience of their newest automobiles. In other Vacationland exhibits we were shown the latest in Pullman car luxuries and modern, streamlined buses with on-board restrooms and seats that reclined for sleeping purposes.

Then there was the National Cash Register Company building atop which was constructed a giant, two-story cash register displaying constantly changing numbers purported to be an up-to-date tally of exposition visitors. In the Electricity and Communication Hall, General Electric displayed many modern marvels, including a talking kitchen of the future, although it wasn't quite clear to me what sort of scintillating conversation one might have with a refrigerator.

I was also fascinated by the Westinghouse robot and a keyboard-operated talking machine displayed by Bell Telephone Laboratories. In the Hall of Science, the University of California showed off a model of their gigantic cyclotron along with an explanation of how it smashed atoms. Unfortunately, they didn't make clear why anybody would want to smash atoms in the first place. I guess the scientists felt it was enough just to show they could do it.

During the lunch hour the crowds visiting the Food and Beverages Building increased considerably with folks drawn in by an almost overwhelming symphony of delicious food smells, although the free samples may have added to the attraction. Inside, I was offered samples of Junket Custard, Rancho Soup, Hills Brothers Coffee, and See's Candy, just to name a few of the available temptations.

There was also plethora of free souvenirs, like the miniature Heinz pickle pin I accepted so as not to offend the earnest young woman charged with distributing them to visitors. Then at the very center of all this culinary excitement I came upon what was, depending on how one viewed such things, the tastiest or most disgusting item in the entire building. It was a one-thousand-pound fruitcake created from fifty dozen eggs, sixty pounds of butter, a hundred pounds of flour, and more than four hundred pounds of dried fruit, all blended with ten gallons of sherry. As one who has never been particularly enamored of fruitcake, my reaction to this ultimate demonstration of the baker's art was that it would make a fitting snack for the eighty-foot Dog Woman I passed on my way into the exposition.

With the exception of the half-ton fruitcake, the sights and smells of the Food and Beverages Building had the not-so-surprising effect of putting me in the mood for lunch. So with an empty stomach and feet that needed a break after two hours of hiking all over Treasure Island, I set out in search of a refill. Not far from the giant cash register I found a stand wherein a cheerful young woman with hazel eyes, naturally curly hair, and a decidedly outdoor-girl look about her was purveying sandwiches. Her name, according to the GGIE concessionaire badge pinned to her apron, was Lorraine, and she promptly sold me on the idea that a tuna salad sandwich on whole wheat was the perfect answer to my lunchtime needs. Thus, with my wax-paper-wrapped sandwich and a cardboard cup of coffee in hand, I settled onto a bench in the park-like setting along the Avenue of Olives and enjoyed my lunch.

EIGHT

Munching away on my sandwich, I found cause to contemplate the rather philosophical question of why goons and other nefarious characters of the gangster ilk seem incapable of understanding that if they didn't dress like goons, they wouldn't stand out like sore thumbs. The reason for this particular line of contemplation was sitting diagonally opposite me on the Avenue of Olives. The fellow was short, slender, and looking very sporty in a dove gray and charcoal pinstripe suit with one of those jackets that's pinched at the waist. The rest of his snazzy ensemble consisted of a wide-brim, gray fedora and a tie of the paisley persuasion in shades of orange that might actually glow in the dark.

While it was his get-up that initially caught my attention, there were other reasons for my interest in this particular goon. For one, he'd been dogging my trail ever since I left the Chinese Village. For another, the fellow was Oriental and a dead ringer for the guy in the passenger seat of the sedan I'd seen beating a hasty retreat from Tang Fan's warehouse the night before. Also suspicious was the fact that he was putting a great deal of effort into looking like he wasn't the slightest bit interested in me.

While the fellow wasn't actually bothering me and I certainly wasn't engaged in any top secret activities, it just seemed bad form for a crafty private detective such as I to let goons follow me around willy-nilly. Thinking thusly, I decided it was time to demonstrate some of my craftiness.

In my experience, the most effective way to deal with goons in public places is to confront them. Being confronted tends to make them very nervous. So I stood up, casually dropped the wax paper from my sandwich and my cardboard coffee cup into a handy trash bin, and headed straight for my new friend.

When the goon looked up and saw me, we made eye contact and he knew the jig was up. Predictably, he jumped up from his bench and started walking swiftly in the opposite direction. I stuck behind him, following at a distance of twenty to thirty feet as he made a right turn and headed south on a wide walkway called Pacific Promenade. He looked back over his shoulder several times to see if I was still following as we hotfooted it past the Columbian and Javanese exhibits. After another hundred or so feet, the goon, who was almost trotting by this time, made a sharp left turn into the Japanese Pavilion.

I stopped just inside the entrance to watch him take one last, anxious look over his shoulder before disappearing into a traditional Japanese-style building labeled, "Samurai House." I stood there for a few minutes, nonchalantly leaning against a wall with my hands in my trouser pockets, waiting for him to show up again. After several minutes passed with no further sign of the guy, I casually strolled back out to the Pacific Promenade and sauntered up to a public telephone booth outside the Netherlands East Indies exhibit.

I already intended to call Sergeant Bailey, the homicide detective I met at Tang Fan's, to find out how his investigation was going, and this was a good time to make that call because I now had something to trade for information I knew he wasn't going to share willingly. After dialing a number on the business card the sergeant gave me, I leaned against the telephone booth wall and waited for the flunky who answered my call to track Bailey down. To say the sergeant didn't express great joy at hearing from me when he finally picked up the phone would be something of an understatement. "Okay, Spicer, I'm here. What the hell do you want?"

"Hello, Sergeant, I'm just checking in to see how your investigation of Tang Fan's murder is coming."

"It's coming along just swell. Now get off this telephone and stop bothering me. I'll let you know if I need anything from you."

"Actually, Sergeant, I was hoping you might tell me what you've found out so far."

"Now why the hell would I do that? You're the hot-shot detective; do your own legwork."

I thought about saying that one good reason for telling me what he'd found out was that guys like me help pay his damned salary, but I decided on an answer I hoped would be more likely to engender a spirit of generous cooperation. "As it happens, I have something for you, and I thought we might exchange information."

That derailed his annoyance somewhat. "Is that so? Okay, you tell me what you've got. If it's worth anything, I'll think about giving you some of what we've come up with."

It wasn't exactly the response I was hoping for, but I went with it anyway. "What I have for you is that I just found the guy who was in the passenger seat of the getaway car last night."

"Oh, yeah? What makes you so sure it's the same guy?"

"For one thing, I got a pretty good look at him as they went around the corner, and for another thing, this guy just spent the past two hours shadowing me. Since I can't think of any other Japanese gentlemen who would have a reason to do that, the odds are pretty good it's the same fellow."

"Where'd you see this guy?"

"Out here on Treasure Island. When he realized I'd made him, he took off for the Japanese Pavilion like a scalded dog. That's where he is right now."

There was a moment of silence on the line, and I guessed Bailey was writing down what I just told him. Finally, he said, "Okay, Spicer, I'll grant that it might be the same guy, but that's not worth much and . . . ."

"It could be worth a lot if I gave you a description of the flashy goon suit the guy's wearing and you called exposition security to have someone keep an eye on the Japanese Pavilion until you can get out here to collar the guy for questioning."

I had him there. If he was any kind of cop, he already intended to do what I suggested. Finally, he said, "Alright, describe the guy."

I gave him a detailed description of the goon right down to his bright orange tie and finished with, "Now, why don't I hang on the line for a minute while you call the security folks out here, and then you can tell me what you've got so far on the Tang Fan case."

Bailey grudgingly agreed and I cooled my heels in the booth for another four or five minutes before he came back on to say, "Okay, Spicer, security is on their way over to the Japanese place there, and I've got a detective headed in that direction. Now just what is it you want from me?"

"I want the lowdown on what you know so far on Tang Fan's murder."

He was silent for another moment, then he said, "I'll tell you this much; you're way off base on the reason Tang was killed. It had nothing to do with any missing Chinese dames. If you want more than that, you can get it the same way we did, by talking with Tang's son, Tang Hong."

Letting that piece of news sink in, I thought about pushing for more. I decided against it, figuring I could get the rest of the story by either talking with Tang's son like Bailey suggested or by talking to Liang Chao, or both. "Thank you, Sergeant Bailey. I appreciate your cooperation."

He grunted a reply and I hung up the receiver. As I left the telephone booth, a glance back toward the Japanese Pavilion confirmed that Bailey had some pull with the exposition security people. A young fellow in a black uniform was just arriving at the Japanese Pavilion entrance. I was willing to bet I'd find the other entrances similarly guarded if I took the time to check. Since it was already quarter past two, however, I started back to the Chinese Village for my two-thirty rendezvous with Susie Yang.

As I rounded the corner onto Nanking Road, I was met with loud shouts and the sound of gunfire. Since all this uproar was accompanied by music—which often happens in radio dramas, but seldom in real life—I concluded I hadn't stumbled onto a shootout at the Nanking corral. With a few minutes to spare, I indulged my curiosity to know what all the ruckus was about. It was coming from a large fenced-in area directly opposite the Chinese Village, so I walked over and peeked through an entrance set in the fence.

What I saw was a large crowd sitting on bleachers watching an amazing spectacle taking place on a stage that had to be at least four-hundred feet wide. The backdrop was a painted diorama of what I took to be the Sierra-Nevada mountains. The unusually large stage was necessary to accommodate all the stuff on it, which included two full-sized locomotives facing each other on a railroad track. There were also some buildings and about forty mounted cowboys, all whooping and hollering while a golden spike was pounded into the railroad track.

According to a sign next to the entrance, I was looking at the Cavalcade of the Golden West—the story of how the great American west was won, which at that moment seemed to be recreating the completion of the transcontinental railroad. Also according to the sign, admission to the spectacle ranged from twenty-five cents to a buck depending on the age of the customer and whether the performance was a matinee or a nighttime show. I took it all in for a moment until a nearby ticket taker looked about ready to come over and remind me that if I wanted to witness the winning of the west, I had to buy a ticket.

Susie Yang was already waiting for me at the base of the Pagoda Tower. I recognized her at a distance from her brother's description even though he hadn't mentioned the dark blue beret she wore at a jaunty angle. Miss Yang was slender and about five-three or five-four, although her erect posture made her look taller.

When I got close enough to see such things, I noticed Susie wore very light make-up and her black hair was done in a bob-style that came into vogue back in the 1920s when it was sported by popular motion picture actresses like Clara Bow and Louise Brooks. It still looked good on Susie Yang.

Apparently Jeff had described me to his sister as well, because as I walked up she smiled and said, "You must be Mister Spicer."

"I am, and I'm betting you're Susie Yang. Please call me Johnny."

I shook the dainty hand she offered, and the firmness of her grip surprised me. Clearly Miss Yang was a thoroughly modern American woman who made no bones about the fact. She said, "Okay, Johnny. Jeff said you had some questions about Sun Ling."

"That's right. Is there someplace quiet around here where we can sit and talk?"

"Sure, there's a nice little spot over by the water. I'll show you."

I followed Susie around a small lake just north of the Pagoda Tower. We crossed over a steeply arched bridge and sat on a bench under a small grove of trees next to the lake. A scaled-down san-pan with bright red sails and delicate carvings drifted by no more than twenty feet away.

Leaning back on the bench, I said, "Susie, thank you for giving me your time this afternoon. I know it's already been a busy day for you."

She turned to look at me, saying, "I am more than willing to give up the time if it will help you find out what's happened to Sun Ling. I take it there is no news of her yet."

Susie Yang's voice was higher pitched than most and had an almost bell-like quality to it that put me in mind of the wind chimes someone hung in the forecourt of my apartment complex down in Hollywood. I said, "Nothing positive. Jeff found out that all six of her bodyguards left for China this morning on the Pan American Clipper. I'm not sure what that means other than it leaves me the only one actively looking for Sun Ling."

She cocked her head and frowned. "That does seem odd. I would have expected them to continue searching for her. After all, they were the ones responsible for Sun Ling's safety."

I gave her a nod of agreement and moved on to my questions. "Tell me, Susie, what are your impressions of Sun Ling? How would you describe her?"

Susie hesitated only a moment. "Sun Ling is a wonderful person. She is intelligent, well educated, and as I'm sure my brother told you, she is very beautiful."

I smiled. "Yes, he did mention that. Have you had much opportunity to talk with her personally?"

"We have talked, but not a lot. Except during her daily appearances here in the village, Sun Ling seems . . . withdrawn, or maybe distracted is a better word. I suppose that is to be expected, though. She is in a strange land many miles across the Pacific Ocean from her home, and I'm sure she is concerned about her friends and family in China, what with the Japanese threat and all."

I said, "I'm sure that must be part of it. If you don't mind me asking, on those occasions when you did speak with Sun Ling, what did you talk about?"

She laughed a tinkling laugh. "I'm afraid it was just girl talk. She is fascinated by the American culture and has many questions about what it is like to live here as a Chinese-American."

"What sort of questions?"

"Well, Sun Ling wanted to know how Americans feel about those of Chinese descent who live here. Are we accepted? How are we treated? Things of that nature. She also asked about popular fashions and the best stores in which to shop. As I said, we mostly talked about girl things."

Smiling, I said, "I guess women really are the same the world over."

"As are men," she promptly added. "The fact that Sun Ling is from the other side of our planet doesn't keep my brother from having a crush on her. Unfortunately for Jeff, Sun Ling is all business with no interest in romantic nonsense."

I paused a moment to review my notes. Other than the subjects Susie and Sun Ling talked about during a few conversations, I had nothing new so far.

"Can you tell me how Sun Ling felt about her bodyguards? Was she friendly toward them or did she seem to resent having them around?"

"She was neither friendly nor unfriendly toward them. Like her, they were here to do a job, and she seemed to accept that, although I can't imagine she enjoyed the lack of privacy."

"I understand you play a role in Sun Ling's appearances in the village."

"Yes, I act as one of her handmaidens. It's really kind of fun to get all dressed up in those beautiful costumes and observe the old customs. I enjoy it."

"I'd like you to think about her appearance last Sunday, the night she disappeared. Do you recall anything at all unusual happening that night?"

Susie stared out over the lake as if she was mentally replaying the events of that Sunday evening. Finally, she turned back to me and said, "I really can't think of anything. The crowds in the village might have been a little larger than usual, and she was kept quite busy answering their questions, but that's probably not what you're looking for."

"Truthfully, Susie, I don't know what I'm looking for. I'm just trying to put myself here that night through your recollections. Would you mind going through the last part of the evening step by step?"

"Well, because of the larger crowds, we might have been a little later than usual leaving the booth, but not by more than a few minutes. Afterwards, we walked to the dressing rooms just as we always do."

"Who, exactly, walked to the dressing rooms?"

"Besides Sun Ling, there were the two boys who portray warriors and me and Annie Lee, she plays the other handmaiden. And, of course, one of Sun Ling's bodyguards."

"What about Jeff?"

"Oh, he always stays behind to draw the curtains in Sun Ling's booth and turn out the lights. Jeff follows along a few minutes later."

So far, Susie's description of the night's events jibed perfectly with the account Jeff gave me earlier. I continued in the same vain just to be sure Jeff hadn't missed anything. "You said just one of Sun Ling's bodyguards accompanied you back to the dressing rooms. Didn't they work in pairs?"

"Yes, usually they did, but when we finished our nightly appearances, one of the bodyguards went to bring Sun Ling's car closer so she didn't have to walk so far in the cold. The other bodyguard stayed with her."

"Okay, got it. Now, Jeff said the front doors to the dressing room building are kept locked. If Jeff stayed behind, who let you into the dressing room building?"

"Oh, Sun Ling's bodyguards had a key to the building."

"I see. There are three sets of doors on the village side of the dressing room building. Which set did you use Sunday night?

"The green ones at this end of the building. We always use them because they are closest to Sun Ling's booth."

"What about the doors to the dressing rooms? Did Sun Ling's bodyguards have a key to them as well?"

"No, I don't think so. Jeff always left those doors unlocked so we could get in. Then he locked the dressing rooms after we left."

"Alright, now I have the picture. What happened Sunday night once you were inside the dressing room building?"

"We went to the dressing rooms and changed back into our street clothes."

"How many dressing rooms are there, and which ones do you use?"

Susie gave me a little frown and asked, "Didn't Jeff tell you all of this?"

"Most of it. I just want to be sure I have all the facts straight and that Jeff didn't forget any little details that might be important."

She nodded her understanding, but Susie's expression said she knew what I was up to. "There are three dressing rooms—Sun Ling's plus one for male performers and one for the women. The men's dressing room is the first one you come to at this end of the building, and then comes the women's dressing room. Sun Ling's is the third dressing room down the hall."

"Did you actually see Sun Ling go into her dressing room?"

"Oh, yes. We stopped outside the boys' dressing room, and while Annie and I said goodnight to them—Annie sort of likes one of the boys—I watched Sun Ling go into her dressing room, and I saw the bodyguard close the door behind her. Then Annie and I went into our dressing room and changed."

We were now at the critical part of the evening, the part when Sun Ling disappeared, so I asked every question I could come up with in the hope of triggering some memory Susie might not otherwise think of. I said, "So you and Annie were in the dressing room right next to Sun Ling's. Is that right?"

"Yes."

"And with those thin walls, you would have heard any unusual noises from her room?"

Susie shook her head. "Not necessarily. There is always a lot of noise from the Gayway right behind the dressing rooms. For us to hear anything from Sun Ling's dressing room over that racket, it would have to be pretty loud."

"So did you hear any unusual noises while you were changing that night?"

"Not that I remember."

"Alright, what happened next?"

"Annie and I changed and went back out into the hall. The boys were already there. They always finish changing first because their costumes aren't as complicated as ours and they don't have a lot of makeup to remove.

"Jeff was also there by then, and he walked with us to the dressing room building doors—the green ones again—and let us out."

That was a little detail Jeff failed to mention. It meant he wasn't outside Sun Ling's dressing room the entire time she was supposed to be changing. And that might be significant. I said, "So Sun Ling was still changing when you and Annie left your dressing room?"

"I guess so. Her bodyguard was still in the hall, so that would mean Sun Ling was still in her dressing room. There's nothing unusual about that, though. Sun Ling's costume has more parts, like her headdress and so on, so it takes her longer to change."

"What time do you think you left your dressing room?"

"Gee, I'm not sure. It usually takes us about twenty minutes or so to change, so it must have been around nine-thirty or a little after."

"What did you do then?"

"Well, after Jeff let us out of the building, Annie and I said goodnight to the boys and walked to the parking lot where my car was. I always pick Annie up and we ride to Treasure Island together. Then I drop her off at home after."

"And that's what you did Sunday night?"

"Yes, I dropped Annie off at her parents' home on Mason Street up in North Beach, then I drove home to my apartment above my father's restaurant on Stockton, and I went to bed."

"Did anything else happen after that on Sunday night?"

"Yes . . . well, it was after midnight, so I guess it was technically Monday morning by then. Jeff woke me up, knocking on my door. He told me about Sun Ling's disappearance, and we talked about it for a few minutes. He asked me some of the same questions you asked—if anything unusual had happened during Sun Ling's appearance in the village and questions like that.

"Then Jeff went to his apartment and I went back to bed. It took me a while to get to sleep again, though, because I was worried about Sun Ling."

As I added notes to my notebook, I noticed Susie pulling her jacket tighter around her and folding her arms as if she was cold. It wasn't until then that I realized a stiff breeze had come up. The wind was cold and strong enough to raise ripples on the lake. I said, "Okay, Susie, that's enough questions for now. Let's go wait for Jeff in the administration building where we can get warm. It's after three, so he should be showing up pretty soon."

She nodded eager agreement and we hiked back over the bridge. That's when Jeff met us on the path, saying, "There you guys are! I've been looking all over for you!"

Shaking Jeff's hand, I said, "Susie found us a quiet, out-of-the-way place to talk back there. We were just on our way to your office to wait for you."

Jeff said, "Swell. Did you get all the answers you needed from my observant sister here?"

Nodding, I said, "I sure did. Susie's been very helpful in spite of nearly freezing to death out here."

Susie smiled and Jeff said, "Good. What's next?"

"Well, if Susie doesn't mind, I would like her to join us for another look at the dressing room building."

Susie chimed in with her tinkling voice and said, "I don't mind at all. At least we'll be out of this wind!"

NINE

This time we entered the dressing room building through the northernmost of its three facades—the same route into the building Susie said Sun Ling and her party used Sunday night. Beyond the pair of vibrant jade green doors decorated with intricately carved blossoms, however, the building layout was the same as I'd seen when Jeff took me through the red doors at the other end of building that morning.

Carpeted plywood panels bridged the exposed floor joists to the north-south walkway that ran the length of the building and provided access to the dressing rooms. The biggest difference I noticed now was the noise level. The Gayway racket was much more apparent than it had been earlier in the day. The music, barkers' shouts, and crowd noises were easily loud enough to drown out all but the loudest sounds from within the building.

At the north-south walkway I turned left and went about fifteen feet to the north end of the building where the walkway turned right and ended at a sturdy door in the wall surrounding the Chinese Village. This door looked identical to the one Jeff and I used at the other end of the building on our way to the Gayway doughnut shop.

Turning to Jeff, I said, "Does this door open onto the Gayway like the one at the other end of the building?"

"Sure does. Want me to open it?"

"No, I'll take your word for it."

I walked back to the first of five interior doors opening off the north-south walkway and stood there for a moment studying the spider web of studs and beams that filled the vast open spaces opposite and above the dressing room walls.

Finally, Jeff's curiosity got the better of him. "What are we looking for, Johnny?"

"Some clue as to how Sun Ling disappeared from a room with no windows and only one door—a door that was closely watched by her bodyguard."

Jeff added, "And me, too."

I looked at Jeff and said, "Yes, and you, too, part of the time. This morning you forgot to tell me you left the door to Sun Ling's dressing room while you let Susie and the other performers out of the building."

"Yeah, but I could see across the open part of the building the whole time, except for maybe fifteen or twenty seconds while I was on the other side of the entrance curtain opening the outside door. That wasn't long enough for anything to happen!"

Susie quickly added, "That's true, Johnny. We would have noticed if anyone went in or out of Sun Ling's dressing room."

I held up my hands as if fending them off and said, "Simmer down, kids; I'm not accusing Jeff of anything. I'm just pointing out how easy it is to forget little details that could make a big difference."

Jeff still looked a little hurt. He said, "Yes, I forgot that part, but . . . ."

I interrupted him, eager to get back to the question at hand. "We know from Susie that Sun Ling actually entered the dressing room. Susie's friend, Annie, and the two boy-warriors probably saw that, too. We also know Sun Ling wasn't in her dressing room a short time later when the bodyguard broke down the door. So how was she taken from the room? There are only a few ways it could have been done.

"One possibility is that Sun Ling was kidnapped between the time Susie and Annie Lee went into their dressing room and the time you arrived after closing up Sun Ling's booth. For that explanation to fit, though, the bodyguard would have had to leave the door unguarded . . . ."

Susie interrupted to tell me why that possibility didn't hold water. "It couldn't have happened that way because Sun Ling's costume is on the clothes rack. She changed before she was taken, and she couldn't have gotten out of her costume and into her street clothes in that short time."

Looking at Susie, Jeff quickly chimed in, "Say, that's right, Sis! Sun Ling couldn't have been in her dressing room for more than six or seven minutes by the time I got here." Turning to me, he added, "You can definitely cross that possibility off your list, Johnny."

I nodded. "Okay, let's assume for a minute there was no time when the door to Sun Ling's dressing room wasn't being watched by you and the bodyguard after she changed her clothes. That means there must be another way out of the room."

Jeff said, "Yeah, but the bodyguard went over Sun Ling's dressing room with a fine-toothed comb and didn't find bupkis."

"True, but you're overlooking one angle on the secret door possibility." From the corner of my eye I saw Susie nod knowingly. I said, "Susie, would you care to enlighten your brother?"

She grinned and in an exaggerated impersonation of Charlie Chan said, "Number One Son not brightest star in heavens." Jeff gave her a sour look, but Susie continued, "What if the bodyguards were in on Sun Ling's kidnapping? If they were, it isn't likely they would give away the secret to how she was taken by finding a hidden door or whatever they used to get Sun Ling out of her dressing room."

I could almost see the light bulb go on over Jeff's head. "Yes! And if the bodyguards were in on the snatch, it would explain why they took it on the lam back to China this morning."

He might have been right about that, except they left without Sun Ling. Why would they go to all the trouble of kidnapping her and then leave her behind? Besides, all six bodyguards would have had to be in on the deal, and that seemed unlikely. Everything I'd heard about them indicated they were all loyal to the Chinese government. And for that matter, what possible reason would the bodyguards have for kidnapping her in the first place? If the Chinese government wanted Sun Ling back in China, all they had to do was say so and she'd have been on the next boat or plane home. No, unless I was missing a big piece of the puzzle, the idea that Sun Ling's bodyguards had anything to do with her disappearance just didn't fit.

I said, "We can figure out the who part of this later. Right now we need to find out if there really is a another way out of the dressing room. Let's start with this room," I gestured toward the closest door, "And work our way down to the other end of the building. If there's anything to find, it will be somewhere between here and there."

Jeff fished the key ring out of his pocket and opened the first door, saying, "This is just a storeroom."

Stepping into the room, he turned a switch mounted on the wall to the right of the door, illuminating a bare light bulb hung from the ceiling by its cord. The room looked to be about sixteen feet long by eight feet wide with the walls, floor and ceiling covered by sheets of bare plywood. It occurred to me that the plywood franchise for this building alone would have been quite lucrative.

The perimeter of the room was stacked with cardboard boxes. A rolling clothes rack with colorful costumes was also in the room, and I remembered Jeff saying he'd moved Sun Ling's costumes into a storeroom because he couldn't lock the busted door to her dressing room.

Walking over to the clothes rack, I said, "Susie, which of these costumes did Sun Ling wear Sunday night?"

She pointed to an elaborate white silk gown trimmed in pale sea green. "This haufu. As you can see, it consists of several layers, all of which must be removed with great care so as not to tear the silk."

It was quite a get-up with enough delicately stitched designs and patterns to keep a roomful of seamstresses busy for months. "Susie, take a good, close look at the costume and see if you can find anything different or out of the ordinary about it."

While she examined the costume, I went around the room poking into the cardboard boxes. Several of them contained stacks of exposition guidebooks like the one Jeff gave me earlier. The rest of the boxes were filled with inexpensive trinkets of the sort fairgoers purchase as souvenirs—stuff like hand-painted fans, miniature plaster dragons, and little wooden models of san-pans.

I said, "Jeff, do the village concessionaires use this room for storage?"

He saw why I'd asked the question right away and said, "No. The things in those boxes are souvenirs we give to special visitors and prizes for little contests we put on once in a while."

Finding nothing else of interest in the remaining cardboard boxes, I began an inspection of the plywood walls, floor, and ceiling. The floor simply consisted of four-by-eight panels nailed to the floor joists. The walls were pretty much the same deal—plywood sheets nailed to studs. Like the floor, the walls appeared to be solidly built with no unusual gaps or other indications they might be concealing something.

The edges of two-by-four headers were just visible above the tops of the plywood wall panels. The four four-by-eight plywood sheets forming the ceiling were arranged in two rows of two aligned so their eight-foot lengths paralleled the length of the room. While I couldn't actually see how the ceiling panels were held in place, I figured they were nailed to the tops of the wall headers and to the top of an eight-foot two-by-four stringer spanning the width of the room at its center. The stringer was simply toe-nailed into the wall headers. The design was crude, but the ceiling appeared to be just as solid as the walls and floor.

Behind me, Susie said, "Johnny, I don't see anything out of the ordinary about Sun Ling's costume. There are a couple of places where the hand-stitching is coming undone, but that is probably just normal wear."

"Okay," I said, "Let's move on."

Jeff opened the next door along the north-south walkway and turned on the light to reveal the first of the three dressing rooms. It was the same width as the storeroom, but not quite as long, and the plywood walls and ceiling were painted white. Also, the plywood floor was covered with the same inexpensive carpeting used outside on the open hallway. I guessed the carpet was there to prevent wood splinters in the event users of the room were barefoot.

A built-in counter ran the length of the room against the back wall opposite the door. Three identical mirrors were hung at equal intervals on the wall above the counter, and a wooden chair was positioned opposite each mirror. A small sink like the one in Sun Ling's dressing room was installed on the wall to my right next to the end of the counter. The only other items in the room were a pair of portable clothes racks pushed up against the wall to my left. They were crowded with more costumes. Pointing to the racks, I asked, "Who wears that stuff?"

Susie said, "This is the dressing room used by the men who wear costumes in the village, like the boys who portray the warriors in Sun Ling's procession." She added, "This is the same as the women's dressing room, except it's reversed. The sink in our room is on the left and the clothes racks are against the right wall."

By this time Jeff had gotten into the spirit of our search. He was thumping walls with his knuckles and stomping on the floor enthusiastically, apparently in the hope of finding a mysterious secret passage. I let him go at it even though I was pretty certain there would be nothing to find until we got to Sun Ling's dressing room. Mainly, I wanted to study the construction of these rooms. I figured knowing how they were built would help me spot anything that might be different about the room Sun Ling used.

The most noticeable construction difference between the men's dressing room and the storage room we'd just come from was the ceiling. Being shorter in length than the storage area, this room's plywood ceiling panels were arranged differently. There were only three of them—two aligned side-by-side with their lengths paralleling the long direction of the room and one spanning its width. That made the dimensions of the room roughly twelve feet long and eight feet wide.

Like the storeroom, this room had a two-by-four stringer spanning its width to help support the ceiling. In here, however, the stringer crossed the room under the point where the two longitudinal panels butted their ends against the long edge of the third panel. This put the stringer slightly to the left of the door, which was centered in the room's west wall.

Noticing the sink put me in mind of another question. I said, "I haven't seen any restroom facilities in this building. Are there any?"

Jeff said, "No. If the actors need a restroom, they use the public ones out in the village or the facilities in our office building."

"Okay, let's take a look at the next room."

We traipsed back out into the open hallway and Jeff opened up the second dressing room. Just as Susie said, it was identical to the first dressing room except everything was reversed. I asked Susie, "This is the room you and Annie use, is that right?"

Susie nodded and Jeff began his wall-thumping/floor-stomping routine again. He looked a little disappointed when I interrupted him before he finished the first wall. I'd seen all I needed to see in that room, so I said, "Alright, let's get on to Sun Ling's dressing room."

The broken door to the third dressing room was ajar, so I pushed it open and walked in while Jeff locked the room we'd just left. Sun Ling's dressing room was still a mess—the floor littered with debris from the bodyguards' frantic search for their charge. Aside from the overturned furniture and the pulled-up carpet, the most obvious difference in Sun Ling's room was that curtains had been hung over the walls to give the place a more finished look.

I said, "Susie, please take a look around in here and see if you can find anything that should be here, but isn't, or anything that is here, but shouldn't be."

While she began looking through the loose items on the floor, most of which appeared to be from Sun Ling's dressing table, I put Jeff to work pushing the curtains aside to examine the walls. I kept an eye on his progress, but figuring the walls were too thin to conceal anything in the way of a secret passage, I focused on the floor and ceiling.

Stepping over and around the mess on the floor, I was crossing the room toward its center for a better view when I felt a momentary coolness on the back of my neck—a whisper of a breeze I'd not encountered in the other rooms. I stopped, but it was gone. I took a step back. Nothing. I turned completely around. Still nothing. I stepped to the left, to the right, and forward again with no results.

Had I imagined the sensation? I didn't think so. I slowly retraced my steps one more time. To Susie and Jeff it must have looked like I was dancing the foxtrot. Jeff said, "Find something, Johnny?"

Ignoring his question for a moment, I thought about what a breeze in this room meant. Given the slapdash construction of the unfinished building, there could very well be air leaks allowing the strong, chilly wind outside to get inside. And the broken door to the dressing room was standing wide open, so any breezes that got into the building could easily enter the room from that direction. The significant point, however, was that for air to move through the room, there had to be another opening—a way for air to leave the room.

Looking up, I spotted a difference between the construction of this room and the other dressing rooms. Instead of using one four-by-eight sheet of plywood across the width of the room at its north end, the builder had used two four-by-four panels. Why?

Had the contractor run out of four-by-eight plywood sheets and simply used what was at hand to finish the ceiling? Maybe. I stepped over for a closer look at the seam between the two four-by-four panels. They appeared to fit together snugly with no noticeable gap, but I wanted to make sure.

Pulling a Lucky Strike from the pack in my shirt pocket, I lit it and blew the smoke upward toward the ceiling. After my third puff I saw it. The smoke was slowly being drawn through the seam between the two smaller panels. That made sense because the edges of all the other plywood sheets were nailed down to the wall headers or to the supporting stringer beam, which pretty well blocked any air movement, but there was no support under the seam between the two smaller panels. Again, why?

I stubbed out my cigarette and picked up the wooden dressing table chair. Positioning it under the seam in question, I clambered up so I could reach the panels on either side. I pushed up against the plywood sheet closest to the door. It was rock solid. Then I pushed on the other panel, and it moved—only a quarter of an inch, or so, but the entire panel definitely moved! I tried pushing harder and got the same result. The plywood couldn't be nailed down along any of its edges and still move like that. Realizing I'd found the anomaly I was looking for, my pulse picked up a beat or two.

My excitement was apparently contagious because I heard Jeff ask excitedly, "Is that it? Is that the secret door?"

Stepping down from the chair, I said, "I'm not sure. If it is, something's keeping it from opening."

I walked out to the open hallway and looked up. With no second story flooring, the space above the dressing rooms was wide open. If I could get up there, it would be easy to climb on top of the ceiling for a look at the moving panel from the other side.

"Jeff, is there a ladder around here somewhere?"

"Yeah, there should be one in the storeroom next door. Want me to get it?"

"Yes, and a flashlight, if you can find one."

Jeff jogged over to the last door along the open hallway, unlocked it, and disappeared inside. Susie had followed us out of the dressing room and was looking up at the space above it as I had. In a quiet voice, she asked, "Do you think they took Sun Ling out through the ceiling?"

"It's a possibility."

"I don't know if it means anything, but there are two items that should be in Sun Ling's dressing room that aren't there."

I looked at her. "What items?"

"Cold cream and facial tissues. We use cold cream to remove our theatrical makeup, and there should be a big bottle of it, along with a box of tissues, in Sun Ling's dressing room, but I didn't see them. I even looked under the rolled-up carpet. They aren't there."

I thought about that for a moment and then asked, "Do you take off your makeup before getting out of your costume or after?"

"Annie and I always do it after. I imagine Sun Ling did it that way, too."

I was pondering the significance of a missing bottle of cold cream when Jeff returned with an eight-foot folding ladder. We set it up on the hall floor just outside the door to Sun Ling's dressing room, and I was about to start climbing when Jeff held up a white candle. "I couldn't find a flashlight. Will this do?"

"It will do just fine. Good thinking."

At the top of the ladder, I swung myself over to the top of the dressing room wall and lit my candle. Figuring the thin ceiling panels wouldn't support my weight, I found the line of nails where the plywood was nailed to the support stringer and followed them out to the center of the ceiling on my hands and knees. By the time I got there, I was certain I'd found what I was looking for.

The first thing I noticed was a simple, wooden ladder lying diagonally across the four-by-eight ceiling panel to my right. It looked to be about nine or ten feet in length—just long enough to reach the floor of the dressing room.

Next I examined the suspicious four-by-four panel. It was hung from the north end by a pair of sturdy spring-loaded hinges of the type used on self-closing doors. The edge at the south end rested on the ceiling support stringer. The trapdoor was secured by the simple expedient of two wooden pegs pushed into holes in the south end of the two-by-fours framing the opening. The pegs were what kept the trapdoor from moving more than a quarter of an inch when I pushed on it from the dressing room side.

Judging by the craftsmanship, the trapdoor was installed by someone who knew what he was doing—a carpenter or a cabinet maker. Finding out who installed it was now a high priority because that piece of information would ultimately point to Sun Ling's kidnappers.

I pulled the wooden pegs out of their holes and the trapdoor practically opened itself because it was pulled up by the spring-loaded hinges. I pushed it all the way open and looked down into Sun Ling's dressing room. Through the opening I hollered, "Jeff, bring that ladder into the dressing room."

With Susie carrying one end of the ladder and Jeff the other, they appeared below me, looking up through the opening with surprised expressions. Jeff set the ladder below the trapdoor and climbed on up to join me. Poking his head into the open space above the ceiling, Jeff said, "Well, I'll be a monkey's uncle! No wonder Sun Ling disappeared without a trace! But who put this trapdoor in here, and how did they get Sun Ling out of the building?"

"Finding out who installed the trapdoor is our next step. As for how they got her out of the building, the simplest way would have been to walk along the edges of the ceiling panels over there next to the back wall until they got to one end or the other of the building. From there they could drop down into the short hallway and leave the building through one of the doors in the outer village wall.

"They could have done that as soon as they secured the trapdoor, but it's more likely they waited up here on the ceiling until the bodyguards gave up the search for Sun Ling and left the building. Either way . . . ."

"But how did they get through the door into the Gayway? The doors at both ends of the building are locked, and only a few of us have keys."

I was holding the candle up to shed some light on what I figured to be the escape route when I noticed something in the shadows I hadn't seen before.

I said, "How they got through the outer door to the Gayway is another question we need to answer. Jeff, climb down and send your sister up the ladder for a minute."

While reluctant to leave the scene of the crime, Jeff did as I asked. A minute later, when Susie's head popped through the opening, I held the candle up again and pointed to the items I'd spotted in the shadows. They were on the next ceiling panel to the north and consisted of a white glass jar and a cardboard box of tissues with a wad of used tissues next to it. "Is that the stuff you said was missing from Sun Ling's dressing room?"

She peered into the darkness and said, "It looks like it. That's definitely a cold cream jar. What's it doing up here?"

That was a darned good question. I added it to my list of darned good questions and followed Susie down the ladder into Sun Ling's dressing room. I was feeling pretty pleased with myself for finding the trapdoor Sun Ling's bodyguards had missed. It was time to show my employer what an excellent choice he'd made in putting Johnny Spicer on the case.

TEN

Jeff Yang's cubbyhole of an office was crowded to overflowing with three of us in there. I sat at Jeff's desk to use the telephone and Susie settled into the guest chair, which left Jeff perched on the corner of his desk. It was cozy to say the least.

When the long distance operator had performed all the necessary gyrations to connect my collect, person-to-person call to Liang Chao, I said, "Good afternoon, Mister Liang. I have some news to report about Sun Ling's disappearance."

"Excellent. Please proceed with your report."

"I spent most of today with Jeff Yang and his sister, Susie, and before I go any further, I want to say that Jeff and Susie have been very cooperative. We made some headway today that would not have been possible without their help."

I winked at Jeff as I sang his and his sister's praises to Liang. Jeff was grinning from ear to ear, and I thought I saw a slight smile cross Susie's lips. Liang said nothing, so I got on with my report.

"The last time Sun Ling was seen Sunday night was when she entered her dressing room after completing her last performance of the day in the village. One of her bodyguards and Jeff Yang waited for her just outside the door. Are you familiar with the building that houses the dressing rooms?"

"Yes, I am familiar with the building."

"Good. Then you know it is unfinished inside and that the dressing and storage rooms are constructed of plywood along the back wall of the building. The dressing rooms each have one door and no windows, so with Sun Ling's dressing room door being watched by her bodyguard, my first problem was to determine how she was taken without being seen.

"After a thorough examination of the dressing room I have the answer to that mystery. One of the plywood ceiling panels is hinged so it can be opened, and in the empty space above the dressing room I found evidence that Sun Ling was taken from the dressing room through that opening in the ceiling."

I paused to give Liang an opportunity to respond to this news. After a moment's silence, he simply said, "I see."

When the enthusiastic praise I was expecting for my brilliant detecting wasn't forthcoming, I mentally shrugged and continued. "From there it was a relatively simple matter for Sun Ling's abductors to take her from the building through one of the two doors that open out onto the carnival area behind the village. So the next step is to find out who turned the ceiling panel into a trapdoor and when they did it. The answers to those questions should put us hot on the trail of the kidnappers."

"Yes, that would seem to be the most logical way to proceed. Do you have any other developments to report?"

"Yes, a couple of items. Around midday I had some time to kill, so I used it to familiarize myself with the exposition grounds. While doing that I picked up a tail. When I got a good look at the guy following me, I recognized him as one of the two men I saw leaving Tang Fan's warehouse last night.

"When he realized I was on to him, the fellow beat a hasty retreat directly to the Japanese Pavilion. I took advantage of the situation to trade the killer's whereabouts for some information from the homicide detective investigating Tang Fan's murder. What I learned from him was that according to Tang's son, Sun Ling's disappearance had nothing to do with the murder. Since the cop wasn't willing to give me anything further, I plan to see Tang Hong tomorrow morning to get the rest of the story. Would you please call him and clear the way for me to interview him?"

The pause that followed my question was long enough to make me wonder if the connection had gone dead. Finally Liang said, "Is such an interview necessary? If Tang Fan's death is not connected to Sun Ling, interviewing Tang Hong would seem to be a waste of valuable time."

"Mister Liang, I only have the homicide detective's word for that. It's always a good idea to verify these things. More important to me, Tang Fan's killers obviously know I witnessed their getaway, and they somehow knew I could be found at the Chinese Village. That makes finding out more about them a matter of self-preservation."

The pause was just a little shorter this time, but not much. Even though it made no particular sense, Liang obviously had some reservations about my looking further into Tang Fan's murder. Finally, he said, "Alright, Mister Spicer, I will place a telephone call to Tang Hong. When do you expect to visit him?"

"First thing tomorrow morning, say about eight o'clock."

"Very well. I'll make the necessary arrangements. Does that conclude your report?"

I'd saved the most bewildering piece of news for last, and now it was time to spring it on Liang. "Not quite. I have one more rather surprising item to report. Are you aware that all six of Sun Ling's bodyguards left for home this morning aboard Pan American Airways' China Clipper?"

That bit of news generated the longest pause of our conversation. When Liang spoke again, I got the definite impression he wasn't being entirely honest with me. Liang's prevarication skills were clearly in need of some polishing.

"No, Mister Spicer, I was not aware of that fact. I do not see, however, the departure of Sun Ling's bodyguards as being of particular importance at this time."

"I disagree, Mister Liang. I think the departure of the bodyguards is very important. After spending Sunday night and Monday looking for Sun Ling, they have suddenly departed the country by the fastest and most expensive means available to them. I take their abrupt departure as an indication something about this case changed within the past twenty-four hours. Whatever that change might be could have a definite bearing on our investigation. You need to call on your contacts within the Chinese government to find out what's going on."

Liang was quicker on the uptake this time, but again, the ring of truth was lacking from his words. "Alright, Mister Spicer, if you insist, I will make some inquiries. Please understand, however, those inquiries may take some time."

On that note we ended the conversation, and I sat back in Jeff's chair for a moment to fix Liang Chao's words in my mind. Something was definitely rotten in Denmark . . . or to be more accurate, in China.

Jeff and Susie were watching me, apparently waiting for some comment on the telephone conversation I'd just completed. My bafflement over Liang's attitude must have shown in my expression because Jeff said, "Something wrong, Johnny?"

I looked up and replied, "Probably not. I was just thinking things over." Then changing the subject, I added, "We need to find out who gimmicked that ceiling panel in Sun Ling's dressing room. When I got here this morning there were a couple of carpenters building a platform of some kind out in the village. Have there been any projects like that in or around the dressing rooms since the exposition opened?"

"Oh, you mean like projects that would have given somebody the chance to build that trapdoor on the sly?"

"Yeah, that's what I'm getting at."

"Well, not that I know of, but you gotta remember I'm not here all the time. I'm mostly only around in the afternoons and evenings when Sun Ling is scheduled to be here, so if the guys who built the trapdoor were here in the morning, I might not have seen them."

Susie said, "How do you know the trapdoor wasn't put in when the dressing rooms were built?"

"I don't know that, but for the trapdoor to have been installed as part of the original construction, it would mean the scheme to kidnap Sun Ling was planned well before the exposition opened. Jeff, do you have any idea when it was decided that Sun Ling would be coming here?"

Jeff thought about my question for a while. Finally, he said, "I can't say exactly, but I first heard about Sun Ling appearing at the exposition from my father when he took sick and asked me to fill in for him as Sun Ling's official escort, and that was back before last Christmas."

"So, assuming construction on the dressing room building wasn't complete by that time, I guess it's possible the trapdoor was installed when the building was built."

Jeff said, "The dressing room building wasn't even started back then. I know that because I came out here a few times to see how the village construction was coming."

While I was still thinking it more likely that the trapdoor was an addition rather than part of the original construction, I figured it wouldn't hurt to find out for sure. "Jeff, can you find out the name of the contractor who built the dressing room building?"

"Sure! Give me about five minutes."

With that, Jeff jumped up and left his office. I looked over at Susie and saw her looking back at me with a curious expression on her face. She didn't look away when our eyes met. I said, "Susie, you look puzzled. What's on your mind?"

Without hesitation her tinkling voice said, "I was just revising my opinion of you."

"Oh? In a positive way, I hope."

"I think so."

"Would you care to share your new opinion of me?"

Susie thought about that for a moment as if she was looking for the right words to explain what she was thinking. "Mister Spicer . . . Johnny . . . I think on the one hand you are a very shrewd operator, and on the other hand you are an essentially honest man. I think in the course of your work those qualities sometimes come into conflict, and I think this is one of those times."

Her comment took me by surprise because it seemed out of character for her to speak so frankly to a relative stranger. Apparently my opinion of her needed some revision also. I said, "Forgive me, but that seems like an odd thing for you to say. What sort of conflict do you think I'm in?"

Without hesitation or any beating around the bush Susie said softly, "Mister Liang just lied to you and you are wondering why, but you don't want us to know he lied."

Susie was just full of surprises. I had no idea how she came to that conclusion, and I had even less of an idea about how to respond.

It seemed Susie sensed what I was thinking and said, "That's alright, Johnny. You don't need to say anything. It was forward of me to express my thoughts. I only did so because I want you to know where my brother and I stand in this situation."

"I see. And where do you and Jeff stand?"

Her dark eyes showed no hint of deception as she said, "We owe no special allegiance to Mister Liang, so you needn't be concerned about what we might carry back to him. Speaking for myself, my only interest is in helping you find Sun Ling. Even in the short time since we met, I have come to believe that, if anyone can find Sun Ling, you can. That belief has earned you my full confidence and support."

While I thought Susie, in all her youthful idealism, was being somewhat overly dramatic, I had no doubt of her sincerity. "Thank you, Susie. I appreciate your confidence in me. I'll do my best to keep earning it."

Another hint of a smile crossed her lips, and she said, "I believe you will."

A moment later Jeff bustled back into the room with a roll of blueprints in one hand and a piece of notepaper in the other. He laid the blueprints on his desk, and reading from the paper in his hand, he said, "The contractor who built the dressing room building is Pedderson Constructors, owned by a guy named Arthur Pedderson. He's down the Peninsula in San Bruno."

I said, "Did this guy Pedderson build all of the buildings in the village or just that one?"

"Just that one. The way I understand how it all happened, Mister Jue and the other guys who raised the money for the Chinese exhibit got a late start, and things were getting down to the wire when they actually started building the village. They weren't sure everything would be finished before the exposition opened, so they hired more contractors to work on different parts of the village at the same time. This guy Pedderson was one of the extra contractors they hired."

Gesturing toward the roll of blueprints on his desk, Jeff continued, "I brought the plans for the building with me, but they show it as it was originally designed, with exhibits and storage on the first floor and the dressing rooms and some offices on the second floor. The plans won't be much help, though, because none of that stuff ever got built."

Frowning, I asked, "How come?"

"I don't know if they ran out of time or money or both, but Pop told me the storage rooms and dressing rooms were moved to the ground floor and thrown up at the last minute so there'd be places to lock stuff up and so volunteer actors would have a place to change. Anyway, here's Pedderson's address and phone number."

I took the note and slipped it into my inside jacket pocket. As I did that, Jeff exclaimed, "I don't know about you two, but I'm starving. Let's go over to Wing's and put on the feedbag."

ELEVEN

Compared with my previous exposition culinary experiences earlier in the day, the Chinese Village's Wing Restaurant was a pleasant surprise. Softly lit by paper lanterns and accompanied by quiet strains of what I imagined was traditional Chinese music, the ambiance of tasteful wall hangings, statuary, and large ceramic vases became an oasis of classy tranquility at the center of carnival-like festivities designed to maximize thrills and excitement.

The tables were set with good quality, glazed ceramic rice bowls, soup spoons, small plates, condiment dishes, and teacups, along with paper sleeves containing disposable wooden chopsticks. Overall, I felt quite comfortable there except when it came to the menu. What I know about Chinese food would easily fit in a fortune cookie with plenty of room left over. That being the case, I relied on sage advice from Susie and Jeff for selecting my dinner.

Susie, for example, assured me that Wing's menu items were all authentic Szechuan dishes, although the spices were somewhat tamed down to better suit western tastes. While I recognized some of the choices—Kung Pao chicken, twice-cooked pork, and deep-fried chicken—from patronizing the China Takee Home joint back home, there were many dishes I hadn't encountered before, like tea-smoked duck and something called Fuqi Feipian. Jeff gleefully explained that the latter was cold beef tripe and assured me it was quite tasty if one went in for that sort of thing.

I finally settled on the twice-cooked pork, and having cleared the menu hurdle, I directed the conversation back to the mysterious disappearance of one Miss Sun Ling. The most pressing question on my mind at that point concerned the key Sun Ling's abductors would have needed to escape into the Gayway through one of the dressing room/storage building's back doors.

Turning to Jeff, I asked, "Do both back doors out of the dressing room building use the same key?"

"Yeah, the same key works in both locks."

"Does that key open any other doors in the village?"

"I don't think so, but it's hard to say for sure. Things were so crazy at the end right before the exposition opened, anything is possible."

That wasn't the answer I wanted to hear. "Okay, how many of those keys are there, and who has them?"

He gave my question some thought and then said, "I think the locksmith made a total of six keys for all the locks in that building. I have one, Jack Chen has one, and Mister George Jue has one—Mister Jue has copies of all the keys in the village."

"What about Sun Ling's bodyguards?"

"No, they didn't have that key. They only had one key—the one that opens the front doors of the dressing room building."

"You said somebody named Jack Chen has a copy of the key. Who is he?"

"Jack is the village overseer. He kind of manages everything when Mister Jue isn't around. But Jack's a good guy. He wouldn't be involved in any funny business."

For the moment I took Jeff's word about Jack Chen's loyalty. "Okay, you've accounted for three of the six keys. Where are the other three?"

"They should be in the administration building's key cabinet."

"Can we check after dinner to be sure they're actually there?"

"Sure, that's easy to do."

When our dinners arrived, we all removed our wooden chopsticks from their paper sleeves. I'd handled these particular instruments of Chinese torture a time or two, so I thought I knew what I was doing, but as I went to pick up a piece of pork from my plate both Susie and Jeff stopped me.

Susie said, "Before you use those chopsticks, rub them together like this." She rubbed the lower halves of her sticks against each other, rotating them as she went. "These restaurant chopsticks aren't always finished smoothly, and sometimes they have splinters. Rubbing them together removes the splinters."

I followed her example and was thinking this case was providing some good lessons in the subtleties of Chinese culture, when Jeff shot that idea down in flames. "Actually," he said, "these are Japanese chopsticks. Chinese sticks are longer and round. The restaurant uses these because they're disposable—nobody has to wash them."

After what proved to be a very tasty and filling meal, Jeff signed the check and I thanked him for dinner. Then we headed for the administration building to count keys.

Outside it was nearly dark, and Chinese lanterns were already casting their glow over the village. I checked my wristwatch and found it was only seven o'clock. Apparently sunsets in these parts were hastened by the arrival of San Francisco's nightly fog.

Susie and I followed Jeff to the administration building and then down a long hallway to a small utility room. There Jeff used one of his keys to open the door of a three-foot-by-three-foot wooden cabinet mounted on the wall. Inside, at least a hundred sets of keys were hanging from numbered cup hooks screwed into the back of the cabinet. Jeff consulted a chart pasted to the inside of the cabinet door and then removed a ring of keys from one of the hooks.

Surprised, he said, "Oh-oh, there are only two keys here."

I wasn't at all surprised. "Is there a sign-out sheet somewhere that shows who has which keys?"

"Yes. The sign-out sheet is on a clipboard in the reception office."

Jeff put the key ring back, locked the cabinet, and led us out to the reception counter at the front of the building. The young Chinese receptionist was busy answering some question or other put to her by a young couple who seemed to be experiencing some difficulty finding whatever it was they were looking for.

Reaching under the counter, Jeff grabbed a clipboard labeled simply "Keys" and flipped through several pages until he found what he was looking for. After studying the sheet for a moment, he held the clipboard up for my perusal. "The only people who are signed out for the backdoor keys are the three I told you about. Looks like somebody pinched one of the extra keys."

Trying not to sound too much like a know-it-all, I said, "That's exactly what I thought you'd find."

"But how could somebody steal a key? The key cabinet is always locked."

"Jeff, the lock on that cabinet is a cheap piece of junk. I could have opened it with a paperclip as quickly as you opened it with your key."

"Well, shoot! With the keys to every darn door in the village in there, they should have put a better lock on that cabinet!"

"It happens all the time. People just don't understand locks. They think if they have to use a key to open something, that's the only way in. The lock on that cabinet just keeps honest people out. To anyone else, the door might as well be wide open."

Susie chimed in, "Jeff, you'd better tell Jack Chen to replace that cabinet lock."

I added, "That's a great idea, but in this situation, it's closing the barn door long after the horse has departed the premises."

Jeff nodded. "Sometimes during the day there's nobody in here but the receptionist. If she leaves her desk for some reason, any mug who knows what he's looking for could just waltz in here easy as pie and take a key without anybody knowing."

"Well," I said, "at least the missing key makes my theory about how Sun Ling was taken from the dressing room building a possibility I can work with until something better comes along."

Jeff said, "It sure does. What do we do next, Johnny?"

I had to smile at his use of the word "we." Jeff, and probably Susie, too, felt as if they were part of my detective team, which was fine with me. I'd already benefited from their help, and I would be needing it again so long as I could keep them out of harm's way.

I answered Jeff's question. "I think we've accomplished about all we can do today. I need to go back to my hotel and think things through. But I want you two to know how much I appreciate all the help you've given me. Thanks to you, we made some progress toward finding Sun Ling. Of course, we haven't found her yet, but we made a good start."

Jeff was smiling at my acknowledgment of his contributions to my detecting efforts, and Susie said, "You're welcome, Johnny. If I can help more, please don't hesitate to ask."

I thought I heard a hopeful tone in her voice as if she really wanted to be included in whatever happened next. I replied, "Oh, I'm sure I'll be calling on your help again soon."

Jeff asked, "Will you be out here at the exposition again tomorrow?"

"I'm not sure. My first stop in the morning will be a visit with Tang Hong to find out what he knows about his father's death. Then I'll be going to San . . . ah . . . ."

Jeff quickly said, "To San Bruno to see the contractor?"

"Yeah, that's it. After those stops, I'll be going wherever the trail takes me. Where will you guys be tomorrow if I should need to reach you?"

Susie reached into her handbag and came up with a business card. She also came up with a fountain pen she used to write a number on the back of the card. As Susie wrote, she said, "I'll be at Father's restaurant. The telephone number is on this card. I'm usually busy until lunchtime, but I expect I will be available after that. I wrote my home number on the back in case you need that, too."

Jeff also produced a business card. "Unless they need me at the restaurant for some reason, I'll be here. Here's my office number."

I shook Susie's hand and then Jeff's, saying, "Thanks again for all the help. You guys have a good night, and I'll be seeing you soon."

Leaving the Chinese Village, Susie and Jeff turned right toward the parking lot, and I went the opposite direction to retrace the route I'd taken from the taxicab parking area that morning. I didn't make it very far, though, before I had to stop and stare in awe at the amazing spectacle the Golden Gate International Exposition became when the sun set.

The walkways were brightly lit by the deco-moderne street lamps, but that was just the beginning. All of the many fountains were ablaze from spotlights that turned the spouting water into shimmering sprays of color. Every piece of statuary had its own illumination, and the exhibit halls glowed blue, green, and gold from even more concealed spotlights. I was surrounded by a scintillating rainbow that danced and sparkled with constantly changing hues.

While I sure wouldn't want to pay the electric bill, I will readily admit to being in awe of the exposition's nighttime persona. What's more, with the sparse crowds on a workday night, I practically had the show all to myself.

Entering the empty Court of Pacifica I had to stop again and stare at Dog Woman's amazing after-dark persona. Her starry metallic backdrop was now illuminated by hidden spotlights that slowly alternated between blue and orange. Pacifica herself, however, was lit with white lights from a low angle that gave her the same ghastly countenance kids like to create by lighting their faces with a flashlight held below their chins. The effect was to create shadows on her upper body and face that gave Dog Woman an even more menacing look—one that might well scare the bejeezus out of an impressionable child.

As I stood there gawking at the colorful, eighty-foot monstrosity before me, I heard the soft scrape of a shoe on concrete. The sound was almost lost in the splashing from the fountain behind me. I half-turned to look back over my shoulder and had just enough time to glimpse an angry Japanese face under the wide brim of a hat worn low on the guy's forehead before the sap in his right hand connected with my noggin.

I staggered forward in a futile attempt to escape my assailant, but the lights went out and I hit the concrete hard with an after-image of Dog Woman in my mind and the thought that the big ugly broad could have at least had the decency to warn me . . . .

TWELVE

Somewhere in the mist clouding my brain a female voice asked, "Mister? Mister, are you okay?"

I opened my eyes just far enough to see Dog Woman looming over me. I thought she had a very pleasant voice for such a disgusting broad. Then I opened my eyes a little further and saw two pairs of sensible women's shoes a few feet away. Since neither pair was nearly big enough to fit an eighty-foot dame, I looked up to see who was wearing them. The shoes closest to me were on a nice-looking brunette wearing a brown wool jacket and a concerned expression. Seeing my eyes open, she asked again, "Are you okay, mister?"

I told her I thought I was and then decided to find out if I was fibbing or not by returning to a vertical position. Pain was pounding in the back of my head like the entire UCLA marching band percussion section was up there.

As I struggled with the arduous task of standing up, the other woman, a second young brunette who bore a strong resemblance to the first except that she wore glasses and a heavy red and white cardigan sweater, asked, "What happened to you, mister? My sister and I were on our way to catch the ferry back to The City when we found you here." Then she added, "Oh, I'm Dot and this is my sister, Flo."

I avoided answering her question about what had happened to me by introducing myself. "Hi Dot and Flo. I'm Johnny."

Dot observed that I was still a little wobbly on my pins and said, "If you don't feel well, I think there's a first aid station around the corner next to the parking lot. We could help you over there if you'd like."

I faked a smile I didn't feel and said, "That's very kind of you, but I think I'm okay."

Then sister Flo held out two objects and said, "I think these must belong to you. They were on the ground over there next to the fountain."

I accepted the fedora and billfold she offered, recognizing both as mine. A quick look in the wallet told me a few things had been moved around, like my P. I. license, but everything was still there except ninety-some dollars.

Since the good Samaritans who'd come to my rescue seemed like honest types, I concluded the guy who'd sapped me was the villain who made off with my ninety bucks.

Pushing a dent out of my hat, I said, "Yes, these are mine. The billfold must have slipped out of my coat pocket when I fell. Thank you for returning them."

Flo said, "Oh, you're very welcome. Now, if you're sure you don't need help to the first aid station, we better hurry or we'll miss our ferry."

"Then you'd better run along and catch your boat. I'll be fine. And thank you for coming to my rescue."

They both told me they were glad they could help, and I watched them trot off through the Northwest Passage toward the ferry docks. When they were out of sight, I sat on the edge of the fountain and took inventory of my situation. Physically, my head hurt like hell, but my vision was clear and all my extremities seemed to be in working order, so I probably didn't have a concussion.

My Smith & Wesson revolver was still tucked into its holster, my watch was still on my wrist, and my keys were still in my pocket. So the only thing missing was the cash. That fit because I was pretty sure the Jap who'd mugged me wasn't your run-of-the-mill thief. That would be too much of a coincidence. He simply took the money to make the attack look like a robbery. The cash was sort of like frosting on the cake.

But if robbery wasn't his motive, what was? The odds were highly in favor of his being part of the bunch that bumped off Tang Fan, which gave the guy plenty of motive. After my run-in with another member of the gang that afternoon, they probably wanted a look at my identification to find out just who the hell they were dealing with. If that was the case, they now knew the witness to Mister Tang's murder was a private dick from L. A. who was carrying a piece. Since that wasn't likely to be good news from their point of view, I took the whole incident as a warning to be a whole lot more careful from this point on.

Walking the rest of the way back to my car, I pondered a couple of questions, like how Tang's killers knew where to find me. The goon who'd followed me around the exposition earlier picked me up just outside the Chinese Village, which only meant they'd made a connection between the fact that I'd been at Tang's warehouse and his involvement in the Chinese exhibit. But the goon was there waiting for me, so how did they know I'd be at the exposition today?

The minute I saw my car sitting by itself in the empty taxicab parking area, I knew the answer. My Chrysler isn't gaudy, but it is distinctive enough to standout from other cars. And since it was clearly visible from the main road into the exposition grounds, I concluded the killers spotted it on their way into the exposition and recognized it as being the same car that was parked in front of Tang's warehouse the night they killed him. That might be an oversimplification, but it would do for the moment.

The next question I pondered had to do with exactly who the hell these guys were. The fact that the goon who'd followed me around the exposition took refuge in the Japanese exhibit when I tried to confront him leant credence to what FBI Agent Tom Kendall told me about the Japanese having an official interest in what Sun Ling was up to in the U.S. That would make the goons secret agents of the Japanese government. All the conjecturing I was doing made my head hurt worse than it did to begin with. Hopefully, I would have some hard facts to go on after talking to Tang Hong in the morning.

Back at the Sir Francis Drake, I turned my car over to the parking valet, picked up my room key at the desk, and made a beeline to the elevator. Once in my room I went straight to my suitcase and pulled out my well-worn leather shaving kit. It has a double plastic lining in the bottom to keep moisture from something like a wet toothbrush from soaking through the leather. When traveling, I make it a point to stash some of my cash under the plastic lining as a contingency against the possibility of something happening to my billfold.

With relief I pulled out the ten twenties and the blank emergency check I'd concealed there before leaving home. Losing ninety bucks wasn't something I could afford to do very often, but at least I wasn't destitute, especially since Mister Liang arranged to have my hotel bill sent directly to his office when he made my reservation at the Drake. I figured to get the ninety clams back as part of my expense reimbursement.

I put five of the twenties into my billfold and returned the rest to their hiding place. Next I picked up the telephone and told room service to send up a bucket of ice and a bottle of Gilby's Spey Royal Scotch.

When my order arrived, I dropped two cubes from the ice bucket into a hefty glass tumbler bearing a gold replica of the Sir Francis Drake's crest and rolled most of the remaining ice into a hand towel from the bathroom. Then I poured a healthy slug of scotch, made myself comfortable in one of the room's frou-frou chairs, and applied the ice-filled towel to the bump on my noggin.

Once comfy, I lit a Lucky, took a long pull on the scotch, and thought about bell-ringers. "Bell-ringers" is my pet term to describe pieces of a case puzzle that don't seem to fit the overall picture. That makes them bell-ringers because they set off alarms in my head that tell me something is out of whack with my working theory about what happened to whomever it happened to. During what now seemed like a very long day, I'd latched onto four bell-ringers in the mysterious case of the disappearing Sun Ling, and they were doozies.

First, there was the abrupt departure of Sun Ling's bodyguards. As I'd told Jeff, I could only think of a few reasons the six Chinese gentlemen left in such a hurry. One was that they'd found Sun Ling, but if that was the reason, where was she and why didn't they tell anyone connected to the Chinese Village they'd found her?

Another reason for them leaving might be they'd learned something that told them they were never going to find Sun Ling. Aside from the possibility they found her dead body, I couldn't imagine what that something might be.

The third possible reason for the bodyguards' hasty retreat could be that the Chinese government didn't want six of their countrymen wandering around the U.S. looking for Sun Ling. Their reason for that might be that the San Francisco Police Department now knew at least a little about Sun Ling's kidnapping, and the Chinese big-shots could be afraid that if questioned, the bodyguards might spill the beans about Sun Ling's real mission to this country. While that theory seemed a little farfetched, it still had to be included with the other possibilities.

The second bell-ringer had to do with the actual kidnapping of Sun Ling from her dressing room. It would have taken the kidnappers a minute or so to open the trapdoor, lower their ladder, and climb down into the dressing room. That was more than enough time for Sun Ling to realize something bad was happening and call out to her bodyguard or even run over to open the door so her bodyguard could fend off the kidnappers. So why didn't she do that?

The cold cream jar I found on top of the dressing room ceiling also bothered me. I could understand the kidnappers getting nervous about the length of time it was taking Sun Ling to change and deciding to grab her before she removed her makeup. I could also imagine them being smart enough to know Sun Ling's makeup would have to be removed before they took her through the exposition grounds so she wouldn't stand out like a preacher at a crap game. What I couldn't imagine was kidnappers who were savvy enough about women's cosmetics to know they had to take the cold cream and tissues with them in order for Sun Ling's makeup to be removed.

My third bell-ringer was the honorable Mister Liang's response to my telling him the bodyguards had flown the coop, or maybe he was responding to my learning about their departure so quickly. Either way, I was certain he was lying when he told me he didn't know the bodyguards were on their way back to China. I suppose I could be off the mark on that, but years of being lied to by everyone from gangsters to society folks have sharpened my sensitivity to prevarication. I know a lie when I hear one, and Liang was lying through his honorable teeth.

Besides the fact that fibbing to a detective you've hired to do a job just isn't nice, Liang's lie rang alarm bells because it didn't fit the big picture. It told me finding Sun Ling wasn't as important to him as he first indicated.

Something else was more important. I had no idea what that something else might be, but the puzzle pieces weren't going to fit until I found out.

My last bell-ringer centered around Tang Fan's murder and my subsequent encounters with his killers. Detective Sergeant Bailey told me Tang's murder had nothing to do with Sun Ling's disappearance, but if that was true, I had one hell of a coincidence on my hands. I tend to be very suspicious of coincidences, especially when they show up in the middle of a case full of other bell-ringers. Again, I had no idea what was really going on, but I was pretty sure whatever it was would change the puzzle picture when I figured it out—if I figured it out.

Over the course of thinking things through, my earlier feeling that I'd made some good progress toward finding Sun Ling gradually evaporated. Now it seemed as if all I'd really accomplished was to open a can of worms, and the worms weren't talking. On that happy note, there came a tap, tap, tapping at my hotel room door.

By this time all the minor aches and pains resulting from hitting the concrete after being conked on the noggin were showing up to compete with the pain in my head. That made getting out of my chair a slower than usual process. Whoever was at my door had time for a second knock before I got there. Due to the lateness of the hour and in keeping with my new policy of avoiding situations that might prove hazardous to my continued well being, I drew my Smith & Wesson, stood off to the side of the doorway, and opened the door a few inches with my left hand. Through the narrow opening I saw that my visitor was a fellow in a dark blue suit. He was a few inches shorter than me, clean-shaven, and smiling a friendly smile. That alone was enough to make me suspicious.

He gave me even more reason to be cautious when he said, "Good evening, Mister Spicer. I'm Park Atkins. I'm a radio news reporter, and if you don't mind, I'd like to ask you some questions about a story I'm working on."

In spite of my belief that reporters are only slightly less loveable than smart alec cops, I returned my revolver to its holster and opened the door wider. His eyes went straight to my shoulder holster, and I said, "That would depend on the subject of your story."

From the way he took my revolver in stride and the way he looked me straight in the eye, I was pretty sure Mister Atkins was carrying some street experience under his belt. He said, "Rumor has it that a member of the Chinese delegation to the Golden Gate International Exposition—a Miss Sun Ling—has disappeared and may be a the victim of a kidnapping.

"That rumor also says an L. A. private cop named Spicer is up in our fair city trying to find Miss Ling. May I come in and talk with you about that subject?"

My first inclination was to tell this character to take a hike, but my curiosity got the better of me. What I was curious about was who'd spilled the beans about Sun Ling and my involvement in the case to a news reporter. Since that question was another bell-ringer, I invited Mister Atkins in and offered him a drink.

Something subtle in the way he declined my offer of scotch told me Atkins and booze were old friends and he was dead set on avoiding a reunion. I then offered him a seat, which he accepted. Pulling a notebook and pencil from his pocket, Atkins said, "That's quite a bump you've got on the back of your head there. That happen in the line of duty?"

"Atkins, I'm gonna be frank with you. I have no intention of telling you a damned thing about why I'm in your fair city. The only reason you're in this room is to tell me where you heard that rumor."

He smiled his friendly smile again and said, "Then we're both wasting our time. You know as well as I that a reporter never reveals his sources."

"Then you might just as well hike your butt out of here because it's been a long day and I'm tired."

Atkins looked down at his notebook for a moment and then looked back up at me and said, "Johnny, we got off to a bad start here. Let me try this again. Do you know an L. A. homicide cop by the name of Don Chambers?"

"Yeah, I know Chambers. So what?"

"Well, I'm a former L. A. cop. Don and I were partners before I left the force. He'll tell you I'm on the level."

"Okay, fine. I'll give your regards to Chambers next time he rousts me for no reason at all."

Atkins turned his smile up a couple of notches. "Yeah, you know Don alright. My point is this: I've been in San Francisco for a few years now and I've made some pretty good contacts. Those contacts and my experience as a cop might just be of some use to you in exchange for an exclusive story on the disappearance of this Chinese gal. What do ya' say?"

I had to give Atkins credit. The guy had spunk. Softening my tone a little, I said, "Look, Atkins, I'm between a rock and a hard place here. As much as I would welcome the help of an experienced hand who knows the territory, my clients gave me very specific instructions about publicity; they don't want any, period. And as you well know, my first obligation is to the people paying for my time."

"Okay, then, how about an exclusive when you crack the case? With any help I can give you, of course."

"Unless the outcome of this caper is a whole lot different than I'm expecting it to be, I still won't be able to tell you a damned thing."

"It's that sensitive, huh?"

"Yeah, it's that sensitive."

He sighed and said, "Alright, I'm sorry we couldn't work something out." Atkins offered me a business card and said, "Here's my number. If things change or you get stuck or you just want to know where to get a decent fish dinner, give me a call."

I took his card and said, "Okay, I'll keep that in mind. In case it matters, I think it's a shame we can't work together. I think you're an alright guy."

Atkins grinned and said, "I think you're alright, too, Johnny. Maybe when this is all over we can get together over a pot of bouillabaisse and shoot the bull."

We both stood, and I offered a handshake, saying, "I'd like that, Atkins. Before you go, though, I'd like to ask one question."

He cocked his head at me. "Where did I get the word about the missing Chinese gal?"

"Sort of. I wouldn't press you on this if it weren't for the fact that how you got that word could be important to solving the case. Just tell me, did you hear it from a homicide sergeant named Bailey?"

Atkins thought for a moment and then said, "Well, since your question tells me a whole lot more about what's going on than I expected to find out . . . ." He winked at me and continued, "I'll give you a straight answer: No, it seemed to come from a much more direct source. I haven't talked to Bailey in a couple of months. But you can bet I'll be renewing our acquaintance real soon."

We shook hands again, and I locked the door behind him. Most of the ice in my makeshift ice bag was melted, but just the cold, damp cloth still felt good on my head. I settled back in my chair again, took another swallow of scotch, and contemplated what had just become bell-ringer number five.

I knew damned well my question about Bailey would give Atkins a lead that might actually get him somewhere if he knew what to do with it, and I was pretty sure he would. Sometimes you have to give a little to get a little, and his answer that Bailey had not told him about Sun Ling was more than a little. Beside Bailey, who I'd let in on the secret because I didn't have any choice, the only people who knew Sun Ling was missing were the folks in the Chinese Village, so one of them was most likely the bean spiller.

I wondered briefly if it could be Jeff. He loved being on the inside and in the know, but Jeff was also loyal, especially to his family. No, there was another player in the game, and I needed to find out who before he or she botched everything up. Maybe Liang would have some insight on who it was, assuming Liang was through lying to me.

THIRTEEN

⟁

San Francisco - Thursday - April 13, 1939

After a restless night during which I did a lot more tossing and turning than sleeping, I was greeted by another gray San Francisco morning. The only thing I found to be cheerful about was that the swelling on the back of my head was down enough to accommodate the wearing of my hat. I gingerly donned said apparel and left my room to meet the world.

After another breakfast of corn flakes and orange juice in the Drake's coffee shop, I retrieved my car and headed back to the Tang Fan Trading Company on Third Street. The warehouse district was a completely different place by the light of day.

Trucks of every size and description, stacked high with goods arriving from or going to foreign lands all over the globe, rumbled back and forth to the docks. And international trade was a noisy business—brakes squealed under heavy loads, horns blared, and machinery rattled all around me as I bobbed and weaved my way past busy forklifts tending lines of double-parked trucks.

I found a relatively safe parking spot a few doors down from my destination and entered the Tang Fan Trading Company. Inside it was a little quieter, but just as busy. A young Chinese woman sat at a desk rubber-stamping a tall stack of official-looking documents with a rhythm Xavier Cugat would have appreciated. She stopped, rubber stamp held high, long enough to ask my business. I told her my name and said Tang Hong was expecting me.

She brought the rubber stamp down with a smack and turned to a complex-looking telephone console. Picking up the handset, the young woman pushed one of the myriad of buttons and, after a pause, said something in rapid-fire Chinese. Then she hung up the phone and announced that Tang Hong would see me in just a minute.

The gal was deep into her stamping frenzy again when the back door to the office opened and a Chinese fellow about the same age as Jeff Yang stuck his head into the reception area. He asked if I was Spicer, and when I answered in the affirmative, he said, "Come on back, Mister Spicer. We will talk in the warehouse."

The interior of the late Tang Fan's warehouse looked quite different from when I'd last seen it. Brightly lit by overhead fixtures, the cavernous space was a replica in miniature of the chaotic scene outside on Third Street. One fellow was maneuvering a diesel-powered forklift between and around tall stacks of crates at breakneck speed while other chaps used two-wheeled hand trucks to move smaller loads hither and yon according to some plan that wasn't apparent to me. A wooden pallet stacked high with cardboard boxes now occupied the spot where I'd found Tang Fan's bloody corpse two nights ago.

I followed Tang Hong into the small office where I found the telephone I'd used to call the cops. Without offering me a seat, Tang said, "Mister Liang said you would be here to ask some questions this morning and that I should cooperate. So what do you want to know, Mister Spicer?"

Tang Hong reminded me a lot of Jeff Yang, except he was dressed in work clothes and had an air about him that said, "I'm a busy guy, so make it snappy." He also had a more noticeable accent than Jeff.

I said, "Mister Tang, I guess you know I had an appointment with your father Tuesday night, and I'm the guy who found him and called the police. You have my condolences."

The young man nodded a brief acknowledgment of my sympathy but said nothing, so I got on with my business. "What I'd like to know is if you have any idea who killed your father and why."

Anger flashed across Tang Hong's face. "I know exactly who killed Father and why they did it. It was the dirty, stinking Japs who want us to stop shipping supplies to China. They threatened trouble if we did not stop the shipments, but Father would not give into them. Another ship full of supplies sailed Monday morning, and that night they killed him."

"Why do they want you to stop your shipments?"

Tang responded to my question in a way that sounded as if the answer should have been obvious. "The supplies we ship to China help our people fight the Japs who try to take over the country."

"Exactly what kind of supplies do you ship to China?"

An expression I took for suspicion crossed his face for a moment before he said, "Canned food, medicines, and farming tools. Nothing else."

I had no facts to back up my hunch, but the tone of his answer told me the Tang family was supporting the Chinese cause with more than canned beans, iodine, and plows. I was getting tired of being lied to by people who were supposed to be on my side, but I really couldn't blame him. Weapons and ammunition, which were quite likely included in his family's shipments to

China, would be considered contraband by both our government and the Japanese. I changed the subject.

"Mister Tang, can you tell me the names of the Japanese who are behind your father's murder?"

"No, they are cowards who make anonymous telephone calls and slink around in the night. I have heard that some of them hide out at that fair on Treasure Island. The police told me they had information that one of Father's killers was seen there yesterday, but when they arrived, the devil was nowhere to be found."

"Did Sergeant Bailey tell you that?"

"Yes. He told me yesterday afternoon."

I could tell Tang Hong was getting impatient. He had important work to do, and I was keeping him from it. "Okay, Mister Tang, one more question and I'll get out of your hair. Do you plan to continue your shipments of supplies to China?"

Tang Hong's anger sparked again. Emphatically he said, "I do!" Then he glanced out at the busy warehouse through the office windows and added, "Members of the Ping Kun Tong have become our allies, and so we are now prepared to defend ourselves against the Jap bastards who killed my father."

I followed his gaze out the window and saw at least part of the protection he mentioned. A substantial Chinese fellow in a brown and tan checked sport coat who'd easily spin the dial twice on a 150-pound scale stood in the shadows intently watching the warehouse activity. He had the look of a pro that would definitely make me think twice before tangling with him. I thanked Tang Hong for his time, and he muttered something like "You're welcome."

After finding my own way back out to the street, I sat in my Chrysler amid the chaos of international commerce for a couple of minutes to think about what Tang Hong told me and what he didn't tell me. Really, my short interview with Tang Fan's son provided only a couple of facts I didn't have before. For one, I now knew Bailey was on the up-and-up when he said Mister Tang's murder wasn't related to Sung Ling's kidnapping—well, he was on the up-and-up from his point of view. I was still certain both events were closely related. Tang was supposedly murdered because he wouldn't stop shipping supplies to China, and the prevailing theory was that Sun Ling's kidnapping was the result of her mission to gain U.S. support against the Japanese invasion of China. Those were simply two sides of the same coin.

I also learned that Tang Hong was as determined as his father had been to continue supporting China with shipments of supplies, and I now knew the Japanese goon who'd followed me around the exposition was still at large, as was the guy who thunked me on the head last night. The undeniable sum of those facts could only be that the violence connected with this case was far from over.

The next item on my agenda was an interview with the contractor, Arthur Pedderson, who built the dressing room/storage building in the Chinese Village. The address Jeff Yang gave me for Pedderson was in the town of San Bruno. I vaguely recalled seeing a highway sign for San Bruno on my drive into San Francisco Monday evening, so I knew the place had to be somewhere down the peninsula of land that separates San Francisco Bay from the Pacific Ocean.

I followed Third Street south to the point where it intersects Bay Shore Boulevard, otherwise known as the U.S. Highway 101 Bypass. There I pulled into a Shell Oil Company service station where a friendly, energetic young man filled my tank, cleaned my windshield, checked my oil and tires, and handed me the free roadmap I requested of the San Francisco-Oakland area. The gasoline cost me twelve cents a gallon, which was a full two cents more than I pay for it at the Richfield station on Wilcox back home. I had to wonder what made San Francisco gasoline worth so much more than L. A. gasoline.

Before leaving the station, I consulted my newly acquired map and determined that the shortest route to San Bruno involved continuing south on Bay Shore Boulevard past South San Francisco and then jogging west to the El Camino Real via San Mateo Avenue. Half an hour later I awarded myself an A-plus in map reading as I passed a sign welcoming me to the "City of San Bruno."

My next challenge was locating 744 First Avenue, and since my handy-dandy Shell map didn't include the lesser streets of San Bruno, I pulled over next to a dark brown utility truck with the letters "P. G. & E." on it's doors. The two fellows standing next to the truck consulting a diagram of some sort were named Ed and Clarence according to the embroidery on their tan work shirts, and they looked like they might know their way around the area; they did, and I was informed that First Avenue paralleled the El Camino Real a block to the east. Not more than five minutes later I turned in to a construction yard surrounded by an aging board fence with a gate that hung askew from its one remaining hinge.

I knew I was in the right place because a slightly drooping sign attached to the front of the yard's sole building proclaimed, "Pedderson Constructors." The yard was deserted, and judging by the rundown condition of what little it contained, I wondered if Mister Arthur Pedderson was still in business. A brand spanking new Ford pickup truck parked on the far side of the building, however, gave me hope I might find someone inside.

After cautiously climbing two creaking wooden steps, I found the front door unlocked and walked in. The office's lone occupant was a hefty, gray-haired guy with a ruddy complexion and a copy of Popular Mechanics magazine. He grudgingly interrupted his reading long enough to look up and say, "We're closed, mister."

I flashed my official private detective photostat and said, "My name's Spicer. I'm investigating a missing person case, and I need to talk to Arthur Pedderson. You him?"

Momentary apprehension crossed his face before he said, "I'm Pedderson, but I don't know nothin' about no missing persons."

"You might be surprised what you know. You built one of the buildings in the Chinese Village out at the Treasure Island exposition, right?"

Pedderson's eyes narrowed. "Yeah, so what?"

"To be specific, you built the building they use for storage and dressing rooms. Is that correct?"

I was playing with Pedderson, taking my time about getting to the reason for my visit so I could see a little more of his reaction. He clearly wasn't happy about answering questions concerning his work, or at least at least the particular work he'd done at Treasure Island.

He glared at me and said, "Yeah, yeah. I built that building. What about it?"

"Are you aware there's a trapdoor in the ceiling of one of the dressing rooms in that building?"

He leaned back in his chair and trying hard to look nonchalant said, "Is there now? Don't that beat all! I wonder who could have built that there trapdoor."

"It wasn't you?"

"Hell, no. I don't know nothin' about no trapdoors, and I'm busy here, so if that's all you wanted to ask about . . . ."

"Busy doing what? Looks to me like Pedderson Constructors isn't doing much constructing these days."

He stood up and put on a menacing expression. "That ain't none of your business, mister. Now shove off."

Sounding as if he'd hurt my feelings, I said, "Why, Arthur, you're not being very hospitable. Besides, you haven't told me who paid you a big chunk of cash on the side for installing that trapdoor, and I really want to know."

Arthur was bulkier than me, but most of his size was blubber, so when he charged me, swinging his right fist around in a haymaker aimed at my head, I had plenty of time to sidestep the blow. He'd put all of his weight behind the punch, and when it didn't connect, he was left way off balance. I took advantage of that fact by throwing a hard, short jab to the point of his chin.

Pedderson's head snapped back, and his momentum carried him around and down to his hands and knees. His back was to me, and when he started to get up, I planted my foot against his butt and pushed hard, driving him headfirst into the office wall.

After a few seconds, he rolled over and started to get up. Pedderson was dazed, but not so much that he couldn't see the Smith & Wesson revolver in my right hand. "Arthur, stay put. You can answer my questions just fine from right where you are."

Glowering, he said, "I ain't sayin' nothin', you lousy gumshoe!"

Smiling, I turned on my award-winning charm and said, "Arthur, you obviously aren't thinking clearly. Let me explain things to you so you understand the situation here. You just assaulted a licensed private investigator. That alone will get you at least thirty days in the county lockup, which is plenty of time for the FBI boys to charge you as an accessory to a violation of the Lindbergh Act."

Of course, I was bluffing 'til hell wouldn't have it, but the fear on Pedderson's face said he was just dumb enough to buy my line, so I kept going. "Now, Arthur, if you tell me who paid you to install that trapdoor, I can tell the G-men how cooperative you were, and they might just go a little easier on you."

Pedderson shook his head and said, "I can't tell ya' the guy's name 'cuz I don't know it."

"Tell me what you do know."

Speaking slowly, as if he was trying real hard to get it right, Arthur said, "He was just some guy who showed up on the job site. He told me he wanted a hidden panel that opened above the last dressing room, and he'd pay me a grand to put it in and not tell anyone I did it. So I did what he wanted and he paid me in cash."

So far his story was pretty much what I expected, except a thousand bucks seemed like too much money for the job, even for doing it on the QT. Obviously there were some high-rollers in on Sun Ling's kidnapping. That figured. What didn't figure in Pedderson's story came when I asked, "What did this guy look like? Was he Japanese?"

Arthur shook his head again and said, "Naw, he was just a white guy in a suit."

I pondered that detail for a second and then said, "Describe him."

"He was just a guy about your size, maybe a little shorter."

"Come on, Arthur, give me something to work with here. How old was he? What color was his hair?"

"He wasn't too old, maybe twenty-six or twenty-seven. I never saw his hair 'cuz he was wearin' a hat."

"How many times did you see him?"

"Twice. Once when he showed up on the job site the first time. He gave me half the money when I said I'd do the trapdoor for him. Then he came by a week or so later when I'd finished the job. He gave me the rest of the money then."

"Did he give you any way to get in touch with him?"

"Naw. He just said to get the job done in a week 'cuz that's when he'd be back."

"Did you ask him why he wanted the trapdoor put in?"

Arthur thought for a moment as if he was trying to remember a conversation. Finally he said, "Yeah, I asked him that, but he told me it was none of my business."

"What else do you remember?"

"Nothin'. That's the whole story. Really."

I tucked the Smith & Wesson back into its shoulder holster and said, "Okay, Arthur. I'm going to look into your story. If you've been on the level with me, you might just be off the hook on the federal kidnapping rap. Either way, don't be planning any trips out of town in the near future."

Cruising back up Bay Shore Boulevard toward San Francisco, I pondered the surprise in Pedderson's story. He'd introduced yet another bell-ringer into the case: How did a white guy figure in a Japanese plot to kidnap a Chinese diplomat?

My conversation with Pedderson did answer at least one important question. As I'd discussed with the Yang kids last night, the timing of the trapdoor installation told me the scheme to kidnap Sun Ling wasn't hatched at the last minute. The dressing room/storage building was finished before the exposition opened in mid-February. Since Pedderson was hired to install the trapdoor before the building was completed, the kidnapping must have been planned before that time—maybe as early as December of last year, which was when Jeff said he first learned about Sun Ling coming to the exposition. I wondered who else knew she was going to be there.

FOURTEEN

San Francisco, like Rome, is built on seven hills or at least that's what the locals would like us to think. There must be more than seven hills, though, because there aren't more than a few streets in the whole damned town that don't go uphill or downhill. Be that as it may, the Sir Francis Drake's guidebook lists the seven official prominences of San Francisco as Telegraph, Russian, Rincon, and Nob Hills; Mount Sutro; Twin Peaks; and Mount Davidson.

I mention this bit of San Francisco topographical lore only because my third destination of the day was situated squarely atop one of those seven hills. I was headed for the Fairmont Hotel at the very peak of Nob Hill. The Fairmont, according to Jeff Yang, was where Sun Ling was staying during her visit here and it seemed like inspecting her hotel room was something a clever detective would do.

After consulting my trusty Shell road map, I determined that the Fairmont was a mere five or six blocks from my digs at the Drake. Most of those blocks, however, were vertical, and I was soon laboring up California Street behind another San Francisco oddity—the cable car.

Sometime back around the turn of the century, it was decided that the most efficient means of transporting the public up and down San Francisco's hills was a bus-like contraption that rides on rails and is powered by a moving cable under the street. The cable car's operator—called a gripman—uses a long lever extending through a slot between the rails to grab on to the moving cable, thus causing the car to move with it. When he wants to stop the car, he releases the cable grip and pulls on another lever that applies the car's barely adequate brakes.

Now this method of conveyance seems practical until you find yourself driving behind one of these rolling antiques. The thing clanked, rattled, and shook so violently I wouldn't have been surprised to find myself dodging a trail of ancient parts behind it. Worse yet is the crucial moment between the time the brakes are released and the cable is gripped. When on an incline behind a cable car one can never be quite sure the damned thing won't roll backward down the hill, demolishing your car in the process. It is apparently for these reasons that cable cars are equipped with loud bells the grip-man clangs at the slightest provocation, and often when there is no apparent provocation whatsoever, leaving one wondering what unseen calamity is about to befall the cable car and any unfortunate motorists behind it.

Thus, I was relieved when our little caravan reached the top of Nob Hill and I turned right onto Mason Street, leaving the cable car behind and pulling into the circular drive in front of the great granite block of a building that is the Fairmont Hotel. A parking attendant immediately headed in my direction, but I was tired of supporting the parking valets of San Francisco, so I flashed my P. I. photostat, said, "Police business," leaving him standing there with an empty outstretched hand.

Inside the Fairmont I found just about what I'd come to expect from high-class San Francisco hotels. An elaborately-paneled lobby ceiling was supported above a white marble floor by a plethora of Corinthian columns. A few thick area rugs and some rich wood wall paneling helped suck up some of the ambient noise echoing throughout the huge room like an ancient mausoleum.

The overall feeling of the place was overstated elegance. The decor of the Fairmont's lobby was, however, slightly more tasteful than the gaudy red and gold trappings of the Drake. Neither was a place where I would choose to spend any more time than necessary.

At the registration counter I asked for the hotel manager. A discrete telephone call was made, and a few moments later a distinguished-looking gentleman with wavy gray hair and black-rimmed spectacles arrived and introduced himself as Garrison van Owen, general manager of the hotel. I returned the favor by showing van Owen my state license along with the English version of Liang Chao's letter of introduction and explaining I was there to conduct an inspection of the hotel room occupied by Miss Sun Ling and paid for by Mister Liang.

Van Owen made a very thorough job of studying all this paperwork before saying, "You made it just under the wire. In another few minutes there would have been nothing for you to inspect in Miss Sun's room."

"Oh?"

"Yes, Mister Spicer. I spoke with Mister Liang by telephone not more than fifteen minutes ago. He instructed me to pack Miss Sun's belongings and ship them to his office in . . . I believe he said San Pedro, California. I was just about to relay those instructions to our housekeeping staff when you arrived."

"I see. Well, then, I'll make my inspection as brief as possible."

Van Owen said, "Alright, Mister Spicer. I must insist, however, that you remove nothing from the room as we are responsible for Miss Sun's possessions and I certainly would not want Mister Liang to find anything missing."

I agreed to this condition and van Owen summoned a bellboy. He instructed the young chap in a dark blue uniform with gold trim to escort me to room 429 and to be sure the room was left exactly as it was when we arrived. I thanked Mister van Owen for his cooperation and followed the bellboy to a bank of elevators off to one side of the lobby.

On our way up to the fourth floor I thought about Liang's instructions to pack up Sun Ling's room. That certainly didn't speak highly of Liang's confidence in my ability to find Sun Ling. On the other hand, she'd been missing for three days, and I could understand his reluctance to continue paying for an expensive hotel room nobody was using.

After unlocking 429 my escort took up a position near the door and as per his implied instructions, kept a close eye on the disreputable detective from Los Angeles. I didn't blame him; I'd have kept a close eye on me, too.

Sun Ling's accommodations were slightly less spacious than mine at the Drake, but the Fairmont's decorators clearly placed comfort above frou-frou, resulting in a room guests might actually find pleasant and relaxing. The furnishings were simple but sturdy and useful. As a bonus, Sun Ling's north-facing room had a panoramic view of San Francisco Bay from the Golden Gate Bridge to the federal pen on Alcatraz Island.

I began my inspection in the closet. There I found five cotton dresses hanging on the pole, three of which were enclosed in the sort of heavy paper garment covers laundries use for freshly cleaned clothes. There was also a sixth dress—a formal white silk number with a high Chinese-style collar. I guessed Sun Ling packed that particular gown for official receptions and the like. The last item hanging in the closet was a full-length black overcoat with a belt at the waist. I checked its pockets and felt a slip of folded paper in one of them. Since I suspected it was a note of some kind and therefore might be important, I palmed the paper and surreptitiously slipped it into my jacket pocket with the intention of looking at it later.

On the shelf above the hanging clothes, I found two black and two navy cotton skirts carefully folded so as to avoid wrinkles. Otherwise the shelf was empty. The last two items in the closet were suitcases of a sturdy design I had not encountered before. They were built of wood with a canvas covering on the outside and a maroon satin interior lining. I hauled the suitcases out to the bed and searched them thoroughly. They contained absolutely nothing.

Next I turned to the room's four-drawer chest of drawers. The top drawer contained white, practical-looking female unmentionables along with two pairs of nylon hose and several pairs of knee-length black socks. I checked underneath the underwear and found nothing concealed there.

Drawer number two contained three carefully folded cotton blouses—one white with a frilly high collar, one pale blue with a tiny pink floral pattern, and one pink with thin pale blue stripes. In the third drawer I found two items. One was a small canvas drawstring bag containing a pair of patent leather dress shoes with heels of a conservative height. The other item was a soft leather handbag in black. The bag was empty save for one copper penny that had become lost in the lining at the bottom of the bag.

The last drawer held a large paper sack of the sort hotels provide in guestrooms for laundry service. In the bag I found another white cotton blouse, one pair of panties, and one pair of knee-length socks. It appeared that, including whatever she'd worn last Sunday, Sun Ling was traveling with ten outfits for daily wear plus one for formal occasions.

The next stop on my inspection was the bathroom, which contained absolutely nothing. That seemed odd because I couldn't imagine Sun Lin—or any other woman, for that matter—traveling halfway around the world without a toothbrush, comb, and other essential toiletries. Where were they? It was possible Sun Ling had taken them with her to the Chinese Village, but I couldn't imagine any reason for her to do that.

Finally, I went to the writing desk next to the window with the scenic view. It only had one drawer, and that drawer contained a stack of stationery, some envelopes bearing the Fairmont's return address, a color picture postcard of the hotel, and a pencil. The top piece of stationery had some pencil sketches on it. I took the sheet closer to the window for a better look.

I'm certainly no art expert, but the three sketches below the Fairmont's letterhead were, to my eye, quite nicely done with shading that gave the subjects a three-dimensional appearance. The drawing at the top of the page was my old chum, Dog Woman. Sun Ling, or whoever drew the sketches, managed to give the big broad a good deal more charm than she possessed in person.

The second drawing depicted the Chinese Village Pagoda Tower, and I immediately recognized the subject of the third sketch as Susie Yang. Susie was looking off to her left with a slightly quizzical expression. Susie was a thinker, and the artist accurately captured that aspect of her personality.

Then I noticed a fourth image—a short string of lightly drawn Chinese characters running down the lower right margin of the page. Of course, I had no idea what the characters meant, but it seemed like a good idea to find out.

I turned to my escort, who was still keeping a watchful eye on me, and held the stationery up, pointing to the drawing of Susie Yang. "Sun Ling and this young woman became close friends out at the Golden Gate International Exposition. I'm certain Miss Sun would want her to have these sketches as a keepsake."

The bellboy frowned. "I don't know about that. Mister van Owen was quite specific about . . . ."

Drawing a fiver from my billfold, I interrupted him, "I doubt very much that housekeeping would even bother to pack this, so rather than having it end up in the wastebasket . . . ."

Bellboys have a lot in common with Pavlov's dogs. Upon seeing money, their automatic reflex is to reach for it. My five-dollar bill vanished into thin air as the young fellow said, "I guess you're right; nobody will care if a few doodles don't make it into the lady's bags."

I nodded my appreciation of his willingness to overlook a minor violation of the rules and carefully rolled the sketches into a tube, which I slipped into my inside jacket pocket. Then, after one last look around the room to be sure I hadn't overlooked anything, I said, "I'm all done here. We can leave now."

No more than ten minutes later I was negotiating my way back down California Street's steep slope. The clock on my dashboard and my stomach agreed it was getting close to lunchtime, so I zigzagged my way to the San Francisco-Oakland Bay Bridge, heading for Treasure Island and another go-round with the chopsticks at Wing's.

FIFTEEN

⌒⌒

The Golden Gate International Exposition was already open for business when I arrived at Treasure Island, so I had to wait in line behind a few cars at the drive-through ticket booths. When it was my turn, I flashed the Participant Pass Jeff provided and was waved on through by the attendant.

Since I also had an exhibitor parking permit, I bypassed the taxicab area in which I'd parked the day before and entered the huge public lot that covered the northern tip of the island. I liked the idea of parking among other cars because it made my Chrysler less conspicuous to anyone who happened to be keeping an eye out for one Johnny Spicer.

Given that the lot was said to accommodate 12,000 cars, I wasn't surprised to see numerous signs advising drivers to make note of the section in which they parked. I wondered how many hours were spent wandering aimlessly around the lot in search of cars lost by folks who failed to follow that sage advice.

As early as it was on this particular workday, however, the parking area was largely empty, so I found a spot at the south end of an aisle adjacent to the Nanking Road walkway that passed in front of the Chinese Village. I locked my car, took a good look around the area for lurking goons, and set off for the village.

By the time I entered the Chinese Village, my stomach was telling me to head straight for Wing's Restaurant, but I stopped by the village administration building first. The young woman behind the reception counter told me Jeff Yang had not arrived yet, but he was expected soon. I asked her to tell Jeff that Johnny Spicer would be waiting for him in the restaurant next door.

The heaping plate of pork chow mein I ordered and Jeff Yang arrived at my table almost simultaneously. Jeff's costume of the day was comprised of black and white saddle oxfords, pearl gray slacks, a dark gray sport coat, and a black dress shirt sporting a white necktie. In that get-up I thought he might easily be mistaken for one of the local goons, but I refrained from saying so. Instead, I said, "Hi, Jeff. Pull up a chair. Have you had lunch?"

"Yeah, I had a bite at Father's restaurant before I came over here. Looks like you've taken a liking to Chinese food."

I'd just managed to get a chopstick-load of noodles into my mouth, so I simply nodded, and Jeff asked, "How's the search for Sun Ling coming? Have you found any new clues?"

I swallowed and said, "A few."

I proceeded to give him a rundown of my activities since we'd parted company the night before, excluding my encounter with the Jap agent. Instead I began with the radio news reporter's visit to my hotel room. To that Jeff said, " I wonder which blabbermouth let the cat out of the bag about Sun Ling to the press."

"I was hoping you might shed some light on that question."

Jeff thought for a moment. "I don't have any idea. I mean, Jack Chen talked to everyone on the staff last Monday. He said Sun Ling would be away for a while, and we weren't to say anything to anybody about her being gone. Are you sure it was somebody here in the village?"

"No, I'm not. But that reporter, Atkins, said he'd gotten the word from a 'direct source.' That sounds like someone here in the village."

"It sure does, but I can't imagine who it could be."

Next I reported on my morning visit to Tang Fan's warehouse and my conversation with Tang Hong. Jeff said, "It's a good thing you talked to him this morning. Tang Fan's wake begins tomorrow and it will last about a week. After that they'll hold the funeral ceremony, so Hong won't be around the warehouse much for a while."

Describing my trip to Pedderson Constructors, I left out the means of persuasion I'd used and concentrated on what Pedderson told me about building the trapdoor. Jeff asked, "And he didn't know the name of the Caucasian guy who paid him to build it?"

"Apparently not. At least if he does, he's more afraid of that guy than he is of me. But the timing is the important point. He put that trapdoor in before the exposition opened, so whoever kidnapped Sun Ling was planning the caper for a long time before they actually did the deed."

"Yeah, but why did they pick last Sunday night to do it?"

I'd already given that question some thought. "Most likely because some part of their plan wasn't in place until Sunday. They were waiting for something, but I have no idea what that something was. Do you have any thoughts on that? Did anything change around here just before Sunday?"

Jeff shook his head. "Nothing that I can think of right now."

I finished the account of my morning's adventures by describing my visit to Sun Ling's room at the Fairmont. Then I asked Jeff, "Did you know Liang Chao planned to check Sun Ling out of the hotel and have her stuff shipped to his place in San Pedro?"

Jeff was looking glum. "No. That doesn't sound like he holds out much hope of you finding her."

"Either that or he just doesn't want to keep paying for her hotel room until she's found. If he checked her out because he doesn't think Sun Ling will be found, it makes me wonder if he knows something we don't know."

"Why would he keep anything from you? I mean, he's paying you to find her, so it doesn't make sense he would keep something from you, does it?"

"No, it doesn't, but the truth is the honorable Mister Liang hasn't been completely forthcoming about other parts of this case. For example, I had the definite impression our news about Sun Ling's bodyguards leaving wasn't a surprise to him, even though he said he didn't know they'd left. He seemed more surprised that I'd learned about their departure so quickly."

"Yeah, Susie said something about that. I always thought Mister Liang was an alright guy—a little stuffy maybe, but a straight shooter. Now I'm not so sure about that."

Changing the subject, I pulled the sheet of Fairmont stationery from my inside jacket pocket and unrolled it, asking, "Do you know if Sun Ling is an artist?"

At first Jeff looked a little surprised at the question, but something clicked in his memory, and he said, "Yes, I think she is. A couple of times I saw her sitting in the village drawing in a book. I only got a look at what she was drawing once, but what I saw looked just like these pictures. Do you think she drew these?"

"It seems likely she did since I found them in the writing desk in her room at the Fairmont."

Admiring the pencil sketches, Jeff said, "She's pretty good. That picture of Susie looks just like her!"

"Yes, it does. Now, what about these Chinese characters in the lower right margin? Can you translate them?"

Jeff looked a little sheepish. "I flunked that class, man. Pop tried to teach us how to read and draw those things . . . said it was part of our heritage, but I wasn't interested in that stuff." Then his expression brightened as he added, "Susie was, though. She got darn good at it. I bet she can translate 'em, or you could ask somebody else in the village."

"I'd rather keep this between the three of us for now. Those symbols probably aren't important, but we won't know that until we get them translated. Is Susie coming out here today?"

"Yeah. I think she was going to come over anyway, but Jack Chen called all the volunteer performers this morning. He said we needed something colorful to replace Sun Ling's appearances, so he scheduled costume processions for four this afternoon and eight o'clock tonight. Just before I left Pop's restaurant Susie told me she'd be over here with Annie Lee around two-thirty."

Rolling the sketches into a tube again, I slipped them back into my pocket and said, "Good. We'll see what she can tell us then."

"What are you going to do in the meantime?"

"I think I'll talk to some of the people who work in the Gayway. Maybe one of them saw Sun Ling being taken out of the dressing room building Sunday night. It's a long shot, but I'll give it a try."

"You want some help?"

"Sure, if you aren't busy."

Jeff grimaced. "No, I'm not busy. With Sun Ling gone, I don't have much to do around here. If I can help you find her, I might at least get my job back."

I paid for my lunch with one of the vouchers Jeff gave me the day before and left a tip on the table. Then we stood up, and I turned to leave Wing's the way I'd come in, through the restaurant's village entrance. Jeff stopped me, saying, "That's the long way. Wing's has another entrance out on the Gayway so customers can come in that way, too."

I followed Jeff down a hallway that ran alongside the kitchen toward the back of the building. It ended in a small lobby with a set of double doors. We stepped through the doors and onto the Gayway.

I reached into my jacket pocket and pulled out the magazine photo of Sun Ling Liang Chao gave me so I'd recognize her if I saw her. I said, "Let's concentrate on the concessions along the village wall. If anyone saw Sun Ling Sunday night, it would most likely be someone at one of those attractions.

Despite it being a beautiful sunny afternoon, the Gayway wasn't doing much business. That was good for my purposes because it meant the concession attendants weren't so busy they couldn't take a minute to look at Sun Ling's photo and answer my question. Unfortunately, those answers were all along the lines of, "Nope, sorry, pal. I ain't seen that dame."

Near the north end of the village wall the Gayway turned right, and looking in that direction I saw many more attractions, including a merry-go-round, some sort of diving bell ride, and at the east end of the street, a tall tower with an elevator that took visitors up for a look at the exposition from an elevation of about 150 feet.

Directly in front of us, however, was a Ferris wheel and to its right, a rollercoaster. Between these two rides was a short walkway leading out to the parking lot. After learning that neither the Ferris wheel operator nor the rollercoaster attendant had been on duty Sunday night, I took a look down the walkway to the parking lot. It was the most direct route out of the Gayway from the dressing room building's back doors, which made it the most likely path Sun Ling's kidnappers would have taken to avoid being seen.

I noticed a security guard standing near the parking lot end of the walkway. Unlike most of the exposition security guys I'd seen, this fellow wasn't strolling around on patrol, and I got the impression the walkway was his permanent station. What were the odds he was on duty there Sunday night? Probably not very good because assignments for security people at a place like this are usually rotated regularly. Still, it was worth a try.

With Jeff in tow, I strolled down to the guard and introduced myself, showing him my P. I. photostat. He seemed impressed, maybe because being a licensed P. I. was a small step up the law enforcement ladder from his security guard job. Being fraternity brothers of sorts, we shook hands and he introduced himself as Wilbur Harmon, a fact borne out by the GGIE security ID pinned to the front of his uniform shirt.

I said, "Wilbur, by any chance were you on duty here last Sunday night?"

After thinking about my question for a moment, he said, "Yes, sir, I surely was."

Holding out my picture of Sun Ling, I asked, "Did you happen to see this woman pass by here that night?"

Wilbur took the photo from my hand and studied it for so long I began to wonder if he'd slipped into a coma. Finally he said, "You know, I believe I did."

"Do you remember what time you might have seen her?"

After another moment's contemplation, he said, "Well, if it was the same young lady, she passed by here on her way to the parking lot about nine-fifteen. My duty shift goes from seven P.M. to three A.M., an hour after the Gayway closes at two. We all get a ten-minute break every two hours, and I think I'd just gotten back from my first break when I saw her."

The time jibed, and my interest in Wilbur Harmon jumped about ten notches. I said, "Was she alone or was she with someone?"

"There was a fellow with her."

"Did you get any sense that the woman was there against her will?"

"Not at all. I would have looked into it if I'd seen anything to make me think that. She was just walking along with the fellow. I do remember thinking they were in a hurry, though. Most folks who come out to the parking lot this way look kind of tired and walk slower because they're worn out from the exposition, but this couple was moving right along."

"Did they go into the parking lot?"

"No, sir. There was a car waiting for them along North Boulevard over there." Wilbur gestured to the roadway running along between the parking lot and the Gayway. "I noticed it and thought I'd have to tell the driver to move along if he was there much longer. Cars aren't supposed to park on the access roads, but I try not to be too hard-nosed about it. Usually when a car pulls up there, it's just somebody who went ahead to get bring the car closer so the rest of their party doesn't have to walk so far. I don't pester them unless they stay there for more than a couple of minutes."

"What kind of a car was it?"

"I remember it being a black Ford four-door sedan—a recent model. I didn't pay attention the license number because there was no reason to."

"Can you describe the man who walked out with this woman?"

Wilbur frowned in concentration. "All I really noticed about him was that he was Oriental, like the woman."

"What about the guy in the car that picked them up?"

"I really didn't get much of a look at him. I have the impression he was Caucasian, but I can't swear to that."

The alarm bell clanging in my head was so loud I almost didn't hear Jeff ask, "Do you recall what the woman was wearing?"

"She was wearing a short gray jacket over a dress or skirt. The dress or skirt was a dark color—maybe black or dark blue."

I thanked Wilbur, telling him I appreciated the fact that he was so observant. I also handed him one of my business cards and said I was staying at the Sir Francis Drake if he happened to think of anything else he thought I should know.

As we made our way back to the Chinese Village, Jeff said, "The outfit that guy described matches what I remember Sun Ling wearing when she got here Sunday afternoon, so it sounds like the woman he saw really was Sun Ling."

"It sure does. I wish Wilbur could have been more specific about whether the guy with her was Chinese or Japanese."

Jeff grinned. "A lot of you straight-eyes have trouble telling us apart, which is kind of surprising since San Francisco has the largest community of Chinese people outside of China and we've been here since the gold rush days. Seems like you ought to be able to tell the difference by now."

I'd already been chastised by Liang Chao for the same offense, and I understood Jeff's point of view. I said, "He did say the guy was Oriental, like Sun Ling, so that might mean he was Chinese."

"Yup, and what about the guy in that car? Unless the Japs are hiring white guys as chauffeurs these days, we might be on the wrong track about who snatched Sun Ling."

I was thinking we might be on the wrong track about several other points of the case, too. When we got to Jeff's office, I flopped into his guest chair and added the very useful information provided by Wilbur Harmon to my case notes.

Then as I slipped my notebook back into the side pocket of my jacket, my hand brushed the folded piece of paper I'd pilfered from the coat in Sun Ling's closet. After going to the effort of swiping the darn thing, I'd forgotten about it.

I unfolded the small blue piece of paper and discovered it was one of those while-you-were-out forms hotels use to record telephone messages. Under the Fairmont's name at the top, the form reported that a "Mr. Jones" called on April eighth at four-fifteen in the afternoon. He left no telephone number, and his message was short and to the point: "Confirming appointment for tomorrow."

I glanced up at the Bank of America calendar hanging on Jeff's office wall. April eighth had been a Saturday—last Saturday to be specific. That meant the appointment mentioned in the message would have been on Sunday, the day Sun Ling disappeared. So who the hell was Mister Jones, and what sort of appointment did Sun Ling have with him?

In my mind's eye the blue message form in my hand slowly dissolved into the picture puzzle pieces representing the mysterious disappearance of Sun Ling. Suddenly all of those pieces did simultaneous summersaults and formed themselves into a completely different picture—a picture into which all of the pieces fit, even most of the bell-ringers. I studied the new picture for a moment and came to the inescapable conclusion that for the past four days I'd been on a buggy ride to nowhere courtesy of Liang Chao and my FBI pal, Tom Kendall.

SIXTEEN

The sound of Jeff Yang's voice saying, "Johnny? Where'd you go?" made the new puzzle picture in my mind's eye dissolve back into the blue Fairmont Hotel telephone message in my hand. I looked up at Jeff.

"What's wrong, Johnny? You look like you were lost in outer space with Flash Gordon or something."

I smiled. "I wasn't quite that far gone, but I just stepped back from the case enough to finally make all the pieces fit and understand what really happened to Sun Ling."

Jeff's face lit up with excitement. "Really? You know where she is?"

"I don't know where she is yet, but I'm pretty certain I now know what actually happened here last Sunday night."

Jeff was practically jumping up and down in his chair. "Well, tell me! What happened?"

My mind was racing a mile a minute trying to understand all the ramifications of what I now knew, or what I thought I knew. Then my brain screeched to a halt when I realized I was facing a crisis I would need Jeff's help to avoid. "I'll tell you what I think is going on when Susie gets here because I'm going to need help from both of you to wrap this thing up. In the meantime, I need a big favor from you."

"Sure, anything."

"I need you to trust me enough to tell Liang Chao a big fat lie."

That threw him. Clearly puzzled, Jeff asked, "You want me to lie to Liang Chao? What about?"

"If I've got this thing figured right, the next time I talk to Mister Liang, he's going to fire me from the case. I don't want that to happen quite yet, so when Liang calls you, and I'm sure that will happen soon, I want you to tell him I'm not here. Tell him I'm out looking for Sun Ling and you'll give me the message to call him when you see me. Okay?"

Basically Jeff was an honest kid, and the idea of lying to a respected elder in his community didn't sit right with him. "Yes . . . I guess so. But why do

99

you think Liang Chao is going to fire you? I mean, you've been making good progress and . . . ."

"That's just the problem. I've been making too much progress—so much that I'm very close to doing the last thing Liang Chao wants me to do."

Now completely befuddled by my doubletalk, Jeff shook his head and said, "What's that?"

"Finding Sun Ling."

Jeff's jaw dropped about a foot and he said, "Huh?"

Before I could answer him, the telephone on his desk rang. I quickly said, "That's probably Liang Chao already. Go along with me on this for now. You'll understand why in a little while."

Jeff slowly picked up the telephone receiver and said, "Chinese Village, Jeff Yang speaking." Then he looked at me with an astonished expression, nodded, and said into the phone, "Good afternoon, Mister Liang." After a pause, Jeff said, "No, Mister Spicer isn't here. He said he was on his way to find Sun Ling."

After another pause, Jeff said, "Yes, sir, I'll tell him you want him to call you as soon as I see him again. Yes, sir. Goodbye, Mister Liang."

Jeff had been watching me throughout the conversation. He glanced down to replace the telephone handset and then said, "You sure had that one pegged right! Mister Liang wants you to call him as soon as possible."

I nodded, and on that note, Susie Yang poked her head into Jeff's office. She said, "Am I interrupting anything?"

Jeff said, "No. Come on in. Johnny's got something important to tell us about Sun Ling."

Susie turned to look at me and I said, "Yes, but not here. Let's all go out to that spot by the lake where we talked yesterday."

Walking through the village I gave some serious thought to how much of what I now suspected about Sun Ling's disappearance I ought to tell Susie and Jeff. As we crossed the arched bridge, I decided to go for broke and tell them the whole story. I was now up against a deadline, and if I was going to make sense of things and find Sun Ling before Liang took me off the case, I was going to need their cooperation—a lot of it.

Arriving at the bench, I gestured for them to take a seat and said, "What I'm about to tell you is going to sound farfetched to begin with. You may even think I've lost my marbles, but don't jump to any conclusions until you've heard the whole story."

Susie nodded and Jeff said, "Okay, Johnny, shoot. We're all ears."

"What I now know is that Sun Ling wasn't kidnapped. Last Sunday night she snuck out of her dressing room and left the exposition willingly."

Now Susie was frowning and Jeff just looked bewildered. I continued my story. "I know that to be true because there are several pieces of evidence that prove it. First, the exposition security guard Jeff and I talked to a little while ago said he saw Sun Ling leave the Gayway with two men and there was nothing about her behavior to indicate she was being forced to go with them. Now, I think the security guard is a pretty sharp guy who would have noticed any indication that Sun Ling was under duress, and I also believe if Sun Ling was being forced to go with the men, she would have tried to signal that to the guard somehow."

Jeff nodded his agreement with my conclusions, but Susie was still frowning. I went on, saying, "I found the second piece of evidence in the pocket of a coat in her hotel room closet. It's a hotel telephone message form, and it says a man named Jones called Sun Ling a little after four last Saturday afternoon. By that time she was probably already on her way out here, so Mister Jones left a simple message that said 'Confirming appointment for tomorrow.'

"Since the call came in on Saturday, whatever appointment the mysterious Mister Jones had with Sun Ling was scheduled for Sunday, the day she disappeared. Now, taken by itself, the message means nothing more than it appears to mean, but when you consider it with what the security guard told us and the fact that Sun Ling made no effort to call out to her bodyguard from her dressing room that night, even though the opening of the trapdoor and the lowering of the ladder would have given her plenty of warning and time to do so, the telephone message becomes a veiled tip-off to Sun Ling that the date for her planned disappearance was to be Sunday."

Susie shook her head. "I see how you could draw those conclusions, but there could also be other explanations for the telephone message and for the guard thinking Sun Ling was leaving of her own will. I just can't imagine why on earth she would stage a phony kidnapping."

Nodding, I said, "I can't either, but there's more evidence indicating that she actually did do such a thing. For example, when I searched Sun Ling's hotel room this morning, everything that should have been there—clothes, suitcases, and so on—was there except for one thing. The bathroom was completely empty. There were no toiletries anywhere in the room.

"I think it's fairly safe to conclude Sun Ling didn't travel halfway around the world without a toothbrush and other such necessities, so if they aren't in her hotel room, where are they? There's only one possibility, and that is she brought them with her when she came out to the exposition Sunday. And the only reason for her to do that is she planned to be gone for a period of time and knew she would need those items."

I watched Susie's expression change as she listened to what I was saying. Something about Sun Ling's missing toothbrush clicked with her. She looked thoughtful and said, "That reminds me of something. I was here before Sun Ling arrived Sunday afternoon, and I remember noticing she wasn't carrying her usual black leather handbag. Instead she had a bigger bag made out of cloth with a flower pattern—I think they call them tote bags. It had cloth handles and a zipper at the top to keep things from spilling out. That bag was easily large enough to carry her toiletry items from the hotel."

"There you go. And there's more. Do you remember the cold cream jar and tissues we found on top of the dressing room ceiling?"

Jeff and Susie both nodded. "They indicate Sun Ling left the room before she removed her stage makeup. I can understand real kidnappers getting antsy about the amount of time it was taking for Sun Ling to change and snatching her before she took off the makeup, but in their hurry to get out of the dressing room, I doubt they would have thought to bring the cold cream and tissues . . . ."

Jeff finished my sentence for me. "But Sun Ling would have thought of it because she didn't want to stand out like a sore thumb when they left through the Gayway."

"Right, so she would have grabbed the cold cream and tissue box before she climbed up the ladder and through the trapdoor."

I could tell by Susie's expression I'd convinced her I was right about Sun Ling disappearing voluntarily. Susie confirmed that by saying, "And if Sun Ling was planning to stay in this country all along, it would explain why she asked so many questions about how Americans accept Chinese people and where she could buy modern clothes to fit in." After a pause she added, "Sun Ling really did disappear voluntarily! But why? If she wanted to stay here, why didn't she just apply for citizenship?"

Jeff said, "Maybe she was afraid the Chinese government would make the U.S. government send her back. After all, Sun Ling is an important person in China."

Shaking my head, I said, "That's not it because I'm pretty sure the Chinese government, Liang Chao and his buddies, and the FBI are all in on this fake kidnapping caper together."

That little bombshell shocked Jeff into asking, "How do you know that?"

"I don't know it for sure, but I suspect it for several reasons. First, the explanation Tom Kendall gave me for the FBI not getting involved in Sun Ling's kidnapping never made any sense. They claimed it was because Sun Ling was here under false pretenses—that she was on a diplomatic mission rather than just being in the U.S. to represent China at the exposition. That's pure hogwash. Even if the FBI really believed it, they would still have to find her and send her back to China.

"There is some truth, however, in Liang Chao's contention that they want to keep the police out of it to avoid a scandal. The real problem is that the local cops aren't in on the gag like the FBI, so they might actually find Sun Ling and discover the whole thing is a great big hoax. That's the scandal Liang really wants to avoid."

Susie's frown was back. "I know you had doubts about Mister Liang's honesty yesterday when you spoke with him on the telephone, but are you absolutely sure he is involved? It all seems so convoluted and mysterious."

"Susie, those are two sure signs of an undercover FBI operation. From Hoover on down, they all think they're smarter than everyone else, and to prove it, they come up with these complex schemes that are far more complicated than they need to be."

Susie said, "Okay, but just because the FBI is in on it doesn't mean Mister Liang is, too."

I replied, "True, but his behavior says he is. Take Sun Ling's bodyguards for example. When I told Liang they were on their way back to China, he claimed he didn't know they'd left, but he showed no surprise and even tried to downplay their sudden departure as unimportant to the case. Heck, I'd bet money he even made the actual arrangements for the bodyguards to leave the country on the Clipper yesterday. He's been playing the FBI's game right from the start."

This time Jeff had something to say. "That seems kind of dumb to me. I mean, they hardly looked for Sun Ling at all. Having them leave so soon after she disappeared looks suspicious."

"If someone close to the situation really thought about it the way you have, it might look that way, but the bodyguards had already served their purpose. They came here with Sun Ling so their intimidating presence would make things look like the only way Sun Ling could be nabbed was through a major clandestine operation by some foreign government. Then they made a big dramatic show out of Sun Ling's disappearance—knocking the dressing room door down and running around the exposition looking for her. But after their performance convinced everyone Sun Ling disappeared under mysterious circumstances, they became a liability."

Jeff looked puzzled again. "How were they a liability?"

"Simply because the more people wandering around on U.S. soil who were in on the kidnapping hoax, which the bodyguards had to have been, the more likely it was that someone would stumble on the truth. By sending the six bodyguards back to China, Liang eliminated the possibility of the bodyguards unintentionally spilling the beans to the local cops or someone else."

Jeff said, "Well, they sure had me fooled."

"They had us all fooled for a while. And another clue to Liang's involvement in all this playacting surfaced when he ordered the Fairmont Hotel to pack up Sun Ling's stuff and send it to his office in San Pedro. Once he has her suitcases, he can send them on to wherever she is and nobody will be any the wiser. The only problem there is that he didn't call the Fairmont quite soon enough. I got there just before they packed up Sun Ling's stuff and found the telephone message she should have destroyed. That message is what finally got me pointed in the right direction."

Then Susie piped up again with a good question. "If all you've told us is true and Mister Liang really doesn't want Sun Ling found, why did they hire you to find her?"

I gave her a sheepish grin before admitting that, in effect, I'd been duped. "Up until now I've just been window dressing. With the FBI supposedly refusing to get involved and Liang coming up with reasons not to call in the San Francisco cops, it would have looked suspicious if they hadn't done something else to show their great concern over Sun Ling's disappearance. That's why they hired me—so there'd be somebody out looking for her on their behalf. Their problem is they underestimated the detecting skills of one Johnny Spicer. With your help I managed to put the pieces together in the right way to uncover what was really going on.

"I'm also pretty sure Liang and Kendall have been keeping a close eye on my progress—they'd be fools not to. And now that they realize I'm smarter than they thought I was, they're in a panic. I figure that's why Liang left that urgent telephone message with you, Jeff. He wants to get me off the case before I do something to blow the lid off their grand scheme."

Jeff nodded to indicate he understood and said, "But what about that reporter who came to your hotel room last night?"

Now Susie looked puzzled. "What reporter?"

Jeff said, "A radio news reporter showed up at Johnny's room last night asking questions about Sun Ling disappearing. He said he and other reporters had gotten the word she was missing from some 'direct source.'"

Susie said, "Oh. I didn't know about that."

I said, "Don't feel bad, Susie. Things have been happening so fast, it's even hard for me to keep up with it all. As for who tipped off the press, I have no idea. I suppose it might have even been Liang and his chums. They may figure that Sun Ling is safely stashed, and with the bodyguards on their way back to China, it's time to cash in on some propaganda about her being kidnapped by Japanese agents. If they got that story into the papers it would help win the support of the American people for China's war against the evil Japanese. Americans have always been suckers for the underdog, which China would certainly appear to be in newspaper articles about the kidnapping of an innocent and, I might add, very attractive, young Chinese woman."

Jeff chimed in, "But I read the Chronicle this morning, and I didn't see anything in it about Sun Ling."

"I'm not surprised. No real journalist worth his salt is going to print a story with international implications on the strength of a tip. They would want confirmation from Chinese authorities and so far they apparently haven't gotten it."

Jeff said, "This is confusing. I mean, if the papers wrote about Sun Ling being missing, would that mean everybody would find out about her secret reason for being in the U.S.?"

"It could, but the FBI and Liang might figure the propaganda value of newspaper articles about Japanese agents kidnapping Sun Ling would be of more value than continuing to keep her mission a secret. Besides, Liang said Sun Ling was actually here to persuade influential Chinese-American businessmen to lobby for U.S. military support in China. There's nothing illegal or morally wrong with that. The only reason for doing it under the table is that the American people aren't anxious to get into another war right now—a point the Japanese might use to their advantage if they could expose some kind of subversive movement by Chinese-Americans to involve the U.S. in their homeland's fight against the Japanese."

Jeff was shaking his head, and I gathered it was over the complexity of the situation. I said, "Yeah, I know. International politics are confusing. One country is always trying to outsmart another to get the upper hand. I guess it doesn't matter that they all look like a bunch of crooks when they do that stuff."

Apparently tired of sitting, Susie stood up and asked, "So what happens now? Are you going to keep looking for Sun Ling, even if she doesn't want to be found?"

"Mister Liang is paying me good money to find Sun Ling, and that's what I intend to do, if only to learn what's behind this complicated charade he and the FBI cooked up."

"But do you have any idea where to look for her?"

"No, I don't. That's why I've told you two the whole story. If I'm going to find Sun Ling before Mister Liang catches up with me and takes me off the case, I'm going to need some help from you guys. How 'bout it? Are you with me?"

Jeff nodded enthusiastically, and Susie said, "I guess so. I just have the feeling I'm betraying Sun Ling. Now that we believe she left voluntarily, I think she must have had a good reason. I wouldn't want to get her into trouble or anything like that."

"Susie, international intrigue is a serious and sometimes deadly game. It's very possible the not-so-honorable Mister Liang and the FBI have gotten Sun Ling into a situation that's more than they can handle. If that's the case, Sun Ling might be grateful for some help at this point.

"All I want to do is locate her, make sure she's okay, and ask a few questions to find out what this is all about. If Sun Ling doesn't want or need my help, I'm under no obligation to tell anyone but Liang Chao where she is, and he already knows."

That put the situation into a different light for Susie. She nodded slowly and said, "Okay, Johnny, I'm with you, too."

I saw Jeff look at his wristwatch. He said, "We're going to have to get going soon. It's almost time for the volunteers to change into their costumes for the procession."

"Okay, Jeff, I just have one more question." Taking the sheet of stationery I'd found in Sun Ling's hotel room from my inside coat pocket, I unrolled the page and handed it to Susie. "What do you make of this?"

As her eyes scanned down the page, she said, "These are very nice drawings." Then her gaze landed on the sketch of herself at the bottom of the page. "Wait, is that supposed to be me?"

Jeff grinned. "Feel like you're lookin' in a mirror, sis?"

In an appreciative tone, she said, "I do! These are wonderful! Who drew them?"

I said, "Since I found them in Sun Ling's hotel room and Jeff says he occasionally saw her sketching in the village, I'm guessing she did."

Sounding somewhat in awe, Susie said, "Yes, I know she likes to draw, but I had no idea she's this talented."

"Yes, the drawings are good, but what interests me more right now are the Chinese characters in the lower right margin. Jeff said you might be able to translate them."

Susie studied the page a moment and then said, "Well, yes, but what they say doesn't make any sense."

"What do you mean?"

"Well, Chinese characters aren't an alphabet like we have in English. They represent sounds in the Chinese language and tell you how to pronounce the words as well as what they mean. It looks like Sun Ling was trying to write an English word she heard, but the word had sounds in it that aren't used in the Chinese language, so when you say the word back, it doesn't make any sense."

"Give it a try anyway."

"Okay. The word seems to have three syllables, and you would say it 'bu-ling-tan.' See what I mean? I guess it could be a proper noun, but I've never heard of it before."

I repeated, "Bu-ling-tan. Is that right?"

"Yes. That's what it says."

Jotting the three phonetic syllables down in my notebook, and with a sigh of disappointment, I said, "Okay. Thanks, Susie. I was hoping those characters might give us something more to go on, but it looks like they're a dead end." Turning to Jeff, I added, "Okay, that's it. I'm sorry if I made you late."

I returned the page of sketches to my pocket, but as I did so, I saw a little of what I took to be sadness on Susie Yang's face. I made myself a mental note to be sure the page of Fairmont Hotel stationery ended up with her when this caper came to whatever end it was going to come to.

SEVENTEEN

There was already a small group of young men and women hanging around the green door to the dressing room building when Susie, Jeff, and I got there. While Jeff unlocked the door, Susie introduced me to her friend, Annie Lee, the girl who played the other handmaiden during Sun Ling's appearances in the village.

As the kids filed into the building, Jeff said, "Hey, Johnny, I just had a great idea. After I let these kids into their dressing rooms, I'll come back and take you up in the Pagoda Tower. You can watch procession from up there, and you can also catch a great view of the whole exposition. It's really something to see!"

I said that sounded fine to me, and then I killed a few minutes saying "bu-ling-tan" over and over in my head, trying to make it mean something. When Jeff came back, the syllables meant nothing more to me than they had when he left.

The shop occupying the ground floor of the impressive seven-tiered Pagoda Tower was in the business of selling Chinese Village souvenirs, and judging by the crowd of customers inside, the shop appeared to be a profitable venture. At the center of the shop, Jeff unlocked the door to a square room that turned out to be a stairwell housing a steep stairway zigzagging its way to the top of the tower. I followed Jeff up the steps, and as we passed a door on the second-floor landing, he said, "We can watch the procession from this level, but we have to go up another floor to really see the exposition."

The tower's third floor was a square balcony surrounding the stairwell. Jeff wasn't kidding about the view. It was nothing short of spectacular. He said, "I have to go back down and let the kids out when they're through changing for the procession. Then I'll come back here and watch the procession with you. I'll meet you on the next floor down."

He disappeared through the stairwell door, and I wandered over to the north side of the open balcony. From there I had a wonderful view of the parking lot. It was still less than a third full, but there seemed to be more cars entering the lot than leaving it. I could also see my faithful steed patiently awaiting my return.

Moving to the east side of the tower, I got a seagull's eye view of the Gayway. The crowds along its streets had grown since Jeff and I'd been there earlier. The largest concentration of fairgoers was clustered in front of Sally Rand's Nude Ranch. That was no surprise. Beginning in the twenties, Sally earned her stripes—or more accurately, she'd taken them off—in burlesque houses from New York to San Francisco, acquiring the dubious title of the country's most famous stripper. Now it seemed Sally was moving up in the world, capitalizing on her name, and letting other women take off their clothes while she raked in the profits. According to my handy-dandy guide book, Sally's Nude Ranch was a show featuring women clad in little more than six-guns and cowboy hats performing ranch chores. Not exactly wholesome entertainment for the entire family.

As I was about to step around to the south side of the balcony, I spotted a couple of familiar faces in the crowd below me. They belonged to Tang Hong and another fellow I recognized from my morning visit to Tang's warehouse—the hefty Tong bodyguard I'd seen keeping an eye on things there. Tang Hong's presence at the exposition struck me as strange because he didn't seem like the kind of fellow who enjoyed fairs and amusement parks, especially a few days after his father was darn near cut in two by a shotgun blast.

Then I remembered Tang saying Sergeant Bailey told him one of his father's killers was spotted by someone at the exposition, that someone being me. Now Tang's being here with his mountain-sized Tong buddy made sense. They were looking for the guy. Of course they weren't going to find him. Any goon worth his salt, particularly one with a murder rap hanging over his head, would have more sense than to hang around a place where he'd already been spotted. That was just fine by me. We really didn't need any more bloodshed, and even if he was on a wild goose chase, Tang looked like he could use the fresh air.

The best view of the exposition buildings was from the south side of the balcony. In the afternoon sun, shadows were growing longer, emphasizing the height of the towers and elongating the shapes of the statuary. The sun also made all the fountains and waterways sparkle like fields of blue diamonds. I stood there for a couple of minutes taking it all in before moving around to the balcony's west railing.

Now the view included the San Francisco skyline beyond the Cavalcade of the West across Nanking Road from the Chinese Village. The audience for the next showing of the Cavalcade was lining up outside the enclosure, and as I watched them, I was surprised to see what had to be the dumbest goon west of the Rockies. I was obviously wrong about the guy; he didn't have enough sense to stay out of sight because there he was, lurking in the shadows along the Cavalcade's wall.

I turned quickly and looked south again. It took me a moment to spot them, but Tang and his buddy had already turned right out of the Gayway and they were headed toward Nanking Road. Suddenly I had the feeling I was watching two trains heading toward each other at high speed on the same track. If Tang and his pal turned right onto Nanking road, they would be headed directly for the guy they were looking for, and if Tang recognized him as one of the guys who showed up at the warehouse and threatened his father, blood was going to be shed—very likely the innocent blood of exposition visitors.

Now Tang and company were only a few paces from Nanking Road, and from where I was up in the tower, there was absolutely nothing I could do to head off the impending train wreck. I held my breath as they reached the intersection, willing them to keep going straight instead of turning right. The two men stopped in the intersection for a minute, apparently discussing where to go next. Then they started walking again . . . straight ahead toward the Court of Pacifica.

I glanced back at the goon. He showed no sign of having seen Tang and his Tong muscle. I breathed a sigh of relief. A potential disaster had been temporarily avoided. Now I had to figure out how to defuse the situation permanently.

That's when Jeff stuck his head out of the stairwell and said, "Oh, you're still up here. Come on down to the second floor. The procession is about to start."

"Wait a minute, Jeff. I want to show you something."

He trotted over to my side, and I pointed toward the goon lurking just opposite the northernmost of the two openings in the Chinese Village wall. "You see that guy in the spiffy suit down there next to the Cavalcade?"

Jeff looked where I was pointing and said, "Yeah, what about him?"

"That's one of the two guys who killed Tang Fan."

"You're kiddin'! What's he doing here?"

"Most likely waiting for me. He followed me around the exposition yesterday afternoon, and he knows I recognized him as one of the two guys in the car that sped away after Tang Fan was shot. Odds are he's hoping to get rid of the only witness who can finger him for Tang's murder."

"Oh, oh! What are we gonna do?"

"I'm going to use the telephone in your office to call the homicide cop who's handling the murder investigation. If you want to help . . . ."

Excited at the prospect of being in on the capture of an honest-to-gosh desperado, Jeff interrupted with an emphatic, "Yes! What do you want me to do?"

"Go back to the Gayway through the dressing room building and find that security cop we talked to before. Tell him I said there's a murder suspect wanted by the San Francisco P. D. out in front of the Chinese Village. Tell him I've phoned the cops and they're on their way, but he needs to call in some reinforcements and get out there quick so the guy doesn't disappear on us. Be sure to tell him I said the suspect is armed and very dangerous. Got that?"

"I've got it. What do you want me to do then?"

"Come back to the village and stay put. When the cops get here things are likely to get nasty."

"Okay, Johnny. I'm on my way."

We beat it down the stairs double-time, and I headed for the village administration building. In Jeff's office I dialed Bailey's number and waited what seemed like an eternity for him to come on the line. When he did, the sergeant was his usual, charming self.

"What the hell do you want now, Spicer?"

"Just to let you know the goon I saw in the getaway car after Tang's murder is now standing around outside the Chinese Village out here on Treasure Island. I've already alerted the security guys to keep an eye on him until you can get out here."

I had to hand it to Bailey. He was all business when it mattered. "Okay, Spicer, I'm on my way. I just hope that guy doesn't disappear on us again."

With that the telephone clicked and I pondered what to do next. Ideally the thing to do was go back up in the Pagoda Tower and watch the situation unfold from that nice safe vantage point. Unfortunately, Jeff had the keys so the tower was out. The important thing was to make sure the goon didn't disappear again, and the only other way I could do that was to go out on Nanking Road and keep my eye on him from there.

I went to the southernmost opening in the Chinese Village wall and looked up Nanking Road. The goon was still there on the other side of the Cavalcade show line, which was getting shorter as people went in. I needed a concealed spot where I could watch the guy without him seeing me, and the planting area down the middle of Nanking Road looked like my best bet. It had a couple of man-sized trees in it, and I sprinted for one of them.

The last few people in the Cavalcade line entered the show, and then things went to hell in a handbasket. Wilbur, the security guard, came around the corner onto Nanking Road from the parking lot with Jeff in tow. I hadn't figured on the guy wanting to check the situation out for himself before he went for reinforcements—a dumb move because it almost guaranteed a confrontation Wilbur wasn't up to handling on his own.

I looked on dumbfounded as Wilbur walked straight toward the goon with Jeff still tagging along behind him. The goon, of course, wanted nothing to do with cops of any kind, and I saw him look in my direction as if to make sure his escape route was clear. That left me only one option.

I stepped out of my hiding place and started moving toward the goon, hoping he might surrender peacefully when he realized he was surrounded. He spotted me immediately, glanced back at Wilbur, and drew a pistol from inside his jacket. The goon was a fan of large artillery. The gun in his hand was a military-issue Colt forty-five semiautomatic.

I responded by drawing my Smith & Wesson, and the goon did exactly what I would have done under similar circumstances. He chose the lesser of two evils, turning around and heading for the relative safety of the parking lot—a route that was blocked only by a security cop who had yet to draw his weapon.

A group of three middle-aged women between me and the goon were also walking toward the parking lot. One of them spotted the guy's forty-five and screamed, "He's got a gun!" Then all hell broke loose.

Wilbur finally went for his service revolver, which was in a holster on his belt. He fumbled with the leather strap that snapped in place to keep the pistol secure. The goon kept coming at Wilbur.

I sprinted past the middle-aged women so I'd have a clear shot. By that time the goon was no more thirty feet from Wilbur, who finally got his revolver out of its holster. As he brought it up, the goon and I fired almost simultaneously. He got off two rounds at Wilbur from point-blank range before my slug hit him in the hip—I'd aimed low in the hope of disabling the guy rather than killing him.

The gunshots sounded like artillery rounds going off as they resonated in the canyon created by the Chinese Village wall and the Cavalcade enclosure. At that point a whole bunch of things happened at the same time. Exposition visitors on Nanking Road, including the three middle-aged gals, were now screaming and running every which way.

From the corner of my eye, I'd seen Wilbur jerk twice in quick succession before he staggered backward and went down, his revolver clattering to the concrete several feet away. From the way he hit the ground, I was pretty sure Wilbur out of the game—maybe for good.

My shot sent the goon sprawling, but he managed to hang onto his Colt. I ran toward him, pushing a couple of kids out of harm's way as I went by. The guy on the ground rolled over to look at me and found himself staring up the barrel of my Smith & Wesson. Looking down at him over my revolver's sights, I said, "Go ahead; give me a reason to blow your head off right here and now. All it will take is a twitch."

The goon decided he wasn't ready to die. He opened his hand and let the Colt fall to the ground. I ordered him to roll over onto his stomach and not move a muscle. Rolling over clearly caused him some pain, but he did what he was told and I picked up his pistol, slipping it into my coat pocket. Then I took a look around.

The three older gals who'd been doing all the screaming, along with several other folks, were looking back over their shoulders as they ran for the parking lot. The two kids I'd pushed out of the way were still on their hands and knees in the median strip that divided Nanking Road, their eyes as wide as saucers. People were pouring out of the Cavalcade show and the Chinese Village to see what all the fuss was about. A gray-haired man and a woman I took to be his wife were kneeling over Wilbur, trying to revive him.

With the crowd growing, and not wanting to take my eyes off the wounded goon at my feet, I needed some help. I looked around for Jeff and was surprised to see him lying on the ground about ten feet beyond Wilbur. That was strange because I'd seen the security cop take both rounds fired by the goon. A young woman was leaning over Jeff, and whatever had happened to him, it appeared he was fairing better than Wilbur. Jeff was moving and talking to the woman standing over him.

At that point reinforcements finally arrived in the form of three more security cops. Two of them came running around the corner onto Nanking Road from the parking lot end, and the third, an older fellow with sergeant's stripes on his sleeve, came from behind me. He had his revolver drawn, and since I was the only one still standing with a weapon, he pointed it at me. I said in a loud, clear voice, "Private cop! This guy is wanted by the SFPD as a murder suspect. He shot your man over there. A San Francisco homicide cop named Bailey is already on his way over here."

The security sergeant bought my story, at least temporarily, and said, "Okay. Where's this guy's gun?"

Without taking my eyes off the goon, I said, "It's in my side coat pocket. Help yourself."

He pulled the Colt from my pocket and sniffed it to see if the piece had actually been fired, which would help prove my story was on the level. Satisfied, he yelled at the other two security guards. "Cody, get over here and keep an eye on this bird. Eddie, get back to the office and call for some ambulances—it looks like we'll need at least three of 'em—and send some more men over here!"

With Cody now holding his service revolver on the goon, the sergeant took a pair of handcuffs from a leather case on his belt and cuffed the goon's wrists. Coming back to me, he said, "My name's Russo. You got some ID?"

I holstered my Smith & Wesson and handed Sergeant Russo my wallet opened to my P. I. license. He studied it for a minute and then handed it back to me, saying, "Okay, Spicer, stick with me."

It was clear from his demeanor that, unlike Wilbur, Russo was a pro. I guessed he was a retired cop adding a little to his pension by working in the exposition's security department. They were lucky to have him.

We walked over to Wilbur. The elderly man who'd been trying to help the downed security guard looked up and said, "I'm a doctor, but I'm afraid I can't do anything for this poor fellow. He has no pulse at all."

Russo nodded glumly and said, "Thanks for tryin', Doc." The sergeant gestured toward Jeff and added, "Would you mind takin' a look at this other fellow over here?"

As we walked toward Jeff, Susie Yang showed up at his side. She was still in her costume and there was panic in her normally calm voice. "Jeff? Jeff, are you okay?"

Jeff smiled weakly and said, "Sure, Sis, I'm fine." He looked up at me and said, "Tell her, Johnny. Tell her I'm gonna be fine."

The doctor opened Jeff's shirt to reveal what looked to be a bullet wound in his right shoulder. It took me a moment to figure out where the hell that bullet came from. I said, "Yeah, Susie, Jeff will be fine. I think the bullet that hit his shoulder had already passed through the security guard over there and was pretty well spent. It couldn't have done too much damage."

The doctor agreed. "Yes, this wound doesn't appear too deep, so it isn't likely the bullet hit anything critical, but it's still in the boy's shoulder. It will have to be removed at the hospital."

Susie didn't look entirely convinced, but she said, "Okay, but I'm going to the hospital with you. Just to be sure."

While all this was going on several more security cops showed up, and Russo barked orders. "Jennings, you and a couple of guys clear this crowd out of here, and then get maintenance to bring some barricades to block off both ends of this walkway. Collier, you take two men and see if you can find any witnesses who actually saw what happened here. Get their names, addresses, and telephone numbers, and write down what they saw."

I glanced back over my shoulder to be sure the goon was still where I'd left him, but I needn't have worried. Cody was on the job. Wailing sirens then heralded the approach of the ambulances Russo ordered, but Sergeant Bailey got there first. He arrived in an unmarked Chevrolet four-door sedan and pulled up at the parking lot end of Nanking Road. Four uniformed officers piled out of the Chevy with Bailey, who was in civilian clothes. Russo walked quickly toward the cops, and I followed along at a more leisurely pace. I was in no hurry for another dose of the sergeant's charming personality.

Bailey's friendly greeting to Russo seemed to confirm my suspicion that the security sergeant was a former cop. "Hiya, Tony. How've you been?"

With my arrival, Bailey interrupted Russo's response. "Spicer, you're a one-man disaster! Every time I see you the joint is littered with dead bodies."

I knew he was trying to get my goat, but I corrected him anyway. "Actually, only one of these bodies is deceased, and if the guy had done what he was told to do, he'd still be breathing."

Russo started to take umbrage at my criticism of his downed security guard, but Bailey interrupted him again. "We'll see 'bout that. Tony, is there somewhere we can go to sort all this out?"

The security sergeant suggested his office, and after Bailey gave his men instructions on how he wanted things handled, we walked over to Russo's headquarters in the exposition parking lot. What followed was a two-hour grilling during which I repeated my entire story of the afternoon's events at least three times.

While Bailey was putting me through the ringer, my body put me through the adrenalin aftereffects that usually follow a close call with death. I'd smoked half a pack of Luckys before my nerves began to settle and I realized that, in a perverse way, I probably owed my life to Wilbur Harmon. If he'd been a little more cautious and quicker on the draw, it's very likely I'd have gotten the goon's first bullet.

I figured it that way because I was pretty sure the goon was hanging around outside the Chinese Village for the ultimate purpose of eliminating the only witness to the murder of Tang Fan. They'd missed a perfect opportunity to take care of that chore when one of the other Jap agents sapped me Tuesday night in the Court of Pacifica. That detail still bothered me.

Bailey finally ended the interrogation by saying, "Okay, Spicer, it don't seem like you broke any laws, and it's pretty clear to me this fellow Harmon flummoxed things up in the first place, so you're off the hook again. You still stayin' at the Drake?"

"Yeah, but I don't know how much longer I'll be there. I'm pretty sure my client is about to pull the plug on my investigation."

The homicide sergeant raised his eyebrows slightly at that piece of news, but asked no questions. Instead, he said, "Okay. Just be sure I know where to find you. The DA is gonna need your testimony to convict this killer."

I nodded, and after a short pause, Bailey added, "I suppose you expect me to thank you for catchin' one of the mugs who skagged that Chinese guy."

"No, Sergeant Bailey. Having had the dubious pleasure of getting to know you, I have no such expectation."

For the first time since I'd known him, Bailey actually cracked something like a smile. "Well, I'm gonna fool you and say thanks anyway. And it looks to me like you handled a lousy situation as good as it could be handled, so thanks for that, too."

I nodded my acknowledgment of his uncharacteristic outpouring of gratitude and said, "Can you tell me where the ambulance took Jeff Yang, the other fellow who was wounded? I'd like to see how he's doing."

"Sure. They took him to Saint Mary's Hospital."

"What's the best way to get there from here?"

"The best way is to follow me. That's the same place where they took the guy you shot, and I'm goin' there right now to check up on him. After all the trouble it took to catch that bum, I sure as hell don't want to lose him now."

EIGHTEEN

About all I can tell you about the location of San Francisco's Saint Mary's Hospital is it's clear to hell and gone on the other side of the city from the Bay Bridge. I was so busy keeping Sergeant Bailey's tail lights in sight, I couldn't keep track of all the turns we made before pulling into the hospital parking lot.

From there, things got a little easier. Bailey walked into the emergency ward like he owned the place. The goon was still down there, but Jeff Yang had been sent up to a regular hospital room. I left Bailey using the emergency ward telephone to arrange for more cops to keep an eye on the killer, and I took an elevator up to the second floor.

Jeff had a four-bed room all to himself, and he was sitting up in one of those beds talking to Susie. When he saw me, he said, "Hi, Johnny. Did we get that killer?"

Trying to sound cheerful because that's how you're supposed to sound when you visit people in the hospital, I said, "Yup, we got him. More important, how are you doing?"

"Okay, I guess. They gave me some kind of pain pills that make everything kind of blurry. Sis, tell Johnny how I'm doing."

Susie was still in her procession costume, but she'd removed her stage makeup. Other than that, she mostly looked relieved. "Yes, Jeff's going to be alright. The doctor already removed the bullet from his shoulder, and they sent him up here so they can keep an eye on him overnight. The doctor says if everything is still okay tomorrow, Jeff can go home."

Turning back to Jeff, I said, "Kid, I'm sure sorry you got shot. If I'd figured there was a risk of that happening, I'd never have gotten you involved. I just can't figure out what the hell Wilbur Harmon was thinking, showing up like that without any help. You told him what I said, right?"

I could tell the pain medication was making Jeff sleepy because it took him a few seconds to comprehend my question and answer it. "Yes, I told him what you said . . . word for word. But he had to see for himself before . . . before going for help. And he made me go with him to point out the . . . bad

116

guy. What the hell happened out there? All I . . . remember is a lot of shooting."

I gave Jeff and Susie a brief account of the shootout on Nanking Road, but Jeff dozed off before I finished. I said to Susie, "It looks like Jeff is out for the night. Do you want to stay here or can I give you a lift home?"

"I really should go back to the village and change my clothes. I'm afraid I got this costume filthy and it will need cleaning. And I need to bring Jeff's car home."

"Fine, I'll take you back to Treasure Island."

Susie woke Jeff to tell him she was leaving and she'd be back in the morning. Then we went downstairs to my Chrysler, and following her directions, I drove us back to Treasure Island. On the way, I said, "Susie, I really feel bad about Jeff taking that bullet. It was one of those times when a perfectly good plan turned into a disaster."

"Don't feel badly, Johnny. Jeff is going to be fine, and now he has an exciting story to tell his friends. I'm just grateful you weren't hurt. You were very brave to do what you did."

I let the conversation end there. I didn't bother to mention that brave was not high on the list of things I was feeling at the moment.

When we finally got back to Treasure Island, I parked next to the barricades still blocking the parking lot end of Nanking Road and walked with Susie into the Chinese Village. Maintenance men were busy scrubbing blood off the concrete so there'd be no sign of the unpleasantness to spoil the fun of tomorrow's exposition visitors.

Susie produced Jeff's key ring and let us into the dressing room building, where I waited in the hall while she changed. Glancing down the walkway at the broken door to Sun Ling's dressing room, I imagined her bodyguard standing there marking time while she climbed a ladder and disappeared through the ceiling. The whole situation stunk to high heavens, and I cursed Tom Kendall, Liang Chao, and everybody else who'd made a sucker out of me. I also cursed myself for taking a job that was fishy from the very beginning.

Then and there I made up my mind to call Liang when I got back to my hotel room so he could fire me. I also decided not to tell him I was in on the gag. I saw no sense in making him angry and risking not getting paid what I was owed for the wild goose chase I'd been on for the past three days. In the morning I'd drive back to Hollywood and leave all this tomfoolery behind.

When Susie came out, I escorted her out to Jeff's car, which definitely suited him. It was a spanking new Ford Deluxe—a flashy maroon convertible model. Watching Susie get in and adjust the seat so she could reach the pedals, I decided she was more of a Willys sort of gal—practical and efficient with no need of stylish gewgaws. I had to wonder how Susie and her brother turned out to be so different.

Leaving Treasure Island, I looked back over my shoulder for one last gawk at the mythical fantasy world created by the Golden Gate International Exposition's designers. There were no two ways about it; the exposition was something to see, but I'd had my fill of it and was happy to leave the fun and excitement behind.

When the Drake's desk clerk handed me my key, it came with a stack of telephone messages. They were all from Liang Chao except one left by Parker Atkins, the radio news reporter who'd visited me Wednesday night. I dropped them all into the wastebasket and called room service for a ham sandwich and another bucket of ice.

Ordering the ice reminded me of the bump on my noggin, which I'd pretty much forgotten about during the afternoon's excitement. It was still tender, but barely visible in the mirror. Looking at my reflection also reminded me that surviving the incident had a lot more to do with providence than intelligence.

If, as I figured, my assailant was one of Tang Fan's killers or at the very least, in league with them, I should be reclining on a table in the morgue next to Wilbur Harmon instead of waiting for a ham sandwich in my overly elegant room at the Drake. That bothered me. I'm not complaining, mind you, just wondering why the Jap agent didn't finish the job of eliminating the only witness to their crime when he had the ideal opportunity to do so.

My sandwich arrived with the ice, and I poured myself a couple of fingers' worth of Spey Royal. Then I sat down at the room's writing desk to relax and enjoy my dinner. Of course, that's when the telephone rang. Knowing full well who'd be on the other end of the line, I picked up the receiver.

Liang apparently had no time for the customary courtesies. "Mister Spicer, I am extremely disappointed that you have not returned my telephone calls."

"Good evening, Mister Liang. I would have called you by now, but I got a little busy out at Treasure Island this afternoon."

"Yes, so I have heard. I also understand that young Mister Yang was injured in the incident you caused. I trust he will recover."

"Yes, Jeff is doing fine. And I will point out that his getting shot was not my doing. It's also worth mentioning that we captured one of Tang Fan's killers in the process."

"That is all fine and good, Mister Spicer, but capturing Tang Fan's killers is not what we are paying you to do, which brings me to the reason I have been trying to reach you. We have discussed the matter of your progress, or more accurately your lack of progress in finding Sun Ling, and we have decided we no longer require your services."

I continued demonstrating admirable restraint by saying, "I understand, Mister Liang."

"As of this moment you are no longer authorized to search for Sun Ling on our behalf. Is that understood?"

"Yes, Mister Liang. That is understood."

The man was so cocksure of himself I don't think he even expected an argument. Liang continued, "I will instruct my secretary to send you a check tomorrow morning in the amount of four-hundred dollars. With the two-hundred dollar deposit I gave you Monday, that amount pays for five days of your services, including your trip home tomorrow, plus one-hundred dollars for expenses. Will that cover everything, Mister Spicer?"

It didn't cover the ninety-some bucks the Jap agent lifted from my wallet Wednesday night, but Liang didn't know about that, and I'd padded my normal seventy-five dollar daily rate enough that I was still ahead of the game. I said, "That's very generous of you, Mister Liang."

"Then goodbye, Mister Spicer."

I started to reply, but the phone clicked in my ear and Liang was gone. Good riddance.

After finishing my ham sandwich dinner, I spread one of the Sir Francis Drake's hand towels out on the writing desk and commenced to disassembling and cleaning my Smith & Wesson. I'd just gotten the revolver broken down when someone knocked on my door. With no functioning weapon and the knowledge that one of Tang Fan's killers was still out there somewhere, I exercised some sensible caution by asking, "Who is it?"

"It's Park Atkins, Johnny."

Recognizing his voice, I opened the door and said, "Hi, Park. Come on in."

Gesturing toward the collection of Smith & Wesson parts on the writing desk, Atkins said, "I understand you used that revolver with considerable accuracy out at Treasure Island today."

Returning to my cleaning task, I said, "Yeah, although things didn't turn out exactly the way I hoped they would. How'd you hear about it already?"

"Sergeant Bailey over at homicide held a press conference a little while ago. He credited the exposition security cops for collaring the killer, but he did mention that an unnamed private investigator from Los Angeles provided assistance. I presume that was you."

"It was."

"And knowing a little something about how these things work, I'm guessing your role in the incident amounted to somewhat more than mere assistance."

"Good heavens, man! How can you doubt the veracity of an upstanding public servant like Sergeant Bailey?"

"It's easy. I know the guy. Like most cops, he puts the credit where it will do him the most good, not necessarily where it belongs. That's why I stopped by tonight. I was hoping to get a statement from you about what actually happened out there this afternoon. How about it?"

Reassembling my Smith & Wesson, I gave some thought to Atkins' question. There was always the possibility I might return to San Francisco one day and find myself in need of a friend in the SFPD homicide division. That being the case, it seemed prudent to go along with Bailey's version of the story.

"For the record, let's just say I'm happy I was able to provide some assistance to the San Francisco Police Department and the very capable Golden Gate International Exposition security service in the apprehension of a suspected killer. I'm also saddened by the death of the security officer who was shot by the suspect during the incident."

While Atkins scribbled my official statement onto a page in his notebook, another thought occurred to me. I added, "I would also like to commend Jeff Yang, a representative of the exposition's Chinese Village exhibit, for bravery above and beyond the call of duty during the suspect's apprehension. Unfortunately, Mister Yang was also shot, but he is expected to recover fully from his wound."

Atkins finished writing and looked at me with a touch of amusement on his face. "Spicer, you're as full of crap as Bailey. What about off the record?"

"Really off the record?"

Atkins slipped his notebook back into his jacket pocket and said, "Yes, really off the record."

"The simple truth is that Wilbur, the security cop who was killed, thought he was smarter than me. He ignored my instructions on how to handle the situation, and that got him killed. It also darn near got a lot of other people killed, including yours truly."

Nodding his understanding, Atkins said, "I kind of figured it was something along those lines. I'll give your buddy Yang a mention in my broadcast tomorrow night."

"Thanks. He's a good kid."

As I slipped the last round into my revolver and snapped the cylinder closed, Atkins asked, "How's your investigation going? Has the missing Chinese gal shown up?"

Again, I had to think about how to answer his question. If I was right about the FBI being in on the hoax Liang was pulling, there might actually be some issues of national security attached to it. I figured I'd be tangling with Kendall over this case sooner or later, and I sure as hell didn't want to give him anything to throw back at me. If, on the other hand, the whole thing was just more FBI baloney, some unwanted publicity might be a good way to repay Liang for his business—monkey business. Figuring Atkins would want to know more, I said, "No, she's still among the missing, but that's no longer my problem. I've been sacked."

Atkins watched me slip my Smith & Wesson back into its holster and said, "That surprises me, Johnny. You don't strike me as a guy who gets fired very often."

I looked him in the eye and chose my words carefully. "There might be more to the story, but it's not for publication . . . at least not yet. Tell you what, you come on down my way sometime, and we'll have lunch at Musso and Frank. Maybe I'll have more say about it then."

Atkins was no dummy. He got the message between my carefully spoken lines and knew darn well what I was trying to tell him. Thoughtfully, Atkins said, "Yeah, I'm gonna do that. I remember Musso and Frank makes great flannel cakes."

NINETEEN

San Francisco - Friday - April 14, 1939

My last day in the city by the bay dawned in much the same fashion as all the other days I'd been here—foggy with a light drizzle. That was okay by me, though, because I was on my way back to the land of sunshine.

After a quick shower and shave, I packed my bag and headed for the lobby. I informed the desk clerk I was checking out, but there would be one more room charge in the coffee shop. I intended to let Mister Liang buy me a good breakfast.

My next stop was the bell captain's podium where I left my bag and told the scarlet-clad lad I'd be back to retrieve it after breakfast. Then I ordered up a thick ham steak and a couple of eggs sunny-side-up in the coffee shop.

I finished my breakfast and was enjoying the last half of a pretty fair cup of coffee when it occurred to me that Jeff and Susie didn't know I was leaving town. It didn't seem right to take off without saying goodbye and thanking them for their help. Besides, there was something in my coat pocket I wanted Susie to have.

My wristwatch told me it was quarter past eight, and figuring Susie for an early riser, I decided to try giving her a call. I signed the breakfast check and slid into one of the elegant public telephone booths in the lobby. Nobody answered Susie's home phone, so I gave the number for the family restaurant a try.

After a conversation worthy of a Jack Benny radio program skit because the woman's English was only slightly better than my Chinese, I finally got Susie on the line. "Hello, Johnny. You just caught me. I'm on my way to pick up Jeff at the hospital. I would have left fifteen minutes ago, but Jeff insists he wants to go out to the exposition instead of going home to rest. I can't talk him out of the idea, so I had to go up to his room and get him some fresh clothes."

"That sounds like Jeff, alright. I'm glad I caught you, though, because I'm leaving for home today and I wanted to say goodbye before I headed out of town."

Susie sounded genuinely disappointed. "You've giving up on finding Sun Ling?"

"I have no choice, Susie. As expected, Mister Liang handed me my walking papers last night. He clearly doesn't want Sun Ling found, at least not by me. Listen, how would it be if I met you and Jeff out on Treasure Island in an hour or so?"

"I am really disappointed in Mister Liang. He is not the honorable man I thought he was." After a brief pause, she added, "Yes, an hour or maybe a little more at the village will be fine. We'll see you then."

I tipped the bellman a quarter when I retrieved my suitcase, and I tipped the parking valet yet another a quarter for bringing my car around and stowing my bag in the luggage compartment. Pulling away from the curb in front of the Sir Frances Drake, I headed north on Powell Street. The direct route to the bridge and Treasure Island was in the opposite direction, but I had some time to kill so I took the scenic route.

I followed Powell all the way to the bay. When I could go no further, I turned right and ended up on a thoroughfare known as The Embarcadero. This wide boulevard, I found, skirted the waterfront and took me in a generally southern direction past San Francisco's vast port facilities. Each dock had its own warehouse or terminal building with a Spanish Mission facade. I was able to catch glimpses of these facades and the ships moored at their births during brief breaks in the heavy traffic of trucks busily conducting the business of shipping. Like Third Street where it passed by Tang Fan's warehouse, The Embarcadero was a busy place.

Seeking a break from the traffic, I turned onto a street that looked as if it might take me up to an interesting looking circular tower perched atop a hill to my right. The street I'd chosen turned out to be Lombard, but not the part made famous in travelogues for its zigzag course down a residential hillside. Instead, this part of Lombard proceeded straight up one of San Francisco's notorious seven hills—Telegraph Hill, to be specific.

A small sign mounted on a utility pole at an intersection part way up the hill instructed me to turn left if I wanted to visit the Coit Memorial Tower. Since that seemed to be what I wanted to do, I turned left and found myself winding around the top half of Telegraph Hill to its summit, upon which sat the tower I sought. I pulled into a parking place and walked over for a closer look.

A sign informed me the tower was a monument to some rich old gal named Lillie Coit, who according to legend loved nothing more than watching firemen at work. She left a significant part of her fortune for the beautification of San Francisco, which included the memorial tower before me and a second memorial located somewhere else honoring the San Francisco Fire Department.

According to another sign, the paltry sum of twenty-five cents would buy me a ride to the top of the tower via an elevator. I figured if I could pay some fellow a quarter for retrieving my car from the hotel parking garage, I could certainly afford another quarter for such a once-in-a-lifetime experience.

From the circular observation floor, which yet another sign informed me was 180 feet above the top of Telegraph Hill, I could see San Francisco from ocean to bay. In spite of the fog, it was quite a view. I walked around the circumference of the tower looking out at misty views of such landmarks as the Golden Gate Bridge, Fisherman's Wharf, and to the east, the city's newest landmark, Treasure Island. Beyond Treasure Island I could make out the hills of Oakland, which appeared to be bathed in sunshine. Lucky Oakland.

After making a complete circuit of the observation platform, I got tired of playing tourist and returned to my car. From the top of Telegraph Hill, I somehow found the Bay Bridge and crossed it to Treasure Island.

I walked into the Chinese Village administration building a few minutes after nine-thirty and found the Yang kids in Jeff's office. Greetings were exchanged, and Jeff said, "Gosh, Johnny, Susie says you're going home today. I'm going to miss you. This has been a real kick!"

I laughed. "Jeff, I can honestly say you're the first person I ever met who got a kick out of being shot."

He grinned back. "Well, that part wasn't fun, but the rest of it's been neat. I like being a detective."

"I'm glad you had fun, because I couldn't have gotten as far as I did without the assistance you two gave me."

Susie piped up, saying, "It's just a shame it was all for nothing."

Nodding my agreement, I said, "Sometimes the detective business is like that. In this case, we've been the victims of some tomfoolery I still don't understand. And at this point, I really don't have any burning desire to find out what Liang is up to."

Her expression sad, Susie said, "I know, but I miss Sun Ling. I really enjoyed the little bit of time we spent together. She's a very interesting person."

Yeah, I thought, people who make themselves disappear mysteriously are definitely interesting. Changing the subject slightly, I said, "Susie, I have something for you."

I handed her the rolled sheet of Fairmont Hotel stationery on which Sun Ling had drawn three sketches and Chinese characters spelling out the nonsense word, "boolingtan."

As Susie unrolled it, I said, "Since Sun Ling isn't around to tell us different, I'm going to assume she would want you to have that as a keepsake."

"Oh, thank you, Johnny! I'll put this in a frame and hang it on my apartment wall so I'll think of Sun Ling every time I see it."

Turning to Jeff, I offered my left hand to accommodate his good arm, and said, "I'm sorry I don't have anything for you but a handshake and my gratitude for your able assistance."

"That's okay, Johnny. It was a real pleasure helping you out."

"Well, kids, I've got a long drive ahead of me, so I'd better hit the road. When you get some free time, hop on a southbound train and come down to see me. I'll give you the Cook's tour of Hollywood."

Jeff nodded enthusiastically, and Susie said, "I would enjoy that. I've never seen Hollywood."

I gave Susie a fatherly hug and walked out to my car. After starting the engine, I was getting myself comfortable for the drive ahead, when something that struck me as very strange caught my eye.

My Chrysler was parked only a couple of spots from the parking lot perimeter road, and what I saw was a black four-door Ford sedan driving toward the parking lot exit. The strange part was the guy driving the Ford. It was Junior G-man, Tom Kendall. Now what the hell was he doing this far from home? Something told me the answer to that question might prove interesting, so I pulled out behind the Ford and followed it from the parking lot and toward the bridge.

I don't believe in coincidences, so I had to conclude that Kendall's appearance at this particular place and at this particular moment added up to more monkey business. When, after crossing the causeway to Yerba Buena Island, the black Ford stayed to the left—the route that led east across the bridge toward Oakland—the situation got even more interesting.

As I followed Kendall across the bridge, I thought about what business he might have had at the Golden Gate International Exposition. One of those guesses struck me as so obvious I couldn't believe I hadn't thought of it before.

The exposition's exhibit halls included a huge edifice dedicated to the United States government. Inside that building was a plethora of exhibits showing how politicians were spending our tax dollars on projects designed to make us happy and content. What better place to stash a missing Chinese diplomat? That idea didn't jibe with Wilbur Harmon's statement that Sun Ling was headed for the parking lot when he saw her, but that didn't necessarily mean she didn't end up in the federal exhibit building. Had Kendall just visited Sun Ling? Maybe.

U.S. Highway 40 continued straight for about a mile beyond the bridge, at which point the highway turned left onto a street known as San Pablo

Boulevard, and so did Kendall. I'd been keeping a couple of cars between me and the black Ford so as not to be so obvious about following Kendall. If my hunch was right, though, he knew damned well I'd taken the bait and was following along in his wake.

San Pablo Boulevard took us more or less north through the towns of Berkeley, Albany, El Cerrito, and Richmond. By the time we passed through the town for which San Pablo Boulevard was apparently named, I'd been following Kendall for a good half hour, and I was starting to wonder if my Junior G-man buddy planned driving all the way to Washington D. C. for a visit with J. Edgar, himself.

After leaving San Pablo, U.S. 40 turned northeast and traveled through an area of rolling hills studded with oak trees. The scenery was pleasant, and from my point of view, the route had only one problem: It was going the wrong way. While waiting for a traffic signal in San Pablo to turn green, I'd consulted my Shell map and decided to follow Kendall for another ten miles or so to a bridge that crossed a body of water called the Carquinez Strait. If he stayed on U.S. 40 there, I would turn onto a road that headed southeast and eventually connected with U.S. 101 near San Jose.

Meanwhile I kept myself by busy guessing what the hell Kendall was up to. If I was right about my hunch that his perfectly timed appearance in the exposition parking lot was no coincidence, it had to be for one of two reasons. Either he wanted me away from Treasure Island or he wanted me at some other location for a specific reason.

If, on the other hand, my hunch was wrong and his showing up when he did really was a coincidence, following him might lead me to some answers that would make sense out of this crazy caper. I wasn't being entirely honest when I told Jeff and Susie I really didn't care what Liang Chao was up to. I did care, but only out of professional pride. It bothered me to leave a case with so many questions unanswered.

A number of those questions had to do with the antics of the Japanese. Their parts of the puzzle just didn't fit the rest of the picture. For example, I could not believe that whoever the goons reported to actually thought killing Tang Fan would put an end to illicit shipments of supplies and arms from the U.S. to China. China is a damned big country, and a few lousy boatloads of stuff wouldn't go very far there, so it was quite likely others were doing the same thing Tang was doing, probably including Liang Chao. Bumping off one guy couldn't make a difference on that score.

Okay, then, if stopping shipments to China wasn't their motive, why did the Japanese kill Tang? And why did they not kill the witness to their crime—namely, me—when they had the perfect opportunity the other night in the Court of Pacifica? And why, after not killing me when it could have been easily done, did the first goon risk capture by showing up again outside

126

the Chinese Village? Was it really me he was after, or was there another reason for his being there that I wasn't seeing?

Despite what Detective Sergeant Bailey and Tang Hong thought, I was convinced the Japs were players in the Sun Ling game, and as I moved their puzzle pieces around in my mind, I began to see one way in which they might be made to fit the picture. If they did fit the way I was imagining, the convoluted charade dreamed up by the FBI and Liang Chao was about to backfire on them in the worst possible way.

Twenty or so minutes later we were approaching the bridge I'd seen on the map, and a little disappointed that I'd been led on another wild goose chase, I started looking for my turn to the southeast. The way things turned out, however, I didn't have to do much looking—all I had to do was stay on Kendall's tail because he took the very same road.

Since none of the three cars between me and Kendall's Ford made the turn, I pulled over to the side of the road the first chance I got in order to put some space between us. I used the time to get my bearings.

We seemed to be in the town of Crockett, wherein the most prominent industry appeared to be refining sugar. Down a side road to my left there stood a sprawling, nine-story, red brick building bearing a large sign that said, "C & H Pure Cane Sugar." The factory sat between the water and a couple of railroad tracks, which made perfect sense. The raw sugar cane arrived from Hawaii by ship to be refined in the factory, and the finished product left by rail. Very efficient.

When I figured it was safe to continue following Kendall, I pulled back onto the road. Leaving Crockett, the route continued in a more or less southeastly direction and deteriorated into a narrow, winding road with tall eucalyptus trees on both sides. I lost sight of Kendall, but I wasn't concerned because we passed only one turnoff in the first three or four miles. So when the road straightened enough for me to see some distance ahead and there was no sign of the black Ford, I simply made a U-turn and went back to the only road Kendall could have taken.

The fact that he took that road and didn't wait around to make sure I saw him take it made me wonder if I was right about Kendall's intentions. If he really intended leading me to some specific location, he'd just taken an awfully big chance of losing me.

At the turnoff a weathered sign nailed to a leaning wooden post showed a faded arrow pointing to the right and the words, "Port Costa." I made the turn and found myself driving through a sparsely populated residential area with a few small cottages scattered among the trees. A bit further down the road I drove by a school and a couple of churches. Then I was in what passed for downtown Port Costa—two blocks containing a dozen or so wood-frame buildings and a three-story brick warehouse. Small though it was, the little burg boasted two hotels, a post office, some eateries, and at least two saloons, along with the typical purveyors of goods and services.

The street ended at a Southern Pacific train yard and the rotting remains of some long docks poking out into the Carquinez Strait. I wondered what made Port Costa worthy of such attention from the mighty S.P., but my curiosity didn't last long. U-turning at the end of the main drag, I spotted Kendall's black Ford tucked out of sight in an alleyway between the railroad yard and a dilapidated hotel on the west side of the street opposite the brick warehouse. I drove up half a block, turned around again, and pulled to the curb under a shady tree to consider my next move.

Despite the railroad yard, it was quite peaceful in Port Costa. Birds were chirping and a soft breeze gently ruffled the tree under which I sat. There were a few other cars parked along the street, but none of them seemed in a hurry to go anywhere.

The deteriorating docks I'd noticed beyond the switching yard were huge, indicating that Port Costa had been a major shipping center in its day—based on the age of the buildings, probably around the turn of the century. That conclusion, plus the existence of two fully operational saloons in such a tiny town, gave me to suspect things hadn't always been so tranquil here. Likely the men who worked the docks, the train yard, and the warehouse weren't above whooping it up after the five-o'clock whistle blew. In my imagination I could see Port Costa jumping with the best of 'em back in its day.

That led me to think the hotel where I'd seen Kendall's car might have been built to house transient workers. It was a three-story, wood-frame affair festooned with bay windows. Like everything else in Port Costa, the hotel had seen better days. Its gray paint was faded and chipped, and a sign announcing to anyone who cared that it was The Burlington Hotel dangled over the sidewalk at a threatening angle.

As I sat there taking in the sights, Port Costa's peaceful ambiance was lulling me into a stupor until a passing thought jerked me awake like I'd been hit by a bolt of lightning. The damned sign said The Burlington Hotel. Boolingtan . . . Burlington! The mysterious word Sun Ling printed on a sheet of hotel stationery was as close as the Chinese language would let her come to the English name "Burlington!"

TWENTY

I spent a few minutes contemplating the moment of enlightenment I'd just experienced. The name Burlington was important enough to Sun Ling for her to print it—or as close as she could come to it—on a sheet of hotel stationery shortly before she disappeared from Treasure Island. FBI agent Tom Kendall just drove from Treasure Island to the backwater burg of Post Costa and was at that moment visiting the Burlington Hotel. Could it be I was half a block away from finding the missing Chinese diplomat?

On the other hand, I thought, what difference does it make? My former client, Mister Liang, informed me in no uncertain terms I was no longer authorized to search for Sun Ling on his behalf. In other words, finding the missing Chinese diplomat, who might be half a block away, wasn't my problem anymore.

On yet another hand, I had a couple of bones to pick with Tom Kendall. In particular, I wanted to tell him what I thought of the FBI for making a stooge out of a clever, Hollywood detective named Spicer. The third hand won the debate. Slipping the now well-worn magazine photo of Sun Ling into my jacket pocket, I walked across the street to the Burlington Hotel.

The hotel entrance opened onto a short hallway and stairs leading to the upper floors. A door on my right led to a small restaurant. The registration counter was in a small room to the left. An elderly gent with thick eyeglasses and a bushy gray mustache sat at a desk behind the counter leaning close over a copy of LIFE magazine with another old guy in a cowboy hat on the cover. The old guy at the desk squinted up at me and said, "You lookin' for a room, mister?"

"No, actually, I'm looking for this woman." I held up my picture of Sun Ling.

He couldn't see the picture from where he was sitting, so he got up and ambled to the counter where he squinted at Sun Ling, squinted up at me, squinted at Sun Ling again, and scratched his head. "Well, sir, maybe I seen that gal and maybe I ain't, but the hotel don't like me givin' out private information 'bout guests, so I can't rightly tell you if I seen her or not."

Having dealt with a few hotel clerks in my time, I recognized his righteous support of the hotel's privacy policy as a thinly veiled proposition, which I had come in prepared to accept. I laid the five-dollar bill in my left hand on the counter and said, "The young woman in the picture may be in danger. I'm sure she would appreciate your cooperation."

The fiver disappeared instantly, and the old guy said, "Well, sir, now that you put it that way, I do recall seein' that gal. She's a guest here."

I felt the familiar little tingle I usually get when a crucial piece of a puzzle slips into place. "When did she check in?"

He scratched his head and squinted off into space for a moment before saying, "I believe she showed up late last Sunday night."

"What room is she in?"

"She's on the second floor in the room called Ethyl."

"Ethyl? Your rooms don't have numbers?"

"No, sir. All our rooms is named for womenfolk."

"Sounds like a damned whorehouse!"

"That's 'cuz it used to be one. Course they don't allow none of that no more. Things is real tame in Port Costa nowadays."

I shook my head in amazement and said, "A fellow in a suit came in here about half an hour ago. Is he a guest, too?"

"Well, sir, again, the hotel don't . . . ."

I grabbed a handful of the old guy's shirt and dragged him halfway across the counter. "Friend, you're pushing your luck. Unless you want to make me very angry, I suggest you keep answering my questions."

"Okay, okay! Don't get yourself all worked up in a lather. The fella in the suit is stayin' here, too."

I let go of the guy's shirt, and he took a step back to put a safer distance between us. I said, "What room?"

"He's in Kay, right across the hall from that little gal's room."

"Did he check in at the same time?"

"Yes, sir, he did."

Donning my most charming smile, I said, "Okay, old-timer, you go back to reading your magazine, and everything will be just hunky-dory." The old fellow was still squinting at me as I headed for the stairs.

The farther I got up the stairs, the worse things got. The place stunk of mildew, stale tobacco, and other things I preferred not to think about; the hardwood floors were scuffed raw; and what was left of some pale green wallpaper was stained and peeling. The joint hardly seemed suitable for a visiting international dignitary . . . unless you wanted to stash one someplace well off the beaten path. I wondered what Sun Ling thought of the Burlington after her snazzy digs at the swanky Fairmont.

Arriving on the second floor, I had a choice of two hallways. I took a look down the hallway on my left and saw Fanny, Maude, and Ivy, but no Ethyl or Kay. They were opposite each other at the end of the short hallway on my right, and since that hall didn't go all the way to the end of the building, it looked as if the two rooms might connect across the hallway.

I knocked on Kay's door and waited. I heard footsteps on the other side of the door before it opened about twelve inches. Kendall did a good job of looking surprised at finding me on his doorstep. With a nice touch of anger in his voice, he growled, "Spicer, you're off the case! Get the hell out of here and go back to L.A. where you belong."

He intended to slam the door in my face, but just before the latch hit home, I kicked the door hard. It flew open and I followed it into Kendall's room on the run. He was thrown off balance as the doorknob was jerked from his hand, and I slammed him into the wall to the right of the door. He was in shirtsleeves, so it was an easy matter to jerk his service revolver from the fancy cross-hand, quick-draw holster on his left hip and in the same motion flip it toward the bed. The pistol bounced once and clattered to the floor in the narrow space between the far wall and the mattress.

Kendall regained his balance and moved to push me away. I stepped back, and that threw him off balance again. Using his own momentum, I swung him around and pushed him in the direction of the bed. Ancient bedsprings creaked loudly as he hit the mattress.

Kendall glared up at me and sounding a whole lot tougher than he looked at that moment said, "Damn it, Spicer, what the hell do you think you're doing?"

"I want some words with you, Mister FBI Agent."

"Good, we can talk about how you just assaulted a federal officer. You're gonna do hard time for this stunt, Spicer!"

"Not unless you and J. Edgar want to see Sun Ling's story splattered across the front page of every major newspaper in the country."

"Ha! You don't even know Sun Ling's story!"

"I know enough of it to make all the news-hungry editors and reporters between here and New York start digging for the rest of the story. In fact, I've already got a reporter hounding me for my version of Sun Ling's mysterious disappearance. He showed up right after you guys intentionally leaked the news that she'd been kidnapped. You picked the wrong stooge for this caper, buddy."

I watched Kendall's eyes to see if he was going for my bluff. When they narrowed and his theatrical portrayal of a tough, angry FBI agent lost some its conviction, I was pretty sure I had him.

"Look, Spicer, this is a matter of national security. If you blab what you think you know to the press, you'll mess up a plan that came straight down from the White House. You keep meddling in this operation and thousands of innocent Chinese citizens could be killed!"

"To hell with national security! A couple of good people got shot, and one of them is on a slab at the county coroner's office, all because you and Liang have been playing fast and loose with the truth. Now you're going to tell me the whole story—all of it!"

Kendall looked genuinely confused for a moment. Then the light dawned, and he said, "Oh, you mean the exposition security cop and that Chinese kid. Them getting shot had absolutely nothing to do with this."

"Yeah, that's what people keep tellin' me, and I'm not buyin' it. I did for a while, but not anymore. This whole caper is like something Dashiell Hammett dreamed up—full of implausible coincidences and people doing things they just don't do in real life."

The puzzled look returned to Kendall's face. "What do you mean? What coincidences?"

"For openers, how about Tang Fan being killed by a couple of Jap goons right before he's supposed to give me the lowdown on Sun Ling's disappearance?"

"Oh, that. Tang Fan was killed because he was shipping supplies and arms to China and the Japanese wanted to put a stop to it." He grinned a little sheepishly. "That line Liang fed you about the Japanese kidnapping Sun Ling was part of the scheme. Putting the blame on the

Japanese would add . . . . Well, take my word for it, that part was just window dressing.

"The fact that Tang Fan was shot on the same night you showed up really was a coincidence. The timing of his death had to do with a shipment that left for China on one of Tang's ships that morning, not with Tang Fan talking to you about Sun Ling."

"That's what Tang Hong says. And I was supposed to believe the goons I saw leaving Tang's warehouse after the killing were only interested in me because I could ID them, or at least they supposedly thought I could. But that doesn't fit with what happened to me out on Treasure Island the next day."

Kendall was getting pretty good at looking puzzled. He frowned and asked, "What are you talking about?"

"One of Tang's killers—the one who was in the passenger seat of the car that sped away from the warehouse—tailed me all over the exposition. I made him, but when I tried to confront the guy, he disappeared into the Japanese exhibit. I made a phone call and told Bailey, the homicide cop, where to find the goon, but he disappeared before Bailey got there.

"Then, as I was leaving Treasure Island that night, a different Jap goon thunked me on the head. I got a quick look at him before I went out like a busted light bulb. If all the Japs were worried about was me fingering Tang Fan's killers, they would have solved that problem right then and there. But they didn't. All the guy did was go through my wallet. He stole about ninety bucks to make it look like a mugging, but the real reason he attacked me was to find out who the new guy in the game was. I'm sure of that because my P.I. license was in a different place than where I keep it in my wallet. The goon obviously took the license out and studied it before he took off."

Now there was what looked like genuine surprise in Kendall's expression. "I didn't know anything about that."

I didn't believe him for a minute. I wasn't telling Kendall a damned thing he didn't already know, but if he wanted to play it like this was all news to him, that was Jake with me. I went along with the gag. "There's a lot you don't know anything about, Kendall, like the only reason I'm still walking around is because that guy who attacked me was told just to find out who I was and nothing more. They tried to make up for that oversight yesterday. That's why the first goon was back hanging around outside the Chinese Village when we nabbed him."

"Okay, so maybe the Japanese are out to get you. So what? That doesn't prove they have any interest in Sun Ling."

Proving I'm just as good an actor as Kendall, I shook my head in disgust. "That's the problem with you Junior G-men; you expect everyone to go along with the grand schemes you come up with, and when they don't, you just ignore it. You can't see the facts when they're staring you in the face!"

Kendall actually looked a little hurt. "Okay, you tell me what I'm not seeing."

"Think about it. The Japanese aren't stupid. They know Sun Ling being in this country at this particular time isn't a good thing from their point of view because she might actually be successful in getting the U.S. involved in their war with China. It's a sure thing they were keeping close tabs on her.

"Then when she mysteriously disappeared, they had to figure something was up. You guys outsmarted yourselves there. If you hadn't staged the phony kidnapping, the Japs probably would have been content just keeping an eye on her, but once she disappeared, they had to find out what she was up to.

"It was no secret that Tang Fan was involved in bringing Sun Ling here, supposedly for the exposition, and he was handy, so they paid him a visit to find out what was going on. When they'd gotten whatever information they could out of him, they killed him, figuring you guys would come to exactly the conclusion you came to—that Tang Fan was killed in retaliation for his supply shipments to China, even though anyone with a lick of sense would know killing Tang Fan wasn't going to stop those shipments."

Now Kendall was pretending to be deep in thought, as though he was considering what I told him. I ambled over to his window and looked down at the main drag of Port Costa, giving him some time to figure out how he was going to get us from where we were in this charade to where he wanted us to be. I could hardly wait to see exactly where that was.

Finally he said, "Okay, Johnny, let's assume for a minute you might be right and the Japanese are concerned about Sun Ling's involvement with the U.S. government. What do you think they'll try to do about it?"

Kendall's tacit admission that Sun Ling was in some way involved with the government and his newfound interest in what I thought the Japanese might be up to signaled a change in the course of the conversation. I was even beginning to see where all this playacting might be taking us.

I said, "What the Japs do next depends largely on what Tang Fan knew and what, if anything, he told those goons. I'm guessing he knew you planned to make Sun Ling disappear, but he didn't know the details, like where you planned to stash her. If he'd known that and spilled those beans to the goons, you and Sun Ling would both be dead by now."

Kendall looked hurt again. "You don't have much faith in my abilities as an FBI agent."

I laughed sarcastically. "And you haven't shown much faith in my abilities as a detective, but you're the one sitting on the bed with an empty holster, which would seem to indicate my judgment is a little better than yours."

I had him there. "Okay, Spicer, you're right about what Tang Fan knew, but . . . ."

"There are no buts about it! You've created one hell of a mess here. If the Japs didn't find out what they wanted to know from Tang, they're gonna look elsewhere. That puts a lot of people at risk, including a couple of nice kids named Yang who got involved in all this just because they want to help Sun Ling. Tell me, who besides you knows all the details of your kidnapping scheme?"

Acting properly chastised, Kendall quietly answered my question. "Liang Chao is in on the whole thing. Besides him, a few people at the bureau. That's it."

"That makes your first problem Liang. Personally, I don't give a hoot what happens to that lying bastard, but you don't need him spilling his guts right now, so you'd better warn him to expect some visitors of the Japanese persuasion. You might also want to arrange some protection for him. Then you need to get Sun Ling the hell out of here, and the sooner the better."

Kendall stood up and looked out the window as I had done. "Johnny, if what you've said here, or even part of it, is true, I may need some help. The bureau was afraid too many agents milling around would draw unwelcome attention, so since we got Sun Ling off Treasure Island, I've been on my own."

Now we were getting somewhere. Kendall had cleverly maneuvered us through a complete U-turn—going from threatening me with a federal assault wrap to asking for my help. I still didn't know where all this was headed, but at least we were getting closer to the punch line.

Still following his script, but not wanting to appear too eager, I said, "Okay, Kendall, if you're asking for my help, you can have it in exchange for two conditions. First, you have to make sure Susie and Jeff Yang are out of harm's way. The kids have been helping me with my investigation, and the Japs might jump to the conclusion they know something about Sun Ling. Second, you have to tell me why our government pulled a stupid stunt like this."

Kendall came up with a pretty convincing sigh of resignation and said, "Okay, you've got it, but you'll have to wait a few days for the full story—at least until Monday."

I figured Kendall was feeling pretty pleased with himself for successfully manipulating me into agreeing to help him out. That was fine with me because it meant I was now going to find out why he'd lured me to the Burlington in the first place. As far as our bargain was concerned, I wasn't counting on Kendall keeping his end of it. That was okay, too. The truth was I didn't really believe Susie and Jeff were in any great danger. If I thought they were, I never would have for headed home, and I sure as hell wouldn't entrust their safety to Kendall and his crew. I'd simply used concern for the kids' safety as a bargaining chip in a situation that called for some horse trading.

I said, "Alright, Kendall, fair enough. I'll start helping by suggesting you find your revolver under the bed. You might just need it before this is all over."

TWENTY-ONE

$\curvearrowleft \curvearrowright$

While I hadn't actually laid eyes on Sun Ling yet, I was almost to the point of feeling pleased with myself for finally finding her—almost, but not quite. In my business it sometimes seems like every silver lining has a cloud attached to it, and in this case the cloud keeping me from congratulating myself on my cleverness was the undeniable fact that I only found Miss Sun because Agent Kendall wanted me to.

Mister Junior G-man obviously had something up his sleeve—something that required gaining my confidence. Needless to say, the question buzzing around in my head like an angry bee in an empty Nehi bottle was what the devil was he up to? Hopefully, by playing along with the gag I would now learn the answer to that question.

Kendall's manipulation of our conversation eventually led to the hatching of a new plan—one involving my participation—to protect Sun Ling from the threat of Japanese agents. The first step in that plan required Kendall to make some long-distance telephone calls, and since Burlington Hotel guests didn't enjoy the luxury of room phones, he would have to make those calls from the payphone downstairs. Not wanting to leave Sun Ling alone—a concern he didn't seem to have while he went off to Treasure Island for the purpose of luring me to Port Costa—Kendall went through a door that connected Ethyl and Kay to bring Sun Ling back to his room where I could keep an eye on her while he made his calls.

As Kendall ushered Sun Ling into his room, he said, "Miss Sun, I'd like you to meet Mister Johnny Spicer. He's a private detective, and I've enlisted his help because there appears to be a possibility Japanese agents may be looking for us."

The magazine photo of Sun Ling I'd been carrying around for several days didn't begin to do her justice. The doll was absolutely breathtaking despite the fact she'd been holed up in a cheesy hotel for nearly a week. I said, "It's good to finally meet you, Miss Sun."

Sun Ling smiled a little tentatively as if she wanted to be polite, but wasn't really sure that my arrival on the scene was anything to smile about. I could hardly blame her for that because I had some doubts of my own along the same lines.

As he left for the lobby, Kendall said, "Johnny, please brief Miss Sun on our next move."

I said I would, and when he closed the door, I suggested Sun Ling sit in a chair next to the wall, thus keeping her out of sight from either of the room's two windows. Whether or not Kendall really believed the Jap agents posed a threat, I believed it, and I was going to make darn sure nothing happened to Sun Ling on my watch. Then I said, "Miss Sun, the first thing we're going to do . . . ."

She interrupted me with a polite gesture of her hand. "Mister Spicer, the walls of this hotel are quite thin, and although it was rude of me to listen, I overheard your conversation with Mister Kendall. I understand what you and he plan to do."

I nodded. "I certainly don't think you rude for listening. Under similar circumstances, I'd have done the same. It's just unfortunate that you had to hear the unpleasant parts of our conversation. I needed to make Agent Kendall understand a danger he apparently didn't see."

"Mister Spicer, may I be frank with you?"

"Certainly."

After a moment's pause during which she appeared to be organizing her thoughts, or perhaps translating them into English, Sun Ling said, "As you must imagine, the past days have been most unpleasant, and as a result, I fear I now lack confidence in the plan devised by your Federal Bureau of Investigation and Mister Liang. I mean no disrespect, but I also have doubts about Mister Kendall's ability to protect me."

She paused again and then continued, "I believe myself to be a good judge of character, and while I've only known you for a very short time and I base my judgment on words overheard through the wall, I must say to you I am extremely relieved that you have arrived."

Sun Ling wasn't just a good-looking dame; she was also a pretty good actress. I had no doubt that the sincere line of malarkey she'd just handed me was more of the script Kendall devised to gain my confidence. I simply said, "Thank you, Miss Sun. I will do my very best to live up to your faith in me."

We spent the next few minutes in silence while I stood near the hall door to better hear any approaching danger. The performance staged by Kendall and Sun Ling had done nothing to lessen the likelihood that Jap agents were going to break down the door at any moment and start slinging lead. In fact, that likelihood may have been the only thing in the whole cockamamie situation that was real.

Standing there with one ear to the door, I thought of something I needed to tell Sun Ling. "Miss Sun, I nearly forgot; I bring you best regards from Susie and Jeff Yang. They're quite concerned about you. I'm sure they'll be relieved to know you are well."

For the first time since she entered the room, Sun Ling smiled a sincere smile. "Oh, thank you, Mister Spicer. I have been much missing . . . ." She paused to rethink her English and said, "I have missed my conversations with Susie very much. And Jeff, he is a delightful boy, although I fear he was developing what I believe you call a crush on me."

I smiled back at her. "I think you're right about Jeff. You made quite an impression on him. I also want to tell you I took the liberty of giving Susie Yang a piece of paper with some sketches on it I found in your San Francisco hotel room. I hope that's alright with you. She was quite pleased to have them."

Sun Ling looked puzzled, as if she didn't know what I was talking about. Then the light I'd deliberately sparked suddenly dawned. "Oh, I had forgotten making those pencil sketches. Yes, I am glad for Susie to have them." A moment later she figured out why I'd mentioned the sketches. Suddenly frowning, she said, "Oh, my. I should not have left that paper behind!"

"No, that was careless. The Chinese word you printed below the sketches is one of the clues that led me here. Susie translated the characters for me."

Sun Ling appeared to be embarrassed. Her embarrassment might have even been sincere since I couldn't think of any reason Kendall would have put her up to leaving the page of sketches at the Fairmont. She said, "I am most apologetic for being so unwise. I left the room in a great hurry on Sunday, and I forgot those drawings and what I printed on the paper until you mentioned them a moment ago. However, if that paper brought you to my aid, perhaps it was providence which caused me to forget it."

It took great restraint for me to refrain from applauding Sun Ling's quick recovery. I responded to that particular slice of baloney with an equally sincere sounding admonishment that we would have to be much more careful in the future.

Hearing footsteps out in the hall, I instinctively drew my Smith & Wesson. Glancing at Sun Ling, I saw her eyes go wide with fear. The sight of my revolver scared the hell out of her, or so she wanted me to believe. Then Kendall knocked on the door in the pattern we'd agreed on and I let him in.

"Okay, Johnny, everything's set."

Kendall had told me he planned to call Liang and warn him of the danger posed by the Japanese agents. Of course, I didn't know if he actually made that call or not, but in the spirit of the game I asked, "How did Liang take the news?"

"Not well. I offered to arrange a protection detail for him, but he wouldn't hear of it. Said he had his own protection. He did have a lot of questions, though, like where we were taking Sun Ling."

"I hope you didn't answer those questions."

"I didn't. I couldn't, since we don't know exactly where we're going yet."

"Did my name come up in the conversation?"

"No."

"Good. The less anyone knows about the whos and wheres of what we're doing, the better."

After Kendall briefed me on a few additional items of interest resulting from his telephone calls, including the arrangements he'd supposedly made for Susie and Jeff Yang's protection, I said, "Alright, let's get this show on the road. Keep an eye on the main drag out there. I'll signal you when I'm in position."

While Kendall accompanied Sun Ling to her room so she could pack her belongings in preparation for leaving Port Costa, I took a look-see around the Burlington. Mostly the place was eerily quiet. The only sign of life I found was the sound of a radio program coming from a third-floor room on the west side of the hotel. It didn't seem likely a run-down dump like the Burlington was up to providing entertainment for its guests, so I took the presence of a radio as an indication the room's occupant was probably a long-term residential tenant who brought his own entertainment.

On the ground floor I found a back door opening onto the alley behind the hotel. That wasn't good news because anyone with evil intentions could come through that door and up the stairs without being seen from the registration desk, which given the eyesight of the old fellow behind the desk, probably wouldn't make much difference anyway.

The back door had a bolt lock and I slid the bolt home. It was more of a gesture than a real security measure because the rotting wood doorframe looked like it would disintegrate without much encouragement. But with the bolt locked, anyone really wanting to come in through the back door would have to make some noise doing so, and that might be a small deterrent.

I found the hotel's public telephone in the small restaurant across the hall from the lobby. With cracked window glass and its seat dangling by one screw, the booth fit right in with the Burlington's decor. The telephone instrument, however, was functional, which was all that mattered.

Stepping into the phone booth, I gave what I was going to say to Jeff Yang a moment's thought. Even though I didn't hold out much hope that the FBI would actually send an agent out to protect the kids, I had to tell Jeff what was going on just in case they did. Also, I didn't want to scare Jeff, but it seemed like a good idea to remind him that Jap agents played for keeps and a few extra precautions wouldn't hurt.

Deciding to play things more or less straight with Jeff, I dialed "O" for operator and gave his office number to the nasal-sounding female voice that answered. She told me to deposit forty cents for the first three minutes. After the clanging set off by the coins I dropped into the slot subsided, I heard the familiar ring sound indicating Ma Bell was on the job, even in the backwater berg of Port Costa.

Jeff answered on the second ring. "Chinese Village, Jeff Yang speaking."

"Hi, Jeff. This is Johnny Spicer."

"Hi, Johnny. You aren't home already, are you?"

"No, in fact, I haven't even left yet. I'm calling because I have some news for you."

"I hope it's good news."

"Some of it is. First, I found Sun Ling."

I was hurrying the conversation the way you do on a long-distance telephone call to avoid taking more than the three minutes I was allowed and incurring additional charges, but Jeff interrupted. "You did? That's grand! Is she okay?"

"She's fine, Jeff. As I figured, her disappearance was staged by Liang Chao and the FBI. That's all I can say about it for the time being."

"That is good news. Susie will be really glad to know Sun Ling is okay."

"Jeff, the other piece of news I have for you isn't as good. After thinking things through and talking to the FBI agent guarding Sun Ling, I'm convinced the Japanese do have an interest in her and that Tang Fan's murder is related to that interest."

Jeff just said, "Oh, oh."

"The thing is, there is a slight possibility the Japs may also have an interest in you and Susie because of the help you gave me."

"Double oh, oh."

"I'm not trying to scare you, Jeff, but as you already have good reason to know, things get dangerous when those Jap agents are around, even for relatively innocent bystanders."

I thought I could hear a little fear in Jeff's voice when he said, "Yeah, we found that out alright. So what should we do?"

"There's an off chance an FBI agent may show up to give you and Susie some protection, but whether that happens or not, the best thing would be for you and your sister to stick close together and stay out of sight, at least for the time being. I'll call again later in the afternoon to see how things are going, and we can talk about what to do next then. Okay?"

"Okay, Johnny."

"Alright, Jeff, talk to you in a few hours."

Taking care not to break the telephone booth's door off its wobbly hinges, I stepped out into the restaurant. There was no one around except a young woman in a yellow apron refilling catsup bottles. My stomach told me it was in need of sustenance, so I ordered a take-out sandwich. Armed with a roast beef on white and a cardboard container of coffee, I strolled out to the sidewalk and looked up and down the main drag. Port Costa was just as quiet and peaceful as when I'd arrived.

Returning to my Chrysler, I looked up at the window of Tom Kendall's room. He was watching and gave me a wave. I waved back and settled into my car for lunch and a long afternoon. Our new plan called for moving Sun Ling out of the Burlington after dark when we would be less noticeable. Until then, my job was watching the street and the hotel for signs of nefarious characters with evil intentions.

Since sunset was at least four hours away, I was going to be there awhile.

Chewing my stringy roast beef sandwich, I felt a little silly watching for a crowd of Jap agents to show up at the Burlington's front door. I was convinced the Jap threat was real, but I didn't believe for a second Kendall was really relying on me to fend them off. The FBI was there. I didn't know exactly where the agents were staked out, but they were around. Regardless of what Kendall would have me believe, there was no way in hell the FBI would entrust Sun Ling's safety to a single agent.

As for the Japs, if they hadn't shown up by now, it was only because they hadn't yet figured out where Sun Ling was stashed. It was a given fact that the Japs would show up, sooner or later, wherever she was.

It was also a given that I was doing nothing more than killing time until Kendall put the next part of his scheme into play. I still didn't know what that scheme entailed, but I was certain it included no part of the new plan we'd devised in his room.

With nothing better to do, I reviewed that plan because I suspected some of what Kendall told me might be close to the truth. According to Kendall, the FBI's original scheme was to keep Sun Ling under wraps at the Burlington for a week before delivering her to an Army airfield where she would be flown off to some secret location via a military transport plane. I was pretty sure he'd lied about at least part of that because even the FBI would realize it made a lot more sense to leave Sun Ling where she was at the exposition until it was time for her to be picked up at the airfield. If I was right about that, it meant something unexpected happened to force a change in the original plan. I didn't waste any time trying to guess what that unexpected thing might have been.

Kendall told me the base at which Sun Ling would board her flight was Hamilton Army Airfield, located somewhere to the north. Consulting my Shell map, I found that such a place did indeed exist and was situated on U.S. Highway 101 about thirty miles north of San Francisco. My map also informed me that from Port Costa, the shortest route to Hamilton Airfield involved a forty-mile trip which included a ferryboat ride across San Francisco Bay.

Be all that as it may, the plan Kendall and I agreed on consisted of him taking Sun Ling out of Port Costa in his car after dark with me tagging along a short distance behind to keep an eye out for tails. Once clear of Port Costa, I was to follow Kendall to the general vicinity of Hamilton Army Airfield where he would find an out-of-the-way auto court in which we would all hole up until Sun Ling was safely aboard her plane Monday morning.

Of course, none of that was actually going to happen, especially not the parts that involved me. Kendall's stellar performance during our conversation in his room was simply intended to put me off guard so he and his fellow Junior G-men could sneak off and do whatever they were going to do next without any further interference from me. At least that was my current theory on the subject because I couldn't think of anything else to be gained by gaining my confidence.

So having seen Sun Ling in the pink of health, thus technically completing my mission, why the hell was I sticking around where I apparently wasn't wanted? Mostly I was curious as to how Kendall planned sneak off with Sun Ling when I was watching the only road in and out of town. I expected that trick alone to be entertainment worth the price of admission. Beyond that, seeing the thing through might even give me an opportunity for some fun proving to Agent Kendall I wasn't nearly as dumb as he thought.

While my roast beef sandwich was no gourmet delight, I was grateful for the coffee that was helping me stay alert during the warm and uneventful Port Costa afternoon. In fact, I walked across the street for a refill around two-thirty.

About two hours later the level of activity on Port Costa's main drag increased significantly. A Ford panel truck drove by to make a delivery at the railroad yard. A few minutes before five an ancient Ford roadster and a slightly newer Chevy pickup truck showed up, also disappearing into the Southern Pacific yard. About ten minutes later a caravan of two vehicles that were different from the two I'd just seen drive into the yard left, along with the Ford panel delivery, and disappeared up the main drag, apparently signaling a work shift change. A bit later all that traffic was followed by the blue Buick parked a few spaces ahead of me and a light green Plymouth station wagon from in front of the mercantile store behind me. Since both vehicles were there when I first arrived, I figured the drivers for shopkeepers who were headed home after a long and probably not very profitable day.

By six-thirty the sun had set and I'd seen no sign of Kendall, Sun Ling, or the agent's Ford sedan. I left my car and walked across the street. Looking around the corner, I saw Kendall's Ford still parked in the alley alongside the hotel. Something was clearly amiss, so I climbed the stairs to the Burlington's second floor and knocked on Kendall's door.

After standing there more than long enough for him to answer, I tried the door. It opened. I entered the room cautiously, Smith & Wesson at the ready—a precaution that was, as it turned out, unnecessary. Both Kendall's and Sun Ling's rooms were as empty as a politian's promise. The brown leather suitcase I'd seen in Kendall's room was also gone, as were all other signs that either room had recently been occupied.

Turning on the lights, I gave both rooms a quick going-over in search of any clues as to what might have happened to their former occupants. Finding nothing, I went downstairs to the hotel's back door. It was unbolted. That figured because I knew for sure Kendall and Sun Ling hadn't left by either the hotel's front entrance or the restaurant's outside door, both of which I'd been watching all afternoon. Short of climbing out a window, the now unbolted back door was the only other way they could have left the Burlington.

Outside, I walked along the rear of the hotel toward the railroad yard and realized it would not have been difficult for Kendall and Sun Ling to disappear into the yard without me seeing them if they had a mind to do that. Of course, I couldn't say for sure that's what happened. I couldn't rule out the possibility someone surprised Kendall and took them out of the hotel by the back door to a waiting car, but there were no signs of violence in their rooms, and it seemed unlikely kidnappers would have bothered to take Kendall's suitcase along. Besides, I'd seen no cars arrive at or leave the hotel on the only road out of town. But I had seen three vehicles leaving the Southern Pacific yard—one of them a panel delivery that could have easily hidden the agent and his charge.

Well, hell. I'd expected Kendall to pull something, so finding him and Sun Ling gone came as no great surprise. I was just hoping to catch him at it. Instead, he'd successfully ditched me while I was biding my time out front.

Returning to the Burlington's public telephone, I placed another long-distance call to Treasure Island. When Jeff Yang answered his phone, I said, "Jeff, this is Johnny. How are you and Susie getting along?"

"We're fine, Johnny, but the FBI never showed up."

That news came as no more of a surprise than discovering Kendall and Sun Ling had given me the slip. I was contemplating my next step when Jeff said, "Oh, and I almost forgot. The San Francisco cops are looking for you. Some guy named Bailey called and said if I saw you to have you call him right away. He sounded real anxious to find you."

"Oh, swell. Bailey's just what I don't need right now."

"Why? What's wrong?"

"Sun Ling's disappeared again, along with the FBI agent protecting her. I kind of expected that. The FBI is playing more games, and I really don't know what they're up to."

"Well, should Susie and I go home or what?"

"No, don't go home yet and don't leave the village. I'll be on my way over there as soon as I call Bailey. I shouldn't be more than an hour, so just stay put. Okay?"

"Sure, Johnny. We'll be in my office."

I was out of coins, so I had to get the registration clerk—now an elderly woman—to change a buck. Then I placed yet another long-distance call to San Francisco. Ma Bell was making a fortune off me today, and to make matters worse, one of my three long-distance minutes was wasted by the cop who answered my call and took his time finding Bailey.

When the homicide sergeant finally picked up the phone, he said, "Spicer, where the hell are you? I thought I told you to stay in touch. I've been calling all over hell and gone trying to find you."

"I'm still up here in your neck of the woods. What's all the fuss about?"

"I'll tell you what all the fuss is about. A person or persons unknown showed up at Saint Mary's hospital and executed your Jap goon. That's what all the fuss is about!"

"Executed him?"

"Yeah, they shot the patrol cop I had on guard there, and then killed the goon with one bullet to the forehead. Nobody at the hospital saw or heard anything, so they must have had a silencer on the gun they used. This thing has all the earmarks of a professional hit."

"It sure sounds that way." It also sounded like the Jap agents were still in business. That gave me cause to wonder if Jeff and Susie were really as safe as I thought they were.

"Yeah, and that's why I've been lookin' all over hell and gone for you. I'm thinkin' maybe you know more about what these Japs are up to than you've told me. How 'bout that, Spicer?"

"I might, but I haven't got time right now to discuss the matter."

Bailey exploded. "What the hell do you mean you haven't got time to discuss it? Listen, buster, if you got any idea what's goin' on, you'd better tell me and fast!"

"Listen, Sergeant, my main concern right now is making sure that kid who got shot on Treasure Island yesterday and his sister are safe. I'm on my way to see them right now. How 'bout I call you when I get back to San Francisco? Then we can meet up and have a talk."

Bailey sounded like he was about to blow a gasket. "Damn it, Spicer, protecting the citizens of San Francisco is my job, not yours . . . ."

"Yeah, and you're doing a really a dandy job of it, aren't you, Bailey?"

"Don't you get smart with me, you son of a . . . ."

I hung up on him and headed back to my car. Bailey could yell at me later. Besides, my three minutes were just about up anyway.

TWENTY-TWO

I made good time getting to Treasure Island, or maybe it just seemed that way because I used the trip to think things through, but turning onto the Bay Bridge approach, I was no closer to any revelations than I'd been when I started out. That was a shame because I was in need of a revelation or two.

Kendall put on a hell of a show for my benefit, and I still didn't know why. I mean, after all the effort the FBI put into sneaking Sun Ling away from Treasure Island, why would they lead me right to her?

The only answer I could think of that made any sense at all was Kendall figured me for being stubborn enough to keep looking for Sun Ling despite the fact I'd been fired. So he led me to her, pretended to let me in on a big hush-hush government deal, and then snuck away again like a thief in the night, hoping I'd be satisfied with laying eyes on Sun Ling and knowing she was okay.

Sun Ling was in on the deal, too, but she almost overplayed her part with the pretty speech about being so glad I was there because she lacked confidence in Agent Kendall. Of course, she said that to convince me I was doing the right thing by agreeing to help Kendall. That was important because I had to go along with the plan Kendall and I came up with in order for him and Sun Ling to ditch me.

Well, Momma Spicer didn't raise no dummies, and I had enough sense to know when I wasn't welcome. Or more accurately, I had that much sense after being hit over the head with the message a few times. Regardless of how long it took me to get the message, I now had it, and I would have been perfectly happy to just go away like Kendall wanted me to, except for one thing: Bailey's news about the Jap getting bumped off in the hospital. Kendall hadn't figured on that monkey wrench getting thrown into his plan.

The dead Jap agent was a monkey wrench because it meant the Japanese players had upped the ante, and I was in the game whether Kendall wanted me around or not. I had a lot of faith in my version of why Tang Fan was killed, and if I was right, walking away from the table now would be like turning my back on a bullet headed in my direction or at the Yang kids or both. So I had to stay in the game and play the cards I was dealt. The problem was I didn't know if we were playing Five Card Stud or Old Maid.

Hell, the Japs were probably as confused as I was. Should they rub me out me because I might be able to finger Tang Fan's remaining killer, or should they grab me because I might know where Sun Ling is? Either way, the odds in favor of my running into them again were high. And here I was, driving right back into the middle of the mess.

As lousy as the situation was, it struck me as just a little humorous—like those old Keystone Kop movies where everybody was chasing everybody else around in circles. I'd have laughed out loud if three people weren't already dead with a reasonable expectation of that number increasing before the caper was over and done with.

Given the situation and the risks involved, it seemed as if a plan was in order, but turning off the bridge onto Yerba Buena Island, I still hadn't come up with one. It's not easy to think up a plan when you have no idea what in blazes you're planning for.

Crossing the causeway to Treasure Island, I was treated to an impressive electrical display including both the multi-hued extravaganza of the exposition and the twinkling lights of San Francisco across the bay. The long lines of drivers eager to enter the Golden Gate International Exposition reminded me it was Friday night. I had to wait several minutes before I got to one of the drive-through ticket booths. While I waited, I dug my participant's pass out of the manila envelope in which I'd stuffed it that morning thinking I wouldn't be needing it again.

I also grabbed the yellow card given to me by the guard on my first visit to the exposition—the one that allowed me to park in the taxicab zone near the Northwest Passage. Guessing the parking lot was full enough that I'd have a long hike to the Chinese Village, I decided to take advantage of the fact that the taxi parking permit wasn't dated. Once past the ticket booth, I drove straight to the taxi zone and stuck the yellow card up in my windshield.

Across the entrance road an orange ferry boat all decked out in its own array of lights was unloading passengers from San Francisco. I joined a small group of the happy new arrivals as they strolled through the exposition's Northwest Passage entrance. Following along through the Court of Pacifica, I glanced up at Dog Woman. In spite of her spotlights and the constantly changing colors on the screen behind her, she was just as ugly as ever.

I turned left onto Nanking Road and entered the Chinese Village through the southernmost of the two openings in the wall around it. Heading toward the administration offices, where I expected to meet the Yangs, I spotted Jeff standing in front of the green door to the dressing room building. He noticed me about the same time and gave me a wave with his left arm. Seeing his right arm still in its sling jogged my sense of time back into focus. It felt like at least a week had passed since the battle of Nanking Road in which Jeff had taken a stray slug in the shoulder, but all that happened only yesterday. I guess time really does fly when you're having fun.

Approaching Jeff, I said, "How's the shoulder?"

"Oh, it aches some, but not that much. Say, I'm sorry for not sticking around in my office like I said, but Jack Chen scheduled a procession for eight tonight and Susie's supposed to be in it. I figured we were just as safe out here with all these people around as we'd be in my office."

I nodded, not entirely sure I agreed with Jeff's idea about there being safety in numbers. Just then the green door opened. Jeff turned and exchanged a quick word or two with a fierce-looking warrior, and then he waved toward a second floor window of the theater next door where the acrobats performed. About thirty seconds later a voice came over the public address speakers announcing, "Good evening, ladies and gentlemen, and welcome to the Chinese Village at the Golden Gate International Exposition. At this time we are proud to present a traditional Chinese royal procession in which the participants will be wearing authentic costumes of the Ming Dynasty. This procession is an exact re-creation of an event that occurred regularly in China more than 300 years ago!"

The announcer's spiel was followed by a recorded gong and a slow rhythm beat out on a resonant drum. The actors filed out of the dressing room building, stepping slowly in time to the drum beats. A flute or two, along with various Chinese stringed instruments, joined in and added to the authentic feeling of the proceedings.

It was all very majestic, and as the procession wound its way toward the Pagoda Tower, Jeff and I followed along. Soon the announcer's voice came on again over the music to say, "In this pageant, the emperor's daughter, portrayed by the young woman in the white and pale green gown at the center of the procession, is accompanied by four of her handmaidens and eight warriors of the palace guards who protect her. Three hundred years ago such a procession would have taken place prior to a royal ceremony—perhaps in celebration of the emperor's birthday or some other special occasion."

I nudged Jeff and said, "Isn't that gal playing the emperor's daughter wearing the same outfit Sun Ling wore the night she disappeared?"

Grinning, Jeff said, "Yup, and that gal portraying her royal highness is Susie. Didn't you recognize her?"

"Not in all that makeup. Susie got quite a promotion from handmaiden to royal princess."

"She was thrilled about it! That's why we couldn't very well wait for you in the office. It wouldn't have been fair to cheat Susie out of her big chance to be a princess."

I said something along the lines of, "No, we certainly couldn't do that," and continued scanning faces in the crowd, looking for any sign of trouble. A moment later it showed up in the form of Detective Sergeant Bailey. He was easy to spot because his scowl didn't fit in very well with the happy faces of everyone else watching the parade.

Bailey marched up to me like he was Grant and I was Richmond. "Spicer, I've had it up to here with you! You're coming downtown with me right now!"

Keeping my eye on the crowd, I said, "Not unless you think you're tough enough to cuff me and drag me out of here."

The sergeant started sputtering like the fuse on a firecracker, and I said, "Be a little patient, Bailey. We can have our conversation in a few minutes when this procession ends. Until then, I need to keep my eye on this crowd. While I'm doing that, shake hands with Jeff Yang."

Right on cue, Jeff stepped up and offered Bailey a left-handed shake. Somehow that defused the situation, and after shaking Jeff's hand, the sergeant grudgingly joined our happy little group as the procession proceeded around the village and back to the dressing room building.

While Bailey fidgeted impatiently, the procession performers changed, and then we escorted Susie and Jeff back to the administration building, crowding Jeff's office beyond capacity. Jeff offered Bailey the chair behind his desk; Susie sat in the guest chair while Jeff leaned against the wall and I perched on the corner of his desk. Thus situated, I said, "Okay, Sergeant, what would you like me to tell you?"

He looked at Jeff and Susie and said, "Let's have this conversation in private."

"I'd rather have it right here where I can keep an eye on things. Besides, there's nothing I can tell you these kids don't already know."

After a long glare, Bailey growled, "Okay, have it your way. Now quit stalling and tell me what the hell you've been up to and how it ties in with the crime spree I have on my hands."

"Alright, Sergeant, but before I do, I have to tell you there are supposedly some U.S. government secrets involved here. So unless you want to tangle with J. Edgar Hoover, you'd best treat what I tell you accordingly."

That got his attention, but good. I then proceeded to relate the entire story, from my original telephone conversation with Kendall and my initial meeting with Liang Chao right up to and including Kendall's and Sun Ling's disappearance from the Burlington Hotel. I concluded with my current interpretation of what it all meant.

Telling the story took a good twenty minutes, during which Bailey's eyebrows kept going up and down like a yoyo. When I finished, the sergeant just sat there for a while looking like he was trying to digest Thanksgiving dinner. Finally he shook his head and muttered, "Spicer, why the hell didn't you tell me all this to begin with?"

"Bailey, when a big bad FBI agent tells me to keep my mouth shut, I generally do what I'm told. The only reason I'm telling you now is because the Junior G-man trolley has jumped its track, and we—that is, you and I and these kids here—are stuck with the consequences. Besides, if I had told you before, you probably wouldn't have believed me."

Scowling as if it pained him to admit it, Bailey said, "Yeah, I see your point. So what are you gonna do now?"

"To be honest, Sergeant, I have no idea what I'm going to do. The only thing I know for sure is that I need to keep Susie and Jeff here out of harm's way."

Bailey cogitated on my answer for moment before saying, "Well, Spicer, if you're right about all this, and I'm thinkin' you are, the best way you can keep these kids safe is to stay the hell away from 'em. The way I see it, those Japanese fellas are probably lookin' for you, either because they figure you know where this Sun gal is or because they think you can identify them for blasting the old Chinese guy, or maybe both. If they find you and these kids are around, they're gonna be right in the middle of the trouble.

"How about this . . . how about I make sure the kids are safe? I can assign a couple of good patrol cops I know I can trust to watch 'em."

"Forgive me for saying so, Sergeant, but your track record for keeping people safe isn't anything to brag about."

"Damn it, Spicer, that's not fair! How the hell was I supposed to know those federal boys got themselves cross-threaded with the Japanese mafia, or whatever it is? Now that I have some idea what the hell is going on, it's a whole different story."

I opened my mouth to reply, but shut it again when Susie surprised us all by saying, "Excuse me, but don't my brother and I have anything to say about this? We aren't children, you know! I think we should stick with Johnny."

I knew Bailey was right, and while I was thinking up a good argument to convince Susie that sticking with me wasn't a good idea, he beat me to the punch. "Missy, nobody here thinks you and your brother are children, but this is big-league stuff and I've got some experience dealing with professional killers. Maybe Mister Spicer does, too, but your brother's already got one bullet hole in him, and all we're tryin' to do is make sure no more harm comes to you. You're just gonna have to trust me on that, and let me do what I think is best."

Susie was looking at me as if she wanted some confirmation that Sergeant Bailey really was trustworthy. I wasn't sure he was, but he'd made a couple of good points. I gave her what I hoped she'd take as a reassuring nod and said, "The sergeant's right, Susie. I got you into this situation, and I'm sorry about that, but the San Francisco Police Department is far better equipped to protect you than I am."

Susie nodded, but her expression said she was dubious about putting her trust in the SFPD. I couldn't really blame her.

Bailey said, "Okay, that's settled then." Turning to Jeff he said, "If it's okay with you, I'll use your telephone here to line up some officers to take you kids home and keep watch so you'll be nice and safe."

Jeff nodded and Bailey picked up the telephone handset. While the sergeant made his call, I studied Jeff's face. He was being unusually quiet, and I guessed from his glum expression that his shoulder was paining him and he just wanted some rest.

Bailey hung up the telephone and said, "Alright, two of my best officers are on their way over. They should be here in half an hour or so. Spicer, I'm going outside to have a look around. You stay and keep an eye on things in here."

With his dignity and authority restored, Bailey stood up and walked purposefully out of the office. Jeff slumped into his desk chair, and Susie said, "Jeff, are you okay? Is your shoulder hurting?"

The effort it took was obvious, but Jeff put on a weak smile and said, "I'm okay, Sis. Everything is gonna be hunky-dory."

TWENTY-THREE

It was a few minutes after nine when Bailey walked back into Jeff Yang's office with two uniformed cops in tow. They escorted Susie and Jeff out of the office, and as Susie went through the door, she turned and looked back at me over her shoulder. Her gloomy expression gave me the idea she thought I was deserting them. Maybe I was, but I didn't have much choice in the matter.

The office door closed behind them, and Bailey leaned casually against the wall behind Jeff's desk. "Okay, the kids are taken care of. What are you gonna do now?" Before I could answer him, he added, "I mean, it might not be any of my damned business what you do, but I figure if you tell me where you're headed, I'll at least know where to look for the next dead bodies."

The sergeant had a sort of wry smile on his face, which I took to be his way of telling me all was forgiven and we were on the same team now. Lucky me. In answer to his question, I shrugged and said, "I suppose the smart thing would be to find myself a room for the night and get some rest, but I'm not very sleepy."

The telephone on Jeff's desk commenced to ringing and continued to do so for some time. Over the persistent racket, Bailey said, "Tell ya what, I've got a spare room at my place and my wife's off visiting her sister in Fresno, so why don't you come bunk with me tonight? That'll save you the trouble of finding a hotel and give you some time to think on things."

At first Bailey's offer took me by surprise, but after a moment's thought, it made sense. The sergeant saw me as his problem now, and to his way of thinking, the best way to keep tabs on me was to keep me close at hand. I decided to play along with Bailey. At least it would save me a night's hotel bill. "Okay, Sergeant, I'll take you up on your offer. Thanks."

He looked pleased, and we spent a few minutes working out the details of getting my car and following him to his place. As we passed the reception counter at the front of the administration building, the young girl behind the desk stopped us with a question.

"Excuse me. Would one of you gentlemen be Mister Spicer?"

I said, "Yeah, I'm Spicer."

"Oh, good. You just had a long-distance telephone call from a gentleman by the name of . . . ." She consulted a slip of paper, and then continued, ". . . Tom Kendall. He wants you to call him. He said it was very urgent. Here's the number he gave me."

I read the message with Bailey looking over my shoulder. The note simply said to call Tom Kendall in Novato at Tucker 3617. I looked at Bailey dumbfounded, and he looked back at me with more or less the same expression. I wouldn't have been more surprised if the message had been from Bugs Bunny. Bailey said, "Let's go back to that office. I need to make a phone call."

I thanked the receptionist, and we traipsed back to Jeff's office. Bailey took the message slip, sat at the desk, and consulted a list of telephone numbers in his notebook. He picked one and dialed it. When the party answered, he said, "Trace desk. Official police business."

After no more than a ten second wait, he said, "This is Detective Sergeant Bailey, SFPD homicide, badge number 612. I need the physical location of a Novato, California, telephone number. The number is Tucker 3617."

While he waited for the information, Bailey looked over at me and smiled his wry smile again. "See? We cops do have a few advantages over you private dicks."

I didn't bother to tell him I could have gotten the same information. It would have taken a little longer, but I'd have gotten it. Bailey flipped to a blank page in his notebook and wrote what the telephone company trace desk employee told him.

After placing the handset back in its cradle, Bailey said, "Your FBI buddy just called you from the Airway Auto Court at 6088 Redwood Highway in Novato. What do you make of that?"

"Not much, except that Kendall might have been on the level about moving Sun Ling closer to the airfield she's supposed to fly out of on Monday."

Bailey seemed to be studying the note he'd just made in his book. Eventually, he said, "I wonder what he wants. I mean, if the FBI went through all that nonsense you told me about to get you out of their hair, why the hell would he be calling you now?"

I shrugged. "Damned if I know."

The sergeant cocked his head to one side. "You ain't curious?"

"Yeah, I'm a little curious, but not enough to get roped into more of Kendall's shenanigans."

"But supposin' he's got himself into some kind of trouble and needs your help?"

"Hell, Bailey, he's got the whole damned FBI to bail him out. Let him call J. Edgar Hoover."

The sergeant picked up the telephone message, leaned back in Jeff's chair, and studied the slip of paper in his hand for a moment. Then, waving it at me, he said, "I think we oughta look into this."

Angrily, I replied, "You want me to call that SOB?"

"Well, if you don't want to call him, maybe we should take a drive up to this auto court place and size up the situation. It couldn't hurt."

I sighed in exasperation. Whatever he was up to, Kendall was trying to rope me into more of his tomfoolery, and Bailey seemed intent on helping him do it. I had to wonder what the sergeant saw in this situation that I was missing. In the end, though, curiosity got the best of me.

"Okay, Bailey, you win. I don't have anything else to do tonight, so let's go see if we can find out what kind of mess Kendall's gotten himself into now."

Bailey smiled. "That's the spirit! Hell, we might even get a laugh or two out of this."

Somehow I doubted that, but I listened carefully to the sergeant's directions to the SFPD's Northern Division Station on Fillmore Street at Turk. The plan was for me to leave my car there while we went on our fool's errand in Bailey's unmarked Chevrolet cruiser.

As per the sergeant's instructions, I pulled into the parking lot behind the station. I knew I had some time to kill there because Bailey told me he needed to fill up his gas tank and make a telephone call before he picked me up.

While I didn't really expect much from our excursion to the Airway Auto Court, I am a firm believer in the Boy Scout motto, "Always be prepared." With that thought in mind, I opened the Chrysler's trunk and fished around in my suitcase for the box of thirty-eight caliber ammunition I pack on business trips. I counted out a dozen rounds and divided them between my left and right side coat pockets so I wouldn't be lopsided. Thus prepared, I locked the trunk and leaned against my right rear fender to wait for Bailey.

The SFPD's Northern Division Station was a jumpin' joint. The constant flow of arriving and departing prowl cars made me think San Francisco's miscreants must be out in force insuring job security for San Francisco's finest.

The fog was also out in force, making the night air damp and chilly. The airborne mist illuminated by the streetlights was thick enough to be called drizzle in any other part of the world. Here it was just fog.

Bailey's black sedan pulled up behind my Chrysler about quarter after ten, and as I slid onto the passenger side of the front seat, I said, "I was beginning to wonder if you were gonna show. It's damp out there."

"Quit your bellyachin', Spicer. I told you I had to stop for gasoline and a telephone call."

As we pulled out of the lot, I said, "Tell me something, Bailey. Isn't this Novato place a little outside your jurisdiction, or do the cops hereabouts bother about such minor details?"

The sergeant shifted into second as we roared up Fillmore Street. "That's what my phone call was about. I let the Marin County Sheriff's Office know I was headed for their bailiwick. It's just a courtesy thing. We all get along, but the other jurisdictions like to know about it when we visit their territory. It's the same when they come to our neck of the woods."

We continued north on Fillmore until we got to Lombard Street, where Bailey turned left. It occurred to me that I'd now been on both ends of Lombard in the same day, having seen the other end of it that morning when I visited the Coit tower, although after the long day I was having, morning seemed like a week ago. This end of the street was posted with U.S. Route 101 shields, which explained all the motor hotels we were passing. There were dozens of them, most with illuminated vacancy notices below gaudy neon signs displaying quaint names like Sea Breeze Inn and Cable Car Lodge.

Before long the street angled off to the right and we were on the approach to the landmark Golden Gate Bridge. Bailey flashed his tin at the toll plaza and we drove right on through. Then we were crossing the most famous bridge in the world.

The sergeant told me to look back to my right. I did and got an impressive view of the lights along San Francisco's waterfront as they flashed by beyond the vertical cables supporting the roadway. These cables were in turn supported on each side of the bridge by a giant cable that had to be at least three feet in diameter. The bigger cables arched gracefully up from the south anchorage of the bridge to the top of the first of two towers. Then they completed another arch between the towers before curving down to the northern anchorage, thus giving the bridge its well-known shape.

I said, "They just finished this bridge, didn't they?"

"Yeah, they opened it up about two years ago, made a big fuss about it. They had a pedestrian parade—a fiesta, or whatever they called it—out here before they let cars go across, and every nut in town showed up trying to be the first one to do some stunt or other on the bridge. There were two-hundred-thousand of 'em! There was even a guy who walked across on stilts, for cryin' out loud!"

The roadway we were on looked to be about sixty feet or so wide with three lanes of traffic in each direction, and there was a surprising amount of that traffic for the lateness of the hour. Through Bailey's windshield, the entire scene had an eerie amber glow to it from the sodium-vapor lights they put up to cut through the fog. That thought brought to mind another question for my tour guide.

"How come they painted the bridge orange instead of some color that blends into the landscape better?"

"They didn't paint it orange. That ain't paint; it's red lead. They use it to protect the steel from all the salt in the air. If they didn't, this whole monstrosity would rust out in a week and end up in the drink."

"Sergeant, something tells me you don't think very highly of this engineering marvel."

"I don't. It's nothin' but a big eyesore. I liked it a whole lot better when we took ferries across to Marin. It was slower, but better—more natural like. And nobody ever tried to do themselves in by jumping off a freakin' ferryboat."

I assumed Bailey was referring to the numerous suicides I'd read about in newspaper articles. It seemed the Golden Gate Bridge was a popular jumping-off point for people on their way to the next life. I said, "You get a lot of suicides here, do you?"

"Yeah. Eleven since the bridge opened. It's a big pain in the butt. The bridge people keep coming up with schemes to stop 'em, but the crazies always find a way around the barriers and such they put up.

"If it wasn't for all the extra work they make for us, I'd say let 'em jump. If they're nuts enough to think diving 200 feet from this bridge is a good way to end it all, we probably don't need 'em around anyway."

"Your concern for your fellow man is touching."

"Screw my fellow man!"

About a mile beyond the bridge we drove through a long tunnel, and as we emerged, Bailey informed me we were about to pass through the Marin County seat—a town called San Rafael, only he pronounced the second word in the name Ra-fell instead of using the three-syllable Spanish pronunciation, Ra-fay-ell. When I questioned this, Bailey said he grew up in these parts and never heard anyone ever say it the Spanish way. He put an end to this particular topic of discussion by saying, "It's their damned town, so they can pronounce it any damned way they want."

After San Rafael, the traffic thinned out, and we had the four-lane highway pretty much to ourselves. What I could see of the terrain around us appeared to be mostly rolling hills with occasional dark spots, which by their shapes I took to be oak trees. Not much changed beyond the windshield for another fifteen minutes or so, and then civilization reappeared in the form of a little hamlet calling itself Ignacio. A gas station and a couple of stores, all dark, went by so quickly I would have missed them if I'd blinked.

We passed a few more miles of nothing before the lights of another little village appeared up ahead. Bailey said, "That's Novato comin' up. The place were looking for should be on our right at this end of town."

He slowed the Chevy and I spotted the Airway Auto Court almost immediately. It would have been hard to miss the joint's bright pink and blue neon sign featuring the front view of an airplane with an animated propeller that appeared to spin, albeit somewhat jerkily.

Bailey drove right past the place and made a U-turn a short distance up the road. Then he drove back to a closed Texaco service station across the highway from the auto court. The sergeant pulled behind the gas pumps and killed his headlights, saying, "We'll hang out here for a little while and see what's what."

Aside from the convulsive neon display out front, the place was virtually indistinguishable from dozens of other such tourist courts scattered up and down the length of California. Behind an arch-covered entrance drive, it consisted of a dozen or so stucco bungalows arranged in a U shape and connected by carports. A paved rectangular drive provided automobile access to the rooms and surrounded a central patch of lawn in which a couple of eight-foot evergreen trees and some shrubbery were planted. At the center of this greenery a few pieces of metal lawn furniture were arranged around a small burbling fountain lit by pink spotlights.

The Airway Auto Court's office, located to the left of the entrance arch, was identified by a small electric sign that had it been lit would have announced "Vacancy" to passersby. Since only a few of the carports I could see were occupied by cars, it seemed safe to conclude there were vacant rooms, but the management had given up on filling any of them and turned out the light so as to get some sleep.

Half an hour before midnight on this Friday night the only signs of life at the Airway Auto Court were the lit windows of one room at the back of the U and the illuminated booth of a lonely looking public telephone across the entranceway from the office.

Though small and not particularly elegant, the place seemed clean and well maintained. At the moment, it was also the very picture of tranquility. I pointed this out to Sergeant Bailey, and he said, "Yeah, but your FBI buddy called you from here, so he and that Chinese gal can't be too far away. Let's just give it a little more time and see what happens."

So I sat there staring at the hypnotic movement of the neon display across the highway and trying to remember why I particularly cared about what might or might not happen at the Airway Auto Court. True, Kendall had called from this place, but I couldn't honestly say I cared one whit about him. In fact, the only thing I really cared about was getting the Jap goon squad off my back, and I didn't see much likelihood of that happening out here in the Marin County boondocks.

TWENTY-FOUR

The minute hand on my watch eventually dragged itself around to the top of the dial, which meant we'd been sitting at the Texaco station for about half an hour. During that time the most interesting events we'd witnessed were the passing of two automobiles on U.S. Highway 101—one northbound and one southbound.

I stifled a yawn and was thinking about the best way to let Detective Sergeant Bailey in on the news that we were wasting our time when something interesting actually happened. It wasn't much, just a momentary flickering of light off to the left of the auto court that might have gone unnoticed if the thick fog above us wasn't blocking out all the natural light from the moon and stars.

The Airway Auto Court sat between a pair of vacant lots. The structure on the other side of the lot to the north housed an automobile repair business. It was from behind this building that the brief flash of illumination appeared. To my eyes it looked as if a car had pulled up back there and turned off its headlights.

I was about to ask Bailey if he'd seen the light, too, when he said, "You see that, Spicer? Looks like a car just drove in behind that building over there."

"Yeah, I saw the light, but I'm not sure it means anything. Might just be a couple of kids looking for a place to make a little whoopee."

On a dark night your eyes can play tricks on you, so I wasn't sure if another flash of light—briefer and less brilliant than the first—actually happened or if I was imagining it. If I imagined it, Bailey imagined it, too. He said, "That might have been somebody getting out of the car back there."

"Uh-huh."

If the lights behind the car repair joint meant trouble for someone at the auto court, that trouble had to cross the vacant lot between the two buildings. I focused my attention on that black area. A minute passed, followed by another minute, and then a lone figure, briefly illuminated by light spilling from the auto court's neon sign, trotted around the front corner of the auto court and disappeared through the arched opening of the entrance drive.

Bailey and I bailed out of his cruiser and headed across the highway at a run. The sergeant drew his service revolver from its holster on his right hip, and then things really began to happen. First, we heard the distinct sound of glass breaking. This was followed by two pops. They were slightly muffled by the dense fog, and we couldn't see who was doing the shooting, but there was no doubt we were hearing gunshots.

Next, the lights in the bungalow at the back of the auto court blinked off. A second or two later the bungalow's front door opened and a louder pop came from the courtyard. There was a flash of return fire from the bungalow's doorway before the door slammed shut.

Bailey and I were on opposite sides of the entrance drive. From my position on the south side, I could make out the gunman we'd seen enter the courtyard. He was crouched next to one of the evergreen trees between the fountain and the back bungalows. I wasn't sure the sergeant could see the guy from his position on the north side of the entrance, so I said in a loud whisper, "He's next to that tree on the left."

"I see him."

The sounds of three more gunshots came from the bungalow, the muzzle flashes lighting up the drawn window curtains. Now I had the picture. There were two gunmen. One of them was behind the bungalow firing through a back window, which accounted for the breaking glass we'd heard. That guy's job was to flush whoever was inside out through the door so the gunman in the courtyard could pick them off. But the guy in the courtyard fired too quickly when the front door opened. He'd muffed the shot and tipped off the bungalow's occupants to his presence. They'd ducked back inside and were now trapped between the two gunmen.

Since this was Bailey's show, I pulled my Smith & Wesson and waited for him to make our first move. I didn't have long to wait. Raising his revolver, Bailey yelled at the guy next to the tree. "Police! Drop your gun and get your hands up!"

The gunman spun, let off a round in our general direction, and jumped around to the other side of the tree. His shot wasn't really aimed because the guy didn't know exactly where we were. He'd just fired to keep us off balance, and it worked. In his new position, we no longer had a clear shot at him.

With incredibly poor timing, the bungalow's occupants chose that exact moment to make a break for it. The door flew open, a shot was fired into the courtyard from the doorway, and two figures—one much larger than the other—emerged on the run. They were headed for the carport, but they didn't make it.

The gunman in the courtyard fired from nearly pointblank range. The larger of the two figures went sprawling. The smaller figure kept running and was almost to the carport when the gunman took a step forward and fired again. The small figure went down a few feet short of the carport opening.

By taking that step toward his second target, the gunman exposed himself, and the sergeant's long-barreled forty-four revolver roared twice, sending a hell of a racket echoing around the courtyard. The gunman staggered a step and went down hard.

Now that Bailey had everything under control in the courtyard, I ran back out of the entranceway to get the other gunman—the one who'd been behind the auto court firing through a window at the rear of the bungalow. Rounding the corner, I stepped into the vacant lot and paused. Nothing moved back there, and I figured the guy had enough of a head start that he'd already made it to his car. I took off diagonally through the vacant lot's waist-high weeds toward the rear of the car repair place.

I was halfway to my objective when the second gunman suddenly appeared in my peripheral vision from behind the auto court. It must have taken him longer than I thought to figure out what happened in the courtyard, but now he had the picture and was running toward his car for all he was worth.

From where I stood in the middle of the vacant lot, I could see the guy clearly, but he gave no indication of seeing me. I raised my Smith & Wesson and yelled, "Police! Stop and get your hands up!"

Now he damned well knew I was there and acted exactly as I expected him to act. He took one more stride, crouched, and raising the gun in his right hand, he turned toward me. Letting him get a shot off didn't seem like a healthy thing to do, so while he was looking for me among the weeds in the darkness, I fired three rounds in quick succession.

I can usually tell from the way a guy drops after being shot whether he's in or out of the action. I was pretty sure this guy was out of it, but I kept my Smith & Wesson at the ready as I crossed the thirty or so feet to where he'd fallen.

The gunman was on his back, so I could see his face. He looked Japanese to me. Score one for our side. I kicked his pistol—another Colt forty-five semi-automatic, which seemed to be the weapon du jour of Jap agents—away from his body. Then I saw the spots of blood on the front of his shirt. Two of my three shots ended up within two inches of each other in the guy's chest, and judging by the relatively small amount of blood, I'd hit him squarely in the heart. A still-beating heart pumps out a lot more blood than this guy lost. He was dead before he hit the ground.

I stepped back and took a long look at the man whose life I'd just ended. Yes, he'd have done the same to me without hesitation if I hadn't gotten him first. And no, he wasn't the first man I'd killed, but neither of those facts made looking at what I'd done any easier.

After slipping the guy's Colt into my jacket pocket, I walked slowly back to the auto court. I wasn't in any big hurry to see what I knew I'd find there. The two figures I'd watched run from the bungalow's door matched the sizes and shapes of Sun Ling and Tom Kendall, and it occurred to me that maybe I ought to feel guilty about not returning Kendall's call to Jeff Yang's office, but I rejected that notion. Kendall created this situation all on his own, and I'd be damned if I was going to shoulder any of the blame for his stupidity.

A siren wailed in the distance as I walked through the auto court entranceway. The place was ablaze with lights, apparently turned on by the burly guy in slacks and an unbuttoned shirt who was standing just outside the office. At the back of the courtyard Bailey was down on one knee next to the smaller of the two figures from the bungalow. As I approached the sergeant, I asked, "How is she?"

He looked up at me. "Oh, I think she'll make it if the ambulances don't take too long getting here. I'm not so sure about the guy with her. I take it this is the Chinese gal you were looking for, and that guy over there is your FBI pal."

I looked over at Kendall. He wasn't moving. "Yup, that's Kendall, alright."

"Did you get the guy who was around back?"

"I did. He's in the vacant lot and he's not goin' anywhere."

When I glanced at Sun Ling again, her eyes were open. I said, "Hello, Sun Ling. How are you feeling?"

She started to say something, but her eyes drooped shut again and nothing came out. Then a whole lot more illumination poured into the courtyard from the headlights of a black and white sheriff's cruiser that pulled in and drove around the driveway in our direction. Bailey stood and held up his badge so the deputies would know we were the good guys.

The sheriff's cruiser was followed by a second black-and-white and a few moments later by two ambulances. The Airway Auto Court was abuzz with activity. It surprised me a little that Bailey was clearly in charge of the situation. In my experience, local cops don't usually hand over their authority to an outsider so easily. Maybe the deputies knew Bailey, or maybe he won them over with his charming personality. More likely they knew him.

Mostly I just stayed out of the way, answering questions when they were asked and keeping my mouth shut the rest of the time. This was Bailey's show and I left him to it.

While staying out of the way, I did notice one detail that raised a question in my mind. The automobile parked in the carport next to Kendall's bungalow was his black Ford. I recognized the license plate numbers from when I followed him out to Port Costa, but the last time I'd seen that Ford it was still parked alongside the Burlington Hotel. If Kendall and Sun Ling left

Port Costa in the Chevy panel delivery I'd seen go by, how the hell did Kendall's car get here?

The sky to the east already had a hint of gray in it before we finished all of the talking and official paperwork associated with the night's events. Kendall and Sun Ling had long since been taken to the local hospital, and Bailey sweet-talked the sheriff's boys into providing round-the-clock guards for them. The two goons they hauled away in the county coroner's station wagon were well beyond any such need.

According to my wristwatch, it was nearly five o'clock when Bailey and I climbed back into his Chevy cruiser still parked at the Texaco across the street. By six we'd picked up my car from the North Division Station and I'd followed Bailey to his comfy little home west of the downtown area in a quiet neighborhood he called The Avenues.

It wouldn't have mattered to me at that point if his comfy little home had been on the busiest corner in town. As soon as I flopped onto the bed in his spare room, I was off into a nightmare world full of Japanese goons who glared menacingly and waved oversized Colt forty-five caliber pistols in my direction.

TWENTY-FIVE

$$\perp\!\perp$$

San Francisco - Saturday - April 15, 1939

The noon hour arrived and lured me back to the land of the living with whiffs of brewing coffee. Since I'd fallen asleep fully-clothed with the exception of my jacket, shoulder holster and shoes, getting up involved nothing more strenuous than setting out in search of the coffee.

I found it and Bailey in his breakfast nook. He poured me a cup, and in a tone that was much too cheerful, said, "Good morning, Spicer. How ya' doin'?"

I mumbled, "I'm not sure. Ask me again after I get a little of this joe in me."

"Fair enough. While you're doing that, I'll tell what's been going on while you were in dreamland. I talked to the hospital people up in Marin County, and you'll be pleased to know the little Chinese gal is doin' fine. The doctors think your buddy Kendall will recover, but he's going to be laid up for a time. Those forty-fives the Japs carried make a hell of a big hole.

"Also, a few hours ago a troop of FBI agents showed up at the hospital and they've taken over the job of keeping Sun Ling safe. Better late than never, I guess."

The combination of Bailey's strong coffee and the news that Sun Ling was okay gave my enthusiasm for facing the day a good boost. I asked, "What about Jeff and Susie Yang? Are they okay?"

"They're fine. My second shift escorted 'em to Treasure Island this morning, and I'm thinkin' it's probably safe to put my boys back on their regular duties. What do ya' think?"

"I imagine that would be okay. Three of the Jap agents are out of the picture now, and if any remain, they already know where to find Sun Ling, not that it will do them much good. The Yang kids ought to be in the clear."

Bailey nodded. "Now, ain't you glad I dragged you up to that auto court last night?"

"Yeah, I guess so. I sure as hell didn't expect what happened, and if we hadn't been there, things would have turned out a lot differently."

The sergeant grinned at me and said, "You're welcome. Now, I have to get down to headquarters. The Marin County Sheriff's Department is satisfied with things, but I have to explain it all to my bosses."

"You expect any problems with that?"

"Nope. I followed procedures all the way."

"Then you probably won't be needing me to hang around any longer."

"Nah, no need for you to stick around. I know where to find ya if I need ya'. Besides, the sooner you leave the sooner I'll stop finding dead bodies around every corner."

Bailey had his wry smile on again. I gave him a grimace and said, "Then I'll get myself cleaned up and head for Los Angeles. Okay if I stick around here long enough to shave and shower?"

"Sure. Just make sure the front door is locked when you leave."

I said I would and Bailey stood up. Offering his hand, he surprised me by saying, "You know, Spicer, I've never had much use for private dicks, but you handle yourself pretty damned good, especially with the FBI leadin' ya' down the garden path the way they did. You're alright. I hope to see ya' again sometime."

Shaking the hand he offered, I replied, "Thanks, Sergeant. You're not such a bad guy either."

With that, Bailey gave me a grin and left. I finished off my coffee and took a shower and put on my last clean shirt. Before leaving Bailey's place I poured myself another cup of java and spent a few minutes cleaning and reloading my Smith & Wesson. Like my old man used to say, it pays to take care of your tools.

With that chore done, I consulted my Shell map to find a route that would take me back to Treasure Island for what I hoped would really be the last time. Finally, I tossed my suitcase into the Chrysler's trunk, locked Bailey's front door, and got on the road.

A few minutes after two I joined the long lines of Saturday exposition visitors waiting at the drive-through ticket booths. They were the longest lines I'd seen to date, and since I only planned to be on Treasure Island long enough to say goodbye to Susie and Jeff, I took advantage of my taxi area parking permit one more time.

I found the Yang kids in Jeff's office. As I walked in, Jeff said, "Johnny! I wasn't sure when we'd see you again. The San Francisco cops told us they were leaving because we weren't in danger anymore, but they didn't tell us how come we weren't in danger."

Susie was sitting in my usual spot on the edge of Jeff's desk. She got up and shook my hand with a look of curiosity on her face. "Yes, can you tell us what happened last night?"

I gave them a condensed version of my Airway Auto Court experiences and concluded with the news that Sun Ling was expected to fully recover from her wound. Eagerly, Susie asked, "Do you think it would be okay if I went up there to visit her?"

"Well, I can't see anything wrong with that. The trick will be getting past the FBI. I understand they arrived at the hospital in force this morning. But if Sun Ling knows you're there, I imagine she'll insist on seeing you. That should get you in."

"Oh, good! I'll drive up to Novato this afternoon!"

Turning to Jeff, I said, "How's the shoulder, amigo?"

"Better! I hardly notice it anymore, except for this dang sling. I hope they tell me I can get rid of it when I see the doctor again on Monday."

Then, for the second time in the past twenty-four hours, I bid the kids goodbye. Susie shook hands with me and gave me a hug. Thankfully, Jeff just shook my hand. As I walked toward the door, I reminded them of their promise to come down to my neck of the woods for a tour of Hollywood. Susie said they hadn't forgotten and they were looking forward to making the trip as soon as time permitted.

On my way back to my car, I paused in the Court of Pacifica. Looking up at Dog Woman, I thought I saw a change in her expression. I'm sure it was just my imagination, but she almost looked as if she was smiling at me. Chuckling at my delusions, I continued to my car. But just before I stepped out through the Northwest Passage, I looked back, gave Miss Pacifica a little wave, and said, "So long, doll."

She didn't wave back.

TWENTY-SIX

⌒⌒

Hollywood - Monday - April 17, 1939

I got to my office on the second floor of the First National Bank building at Hollywood and Highland bright and early Monday morning. Humble though they were, it felt good to be back among the familiar surroundings of my natural habitat.

And I was raring to go after spending a mostly leisurely Sunday taking care of chores like my laundry and enjoying dinner from the China Takee Home joint with my downstairs neighbor, Tess. The Kung Pao chicken we ordered wasn't served as elegantly as it would have been at Wing's in the Chinese Village, but it tasted just as good at Tess's kitchen table.

The first order of office business was sorting the mountain of mail the postman had slipped through the slot in my outer office door while I was gone. I carried the pile to my desk and began dividing it between my desk blotter and the wastepaper basket, with most of the envelopes and fliers going to the latter destination. When the sorting was done, I was surprised to find I had not one, but two envelopes from Liang Chao's Trans-Pacific Shipping Company in San Pedro. The difference between them was that my address on the envelope postmarked 9:00A FRI APR 14 '39 was typewritten and the address on second envelope, postmarked 5:00P FRI APR 14 '39, was hand-printed.

I opened the envelopes in chronological order. The first contained the promised check for services rendered in the amount of four-hundred dollars, along with a typewritten, detailed accounting of what the check was for.

Picking up the second envelope, I bet myself it was a letter from Liang Chao telling me he'd stopped payment on the check because I'd disobeyed him and found Sun Ling after he'd fired me. I lost that bet. The hand-addressed envelope contained another check—this one in the amount of five-hundred dollars—and a personal note from Liang Chao. Written in a precise hand, the note said:

Dear Mister Spicer,

By now you must be aware that I deceived you in regard to certain information concerning your recent investigation. For this transgression I most humbly apologize and offer the explanation that my deception was made necessary by extenuating circumstances.

I trust you will accept the enclosed check in the amount of $500.00 as at least partial recompense for any inconvenience and/or difficulty caused you by my deception. Contrary to what I was forced to tell you Thursday night over the telephone, I believe you conducted yourself admirably throughout your investigation. Furthermore, I would be most happy to give you my personal endorsement in the event you should need a reference in the future.

Most humbly,
Liang Chao

I dropped the letter on my desk and leaned back to contemplate this unexpected turn of events. I wasn't prepared to exonerate Liang for using me as a pawn in his connivance with the FBI, but I had to think he might not be as dishonorable as I thought him to be, although his second check might have had something to do with my newly elevated opinion of Mister Liang.

Then a picture took shape in my mind. It showed Sun Ling boarding a U.S. Army Air Corps transport ship bound for points unknown. Glancing at my watch, I figured the scene I imagined was probably actually taking place right about then on a taxiway at Hamilton Airfield 500 miles to the north. That, of course, assumed Sun Ling had recovered sufficiently to travel. I had the idea it would take more than a gunshot wound to keep that gal from doing her duty.

At lunchtime, I took Liang Chao's checks down to my bank on the ground floor of the building and deposited them. Then I treated myself to a Reuben at the deli a few doors north on Highland. On my way back to the office, I picked up a copy of the Times from the newsboy at the corner. I was curious to find out what excitement might have occurred in the City of Angels during my absence.

As I worked my way through the national and city sections of the paper, I found things were pretty much business as usual while I was gone. The bad guys and politicians were still up to their usual shenanigans, and Pep Boys was having a tire sale. On the back page of the city section, however, I did find something interesting. The article was only a column wide and nestled between ads for Zenith radios and Thompson's Nash dealership, so if the headline hadn't caught my eye, I would have missed the story entirely.

SANTA MONICA POLICE EXPAND SEARCH FOR MISSING CHINESE MAN

According to Santa Monica Police Chief Charles L. Dice, the department is expanding its search for Liang Chao, owner of the Trans-Pacific Shipping Company of San Pedro. Liang was reported missing on the night of April 14, and to date, investigators have no leads as to his whereabouts.

The brief article went on to provide some vague details of Liang's disappearance and the usual bit about foul play being suspected. If my hunch was right, foul play was definitely involved, and Liang's disappearance provided a possible answer to a question I'd been pondering ever since leaving San Francisco.

The question? How the hell did the Jap goons know Kendall and Sun Ling were at the Airway Auto Court? Logic told me the goons didn't know about the Burlington Hotel in Port Costa. If they had, Sun Ling and Kendall wouldn't have still been there when I showed up on Friday.

My hunch was Kendall planned to move Sun Ling to the Airway Auto Court all along even though he told me he didn't know of a place to stay up near the airfield. That idea was a much better fit with the agent's compulsion for planning each step to the nth degree. So, if one of the telephone calls he made while I stood guard over Sun Ling in his hotel room was to Liang Chao, and if he told Liang he was moving to the Airway Auto Court that night, and if, as I was afraid might happen, Japanese agents in this part of the world grabbed Liang, it would explain how the goons arrived in Novato so quickly when Kendall supposedly had no idea where he was taking Sun Ling.

My theory depended on some fairly large ifs, but the pieces fit. And if I was right, the odds of Liang Chao ever turning up anywhere but on a beach somewhere up the coast were roughly a billion to one.

I had to wonder about the bodyguard, or whatever his official title was, who'd shown up in my office with Liang a week ago. He'd looked fairly competent to me, so if he was on the job Friday night, it meant the southern California contingent of Jap agents was a hell of a lot sharper than the ones I'd encountered in San Francisco.

I tried to feel sorry for Liang because it would have taken a lot of pain to make him spill the beans, but I couldn't work up much sympathy. Liang helped create a ridiculous scheme that was so absurd even an amateur should have had sense enough to realize it would come back to bite him. Plus, he was so cocksure about it all he didn't take the reasonable precaution of accepting FBI protection, or so I'd been told by Kendall. In the final analysis, it seemed to me Liang reaped what he sewed.

TWENTY-SEVEN

⏄⏄

Hollywood - Wednesday – May 9, 1939

Agent Tom Kendall was standing on the front porch of his bungalow on Gower just south of Fountain when I pulled up. He looked like hell. In fact, he didn't look a whole lot better than when I'd last seen him being stuffed into an ambulance in Novato nearly a month ago. That wasn't too surprising, though, because the forty-five caliber slug he'd taken was nearly half an inch in diameter. A round that size does a pretty thorough job of messing up a person's interior plumbing.

What I did find surprising was the telephone call that led me to Kendall's doorstep. After the way he and his FBI cohorts bollixed up the Sun Ling caper, I didn't think Kendall had the nerve to call me anytime soon, if ever. But guilt can make a man do unexpected things, and I got the idea Kendall was feeling guilty as hell, especially after Detective Sergeant Bailey and I saved his bacon.

Kendall called early that morning, saying he needed to talk to me and asking if I'd have lunch with him. He also asked if I'd mind picking him up because he wasn't driving yet. I agreed to the meeting because there were still some loose ends floating around, and I thought I might be able to wheedle some answers out of him. As it turned out, no wheedling was required.

Leaning heavily on a cane, it took Kendall some time to negotiate the three steps down from his porch and the twenty or so feet more to my Chrysler. Once he was in the car and had a chance to catch his breath, I asked where he wanted to go for lunch.

The agent said, "Would you mind if we just drove around some before we go to lunch? I've got some things to tell you, and I'd rather not take a chance on being overheard in a restaurant."

I nodded and drove north on Gower, figuring I'd head up to Lake Hollywood—a peaceful spot that was certain to be free of eavesdroppers. After several minutes, Kendall said, "The first thing I want to say is thank you for rescuing Sun Ling and me at that auto court. I wouldn't be here if you hadn't shown up."

I made no attempt to hide my feelings on the subject. "If it had been up to me, I wouldn't have shown up. An SFPD cop named Bailey talked me into going up to Novato that night. He's also the one who nailed the guy outside your room. So save your thanks for him."

After a moment's pause, he said, "I know your nose is out of joint about what happened, and you have good reason to be angry with me. That's why I wanted to meet with you. I can't undo any of what happened, but I can tell you a few things that might help explain it all."

"Alright, I'm listening."

"Most of what I've got to say is still hush-hush, and I could get the ax or worse for telling you this stuff, but I'm willing to take that risk because I think you deserve the truth. Okay?"

I kept my eyes on the road and my mouth shut. When it finally sunk in that I wasn't going to reply, Kendall continued. "This whole business started in the White House. The way I heard it, FDR was getting an earful from some of the more influential Chinese businessmen in the U.S. He was also secretly corresponding with officials in the Chinese government.

"They all want the U.S. to get involved in the Sino-Japanese war. FDR wants that, too—I guess because he figures we're going to have to fight the Japanese sooner or later, and them having China's natural resources won't make that fight any easier. As you know, though, American voters aren't eager to get into another war, and the politicians are treading very carefully on that subject."

Kendall paused and I made the light at Hollywood Boulevard. Then he said, "Anyway, to make a long story short, FDR invited China to send a representative over here for secret meetings to discuss the situation. He had to keep the meetings under wraps to avoid showing his cards too soon and starting a public uproar. China picked Sun Ling as their representative to meet with FDR, and once that decision was made, Roosevelt called J. Edgar Hoover and told him to set up a plan for getting Sun Ling to Washington on the QT.

"This all happened toward the end of last year. Hoover decided the world's fair they were putting together up in Frisco would be a good cover for Sun Ling's trip to the U.S., so he called my boss, West Coast Deputy Director Ed Whitley, and told him to meet with the Chinese-Americans involved in the fair and work out a plan. You with me so far?"

I nodded and followed the right-hand curve in Gower that ended at Beachwood Drive. I made a left and Kendall went on with his story. "That's when things started getting out of hand. I don't think Whitley has ever actually worked in the field, and he goes in for really complicated plans because he doesn't realize that the more complex the plan, the greater the chances of something going wrong. The Chinese-Americans went right along with him, and together they came up with the god-awful plan that got us into all this trouble.

"The basic idea was fine. Making Sun Ling China's official representative at the exposition was a good reason for her to be in the U.S., and having the Chinese-Americans make the arrangements for her trip kept the FBI out of it. But then Whitley started complicating things. The plan he came up with called for staging an intricate disappearing act to smuggle Sun Ling out of the exposition so she could attend the secret meetings with FDR.

"If that wasn't bad enough, Whitley heaped more complications on the plan, like hinting to the press that Sun Ling's disappearance was the doing of Japanese agents. That was supposed to generate newspaper stories that would explain Sun Ling's disappearance and make the American public more sympathetic to China's situation. That part of the plan failed miserably because when we anonymously leaked the story to the big papers, they weren't willing to print it without confirmation, and since we'd sworn every one involved to secrecy, the papers couldn't get anybody to verify that Sun Ling had disappeared.

"Then Whitley decided we had to have eyes inside the Chinese Village, so he arranged for a Chinese-American cop he knew from Baltimore, of all places, to work in the Chinese exhibit gift shop. This guy was supposed to let us know if anything went wrong. Whitley also stuck the poor guy with some of the detail stuff, like stealing a key to the doors that led from the dressing room building out onto the midway area and helping me sneak Sun Ling away from the exposition when it was time for her to disappear."

I turned west onto one of the Hollywoodland subdivision's twisty roads I knew would take us up to the reservoir. So far Kendall hadn't told me anything I hadn't figured out for myself, except for the part about the FBI inserting a spy into the Chinese Village gift shop. That explained who swiped the key to the dressing room building's backdoors from the administration office's key cabinet and who the Oriental guy was that exposition security guard, Wilbur Harmon, saw leaving the Gayway with Sun Ling the night she disappeared.

I decided I'd better respond to Kendall so he'd keep going and eventually tell me something I didn't know. "Which office does this guy Whitley work out of? I'm asking so I can make sure I don't run into him somewhere along the line."

"Whitley works out of our office here in L.A., but you haven't heard worst of it yet. He also arranged to have that idiot contractor build a secret trapdoor in the ceiling of Sun Ling's dressing room so she could sneak away without being seen. And Whitley is the one who decided we needed to have the Chinese-American businessmen hire a private detective to make a show of looking for Sun Ling. That's how you got roped into all this."

I glanced over at Kendall and asked, "Why me, for heaven's sake?"

"Because Whitley asked me if I knew any private eyes in the area and you came to mind because of the Bellman case a while back. When he told me why he wanted a detective and that the detective wouldn't be in on the plan, I told him you weren't the guy for the job. He needed somebody who wasn't smart enough to figure out what was going on, and that wasn't you. But Whitley didn't hear that part. He just insisted you were the guy to call.

"Another part of his scheme was that Sun Ling had to have Chinese bodyguards with her who were in on the plan so they could pull off a convincing effort to find her without lousing things up. He just kept enlarging the scheme and involving more and more people."

Lake Hollywood appeared up on our left, and I pulled onto a wide area of the road's shoulder that offered a good view of the reservoir. I turned to Kendall and said, "Okay, so this guy Whitley is an idiot, but even an idiot should have figured having Sun Ling hole up in that Port Costa flea trap was an unnecessary risk. Why not just leave her at the exposition until it was time to fly her to Washington or wherever she went?"

Kendall sighed and said, "That was the original plan. We were to wait for word from the White House that FDR was ready to meet with Sun Ling and then take her directly to that airfield for her flight. Unfortunately, an unplanned complication showed up.

"When Whitley originally made up the business about blaming Sun Ling's supposed kidnapping on the Japanese, he never figured on them actually taking notice of her. Then the Baltimore cop working in the village gift shop reported that those Japanese goons, as you called them, were hanging around whenever Sun Ling made an appearance. We did some checking and found out the goons were undercover agents of the Japanese government, which meant the Japs really were interested in Sun Ling.

"At that point, Whitley decided we had to move the schedule up and have Sun Ling disappear right away in case the Japanese had plans of their own for her. He gave me the order to go ahead with Sun Ling's kidnapping as planned and then hide her somewhere until we got word from Washington that her meetings with FDR were set up. The best place I could think of was that Burlington Hotel. I knew about it because of a smuggling case we investigated several years ago. So I called Sun Ling's hotel and told her there was a change in plans and she would be leaving the exposition very soon."

Interrupting Kendall, I asked, "Did you tell her she'd be staying at the Burlington until her flight to Washington?"

He thought about that question for a minute. "I don't remember. I might have. Why?"

"Because when I searched her room at the Fairmont, I found a piece of hotel stationery with some sketches on it, along with the Chinese characters for 'Burlington,' or something close to it. I got Susie Yang to translate the characters, and when I followed you to Port Costa, I made the connection. Also, when I was going through her closet, I found a hotel telephone message in a coat pocket that confirmed an appointment with a Mister Jones on the day she disappeared. That's when I realized her kidnapping had to be bogus."

Kendall shook his head. "Oh, geez. I never thought she'd leave stuff like that in her room. I figured she knew better."

"Well, she didn't." Deciding it was time to get down to brass tacks, I said, "Look, Kendall, your story is all fine and good, but I already know most of it. You want to answer some questions about the parts I don't know?"

He nodded. "I'll try."

"It's pretty clear to me that you showing up in the exposition parking lot the day I followed you to Port Costa was no coincidence, but why the hell did you want me to find you and Sun Ling?"

"Quite frankly, I panicked. I kept getting reports of you showing up in places you shouldn't have been, like at that contractor's office and checking with Pan American to find out if Sun Ling and her bodyguards were on the Clipper for China. That told me you either had everything figured out or you were damned close to it, so I had to get you off the case before you loused up what was left of our plan and . . . ."

I interrupted him again. "So you told Liang to fire me."

"Right, but when you didn't return any of his phone calls, and you shot that Japanese agent at the exposition, I thought I had to do something else right away, and I decided the best thing to do was arrange for you to find us in Port Costa and see for yourself that Sun Ling was okay. Then, to get rid of you again, I pretended to need your help keeping Sun Ling safe from the Japs.

"I made arrangements to have two agents waiting for us in the Port Costa train yard, so Sun Ling and I could go out the hotel's back door and disappear again while you were watching the front of the hotel from your car that afternoon. One of the agents drove us right past you in a panel delivery truck, and the other watched to see what you did. When you left Port Costa, he followed you back to Treasure Island in my car and then drove up to Novato, where he left my car and took the panel delivery back to San Francisco with the other agent."

I laughed out loud. "Kendall, all that rigmarole was completely unnecessary. By the time I saw you in the exposition parking lot, I'd already talked to Liang and knew you guys wanted me out of the picture. I was actually on my way home when you showed up in the exposition parking lot, so your clever scheme to get rid of me just kept me around longer than if you'd just left things as they were."

That piece of information was a surprise to Kendall. Looking glum, he said, "I guess my boss doesn't have a monopoly on complicated schemes. Like I said, I panicked."

"Okay, tell me something else. Did you call Liang Chao that day and tell him you were taking Sun Ling to the Airway Auto Court?"

I didn't think it was possible for Kendall to look anymore miserable about the way things turned out than he already did, but he managed it. Contritely, he said, "Yes, I did. And as you've already guessed, that's how the Japanese agents found us Friday night."

"Uh-huh. And Liang is fish food."

Angrily, Kendall said, "I'm not taking the blame for that one! I told Liang he needed protection, and when he refused, I told Whitley to keep an eye on him anyway, but Whitley didn't think it was necessary. If Liang is dead, which seems likely, that's what got him killed!" After a moment, he added in a softer tone, "And it's what would have gotten me and Sun Ling killed if you hadn't come to our rescue."

"That brings me to the last question that's been bothering me. How come you called me at the Chinese Village Friday night instead of calling your own people?"

"I did call my own people. When I went out to get us something to eat, I spotted the Japanese agents on the street in Novato. I went straight back to the auto court and called the San Francisco field office for help, but nobody answered the telephone—it's not a twenty-four hour office like the one down here. So then I called the L.A. office. They said they would try to contact someone in San Francisco to help me, but I knew that would take some time and I didn't think we had much time left.

"That's when I decided to call you. I knew you were at the exposition because the agent who brought my car from Port Costa to Novato followed you there. But when you didn't call back, I figured I was on my own."

Now that I had all the details and knew exactly how badly the Junior G-men had flummoxed the caper, I mentally went through the litany of choice comments I'd planned to use for the purpose of letting Kendall know exactly what I thought of him and the stinking FBI, but I didn't have the heart to say them. He looked like he'd already been through hell, and I guess he had. Instead, I said, "Okay, Kendall, that's all the questions I have. Where would you like to go to lunch?"

It took him a moment, but he finally said, "I'm sorry, Spicer, but I've lost my appetite. Would you mind giving me a rain check on lunch and taking me back to my place?"

Starting the Chrysler's engine, I just said, "I understand."

On the way back to Kendall's place another question occurred to me. It didn't have to do with the case as much as it had to do with the FBI agent sitting next to me. I said, "Are you going back to your old job when you recover?"

Kendall sighed as if it was a question he'd been pondering, but hadn't yet answered. He said, "That's the plan. It will be a while yet, though."

"Have you considered doing something different?"

"Why? You offering me a job?"

I refrained from telling him I would do that the day after the devil started wearing ice skates. Instead, I said, "I was just thinking you might be better suited for another line of work."

For a long time Kendall stared off into the haze that blankets our fair city on calm days. At last he simply said, "You might be right about that."

- - -

By the time I got back to my office, the mail had arrived. It consisted of one letter bearing the return address of the San Francisco Police Department, Northern Division Station. Inside the envelope I found a carefully typewritten letter on official department stationery from Detective Sergeant Horatio Bailey. If nothing else, I now knew why the sergeant introduced himself by last name only. With a moniker like Horatio, I could imagine the teasing he got in the stationhouse.

Reading the letter, I was taken by the sergeant's formality. It didn't sound at all like the Bailey I knew . . . until I got to the final paragraph.

Dear Mr. Spicer,

The Marin County Coroner's office held an inquest last week to determine the causes and circumstances of the deaths of two unidentified men of Japanese extraction on Saturday, April 15, 1939, on and near the premises of the Airway Auto Court in Novato, California. It was noted during the proceedings that there exists significant evidence indicating that both men were undercover agents of the Japanese government and that they were in the United States illegally.

The finding of that inquest was that during the commission of a crime, one of the men was shot to death in the line of duty by Detective Sergeant Horatio Bailey of the San Francisco Police Department Homicide Division, and the second man was shot to death by Jonathon Spicer, a private investigator from Los Angeles who was acting under the direction and at the request of Sergeant Bailey at the time of the shootings. The inquest further ruled that no legal action against Sergeant Bailey and Mister Spicer was appropriate or to be taken.

Spicer, in case you don't savvy the legal lingo, that means you're officially off the hook for shooting that Jap at the auto court. I was glad for your help, but I have to point out that we haven't had a single dead body show up in The City since you left town.

Sincerely,
Detective Sergeant Horatio Bailey
Homicide Division, San Francisco Police Department

EPILOGUE

Hollywood – Monday – November 6, 1939

I arrived at my office a few minutes before eleven. I was tardy because I spent the morning at the Glendale train depot seeing Susie and Jeff Yang off on their return trip to San Francisco.

The Golden Gate International Exposition finished up its first year of operation a couple of weeks before, freeing the kids up for their long anticipated visit to Hollywood. They arrived Thursday night, and I did it up brown for them with rooms at the Hollywood Roosevelt and a whirlwind tour of all the well known Hollywood landmarks.

We saw the celebrity footprints at Grauman's Chinese Theater, the world famous Hollywoodland sign, the Crossroads of the World center on Sunset, and the quaint shops, vendors and street musicians on Olivera Street—the touristy remains of the old Los Angeles Pueblo. I even took them on a tour of a major movie studio.

I knew the head man at the studio because I did some keyhole-peeping for him just before the Sun Ling caper landed in my lap. When I called the guy, he seemed pleased to arrange a tour of his studio for the kids. There we saw sound stages, back lot sets, and all the other stuff involved in the business of making movies. The kids even got to meet a couple of real movie stars, namely Bette Davis and James Cagney, the latter of whom had just finished making a film called The Roaring Twenties. Both Davis and Cagney personally autographed eight-by-ten glossies for my guests.

For Jeff, however, the highlight of his studio tour seemed to be meeting Mel Blanc, the guy who does voices for the Looney Tunes cartoons. Blanc turned out to be a hell of a nice guy, and he spent several minutes keeping the kids in stitches with the voices of Bugs Bunny, Sylvester the Cat, and Daffy Duck.

I also treated Susie and Jeff to lunches and dinners at a few of the famous eateries in town. We ate at the Pig 'n Whistle, the Musso and Frank Grill, and a joint over in Glendale called the Tam O'Shanter, where Walt Disney and his artists used to hang out back in the twenties.

After three days of playing tourist, the kids were worn out but excited about all the swell stuff they'd seen and done. At the depot they both thanked me profusely and offered to return the favor with a tour of San Francisco. I didn't have the heart to tell 'em I'd had more than enough of San Francisco to last a lifetime.

At the office I found the morning's mail in its usual spot on the floor inside my outer office door. Most of the envelopes ended up in the wastebasket except for a nine-by-twelve manila job postmarked Washington D.C.

Since I didn't know anybody in the nation's capital who might have reason to send me a big envelope, I opened it with curiosity and a small degree of trepidation. I found three items inside. The first was a thin piece of cardboard designed to keep the post office from mutilating the other items.

Next was a sheet of hotel stationery from the Mayflower Hotel at 1127 Connecticut Avenue NW, Washington, D.C. Most of the page was taken up by an artfully done pencil sketch of my old pal, Dog Woman. Below the drawing was a short, cryptic note reading, "Mr. Spicer, thank you for making a miracle possible." It was signed by Sun Ling.

The third item in the envelope was an eight-by-ten glossy photograph, apparently taken in the Oval Office of the White House It showed three people. In the center and seated at his desk was President Franklin Delano Roosevelt. Standing to FDR's left was Sun Ling, looking slim and delectable in a dark-colored dress. On Roosevelt's right was a man in an Army uniform. He wore the insignia of a bird colonel on his epaulets and a bunch of fruit salad on his uniform jacket that said he'd seen more than a little action in his time. Above the campaign ribbons was a shiny pair of pilot's wings.

Turning the photo over, I found a typed caption taped to the back. It said, "Official White House Photo: President Franklin Delano Roosevelt (center) with U.S. Army Air Corps Colonel Claire Chennault (left) and Chinese diplomat, Miss Sun Ling (right).

I studied the image more closely. My guess that it had been taken in the Oval Office was confirmed by standards bearing the American flag and the presidential seal bracketing the center of three windows along a curved wall in the background. The only other clues to the nature of the occasion captured by the White House photographer were the expressions worn by the photo's subjects. FDR looked terribly sincere. The Army guy looked primed and ready for action. And Sun Ling looked pleased.

Based on Sun Ling's expression and what I knew about the discussions going on at the time the photo must have been made, I gathered the outcome of her secret meetings with FDR—the meetings that were very nearly derailed by Japanese agents—was beneficial to China. If that was the case, Sun Ling had good reason to be pleased. So, apparently, did Generalissimo Chiang Kai-shek and the people of China.

THE END

MEET H. P. OLIVER

H. P. Oliver began his career with a degree in journalism from San Jose State University and spent the next thirty-some years writing award-winning entertainment and educational media. Now he applies his creativity and imagination to writing historical mysteries.

About mystery writing, Oliver says, "To be truly engrossing, a mystery needs a little meat on its bones—something more than just figuring out 'who done the evil deed.' Taking a story back in time or even basing it on actual historical events is a great way to endow a good yarn with color and depth. Historical periods and locations give the writer an opportunity to take readers where they've never been before."

H. P. Oliver lives in northern California and spends much of his time working on projects throughout the western states. His interests range from vintage film to restoring classic cars, and of course, history..

For more about H. P. Oliver and his mysteries in history, visit http://www.hpoliver.com.

MORE MYSTERIES IN HISTORY BY H. P. OLIVER

AND THE ANGELS SING

Set in the most glamorous locales of the big band era, *And the Angels Sing* tells the parallel stories of an up-and-coming young singer named Marion Haines and popular trumpeter Teddy Williams. They don't know each other at the start, but like two freight trains converging on the same track, Marion and Teddy are destined to meet head-on in a deadly collision orchestrated by mobster Bugsy Siegel. *And the Angels Sing* will start your toe tapping and leave your heart racing! (Available in digital editions for Kindle and Nook.)

SILENTS!

Lillian Lawrence, the silent film era's fastest rising starlet, is found shot to death in her room at the Hollywood Hotel only days after announcing her plans to leave motion pictures for the less glamorous roles of wife and mother. Lillian's many friends at the studio and her legion of fans across America are all asking the same question: Who could have done such a dastardly deed?

Set in Hollywood during the golden days of the silent film era, *SILENTS!* is a mystery from history capturing all of the action and drama that made Tinsel Town the motion picture capital of the world. (Available in paperback and digital editions for Kindle and Nook.)

THE TRUTH BE TOLD

Hollywood will never forget Peg Entwistle even though she made only one film and it was a dud. No, the scene that made Peggy famous wasn't in a movie; it was in real life, and it was spectacular. Miss Entwistle was the first person to die by falling from the famous Hollywoodland sign. That happened back in 1932, and to this day most people believe she jumped from the sign because her career was failing.

In *The Truth Be Told* H. P. Oliver suggests a fictional alternative to history in which Peggy didn't take her own life, but was sadistically murdered by Tinsel Town's most mysterious villain. Still, after all these years, does any of that really matter? It does to Peggy. *The Truth Be Told* is her story and how she finally told it eight decades after her death. (Available in digital editions for Kindle and Nook.)

www.ingramcontent.com/pod-product-compliance
Lightning Source LLC
Chambersburg PA
CBHW072137170626
46813CB00004BA/1599